"Cora is a wonderful—and funny—curmudgeon. The writing is smooth and the plot moves along nicely.... The puzzles are a small fraction of the fun in these books."
—*Mystery News*

"An enjoyable, easy read, and for a puzzle-lover, ideal."
—*Old Book Barn Gazette*

"Hall's gift for dialogue is never better than in the exchanges between Sherry and Cora.... The pace is brisk, slowed only by the deciphering of the cryptograms.... A treat."
—*Drood Review of Mystery*

A PUZZLE IN A PEAR TREE

"Ideal for the puzzle fan as well as the mystery fan, this frothy, funny and ingenious fourth 'Puzzle Lady' novel has enough plot twists for the most avid mystery reader."
—*Dallas Morning News*

"Crossworders will relish *A Puzzle in a Pear Tree*."
—*Denver Post*

"All will enjoy Hall's nimble wordplay."
—*Booked & Printed*

"The fun for fans of this series consists of the nexus between the plot and the puzzle.... Hall's books involve the reader in the action the way few others do."
—*Richmond Times-Dispatch*

PUZZLED TO DEATH

LAST PUZZLE & TESTAMENT

A CLUE FOR THE PUZZLE LADY

AND A PUZZLE TO DIE ON

A Puzzle Lady Mystery

Parnell Hall

BANTAM BOOKS

New York Toronto London Sydney Auckland

AND A PUZZLE TO DIE ON
A Bantam Book

PUBLISHING HISTORY
Bantam hardcover edition published November 2004
Bantam mass market edition / September 2005

Published by
Bantam Dell
A Division of Random House, Inc.
New York, New York

This is a work of fiction. Names, characters, places, and incidents either
are the product of the author's imagination or are used fictitiously.
Any resemblance to actual persons, living or dead, events, or locales is
entirely coincidental.

Puzzles edited by Ellen Ripstein

Library of Congress Catalog Card Number: 2004045094

Bantam Books and the rooster colophon are registered trademarks of
Random House, Inc.

ISBN 0-553-58435-9

Printed in the United States of America
Published simultaneously in Canada
www.bantamdell.com

OPM   10   9   8   7   6   5   4   3   2   1

For Will,
who knew who to ask

OTHER PEOPLE'S PUZZLES

I want to thank Nancy Salomon, Manny Nosowsky, Cathy Millhauser, and Emily Cox and Henry Rathvon for constructing the puzzles that appear in this book. The ease with which these experts provided what was needed was amazing. I could not have done this book without them.

I want to thank *New York Times* crossword puzzle editor Will Shortz for mustering the troops. Excellent suggestions all, Will!

Last, but not least, I want to thank my puzzle editor, Ellen Ripstein, who has saved me time and again from the folly of my own feeble constructions. I am delighted for once to be able to assign her the easier task of editing the puzzles of people who actually know what they are doing.

AND A PUZZLE TO DIE ON

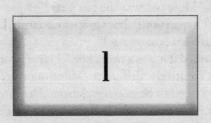

1

"Is it a milestone?" Iris Cooper asked. The Baker-haven First Selectman pulled her sweater around her shoulder with one hand while balancing her coffee and muffin in the other. It was late October, Connecticut foliage season was giving up the ghost, and early winter winds were whipping mini tornadoes of dead leaves along the street.

Sherry Carter, ambushed on her way into Cushman's Bake Shop, shrugged evasively. Sherry wore a baby-blue turtleneck and suede jacket, new for fall. "Cora says at her age they're *all* milestones."

"You mean she won't say?" Harvey Beerbaum asked. The expression on the portly cruciverbalist's face indicated that such behavior was inexplicable, if not downright subversive.

Sherry smiled. "There are two things my aunt refuses to remember. One is birthdays. The other is wedding anniversaries."

"Of course, when you have as many wedding anniversaries as Cora, that's understandable," Iris Cooper

2 / PARNELL HALL

said. No one quite knew how many former husbands Cora had.

"But she only has *one* birthday," Harvey persisted peevishly. "How old was she last year?"

"What a question!" Iris Cooper exclaimed. "It's not polite to ask a woman's age!"

"You asked if it was a milestone," Harvey pointed out.

"That's entirely different. Milestones are important. They need to be noted, celebrated, commiserated with over." Iris frowned. "Is that correct usage? I wish Cora were here to tell me."

Sherry Carter suppressed a smile. If the truth be known, her aunt Cora wouldn't know a grammatical mistake if it stood up on its hind legs, stuck its thumbs in its ears, waggled its fingers, and said, "Nyah, nyah, you ain't got no culture, does you, Miss Puzzle Penning Person?" Sherry actually wrote the nationally syndicated crossword puzzle column her aunt got credit for. Cora merely supplied the sweet-faced, white-haired, grandmotherly picture that accompanied it.

Harvey and Iris didn't know that.

"Come on," Harvey insisted. "What are we going to do?"

"What do you mean?" Sherry said.

"Well, we have to have a party."

"Cora doesn't want a party."

"Nonsense. Everyone wants a party. Isn't that right, Iris? Cora is our town's most famous citizen. She should certainly be celebrated."

"Who should be celebrated?" Aaron Grant said, strolling up. The young reporter had clearly overslept. His shirt was unbuttoned and his tie was untied. He had shaved, but his curly dark hair was dry and un-combed, indicating he hadn't showered.

Sherry's face lit up when she saw him. "Ah, just in time. Aaron, will you please help me explain Cora wouldn't want us to make a fuss."

"Make a fuss about what?"

"It's her birthday," Harvey Beerbaum said.

"Really?" Aaron said. "We should do something."

Sherry groaned at this unexpected sabotage. "No, we shouldn't. Cora wouldn't want us to do anything. She's a very private person."

"Very private people do not do TV commercials," Iris pointed out. "Come on, Sherry. Cora's had a hard time of it lately. I bet her spirits could use a lift."

"Cora's just fine," Sherry retorted. "She was going to get married, it didn't work out. If I told you how many times Cora thought she was going to get married and it didn't work out . . ."

"Nearly as many as the times it did?" Aaron asked mischievously.

Chief Harper came out of the bakery carrying a coffee and a cranberry muffin. He'd already nibbled the top off the muffin, and looked somewhat sheepish about it.

"Eating on the run, Chief?" Aaron asked.

Harper flushed. "Aaron Grant, if you put that in the paper . . ."

"Oh, I think we'll come up with something better, even on a slow news day."

"You could write about Cora's party," Iris Cooper suggested.

Chief Harper frowned. "Party? What party?"

"It's Cora's birthday," Iris informed him.

"Really," Chief Harper said. "Is it a milestone?"

"See?" Iris Cooper told Harvey. "*That's* the way to ask."

"Why? It doesn't get an answer."

"No. But it's the proper form of the question. I thought you were a wordsmith, Harvey."

"Pooh." It was one of the prissy man's strongest epithets. For a second he considered apologizing.

"What's this about a party?" Chief Harper was clearly torn between wanting to finish the conversation and wanting to get to the police station to eat his muffin. The good man seemed just on the verge of jamming the pastry into his mouth.

"We're planning a party for Cora," Harvey Beerbaum told him. "To celebrate her birthday, whichever one it may be."

"I'm telling you," Sherry said, "you can throw a party, but Cora isn't going to come."

Harvey Beerbaum was undaunted. "All right, then. We'll throw a *surprise* party."

"What?" Iris Cooper said.

"Certainly," Harvey said. "That's precisely the thing to do. Plan a secret party as a big surprise."

"Cora likes surprises less than she likes birthdays," Sherry Carter warned.

Harvey Beerbaum was having too much fun to notice. "Oh, this will be delightful. We'll do it in secret. Cora will be the only one in town who doesn't know we're planning it. Then, on the night of her birthday . . . When *is* her birthday?"

"Next Thursday."

"So soon?"

"Sorry it's such short notice. Usually I start discussing Cora's birthday a good month or two before the event."

The irony went right over Harvey's head. "Then we'll have to move fast." His eyes widened at the sight of a jack-o'-lantern in the window of Cushman's Bake Shop. "Good lord. Is that . . ."

"What?"

"Halloween? No, that's Wednesday. Too bad. It would have been a nice theme."

"Nice theme?" Iris Cooper said. "Why, Harvey Beerbaum. I suppose you'd like me to come dressed as a witch?"

"*Not* Halloween." Harvey tugged at his collar uncomfortably, noticing for the first time the First Selectman's nose was rather pointed and she was rather thin.

"Harvey, this is a bad idea," Sherry said.

"Oh, nonsense." Harvey was not to be stopped. "So, the party's Thursday, November first. That's all that matters. We can work out the details later. The important thing is, no one tells Cora."

2

"Harvey's planning a party," Sherry called as she entered the front door. Sherry was surprised Cora hadn't come out to meet her. Even Cora couldn't sleep through the entire afternoon. Sherry wondered if anything was wrong. "Hello?" she called again.

Sherry needn't have worried. Cora came bustling into the living room, bright-eyed and bushy-tailed, clutching her drawstring purse. "Oh, it's you," she said. "I heard the door."

Cora's cornflower-blue eyes were wide. Her cheeks were flushed. She seemed rather agitated, almost flustered.

"Aunt Cora. Are you all right?"

"Of course I'm all right. Why wouldn't I be all right?"

That brought Sherry up short. The reason for Cora Felton not being all right was usually alcohol. Cora had been on the wagon for some time. Still, there was always the danger of a relapse.

"So, what have you been doing?" Sherry asked.

That flustered Cora even more. "Doing? How can I do anything when you drive off, leave me without a car?"

"Where did you want to go?"

"Nowhere. But if I wanted to, I couldn't. I'm trapped here all day long."

"It's three o'clock."

"That's not the point. The point is, we only have one car, so I'm stuck here when you go off to work and leave me."

"I'm a substitute nursery-school teacher. I average two or three days a *month*."

"And on those days, I'm stuck."

"You want me to get my own car?"

"We can't afford another car."

"Maybe you'll get one for your birthday," Sherry ventured tentatively.

Cora's eyes narrowed. "Sherry. Don't you dare tell anyone it's my birthday."

"It's a matter of public record."

"Sure, if you knew to look. If you didn't know it was my birthday, you wouldn't know to look."

"Aunt Cora . . ."

"Why are we talking about this? No one knows it's my birthday. And don't you dare say a word. It's bad enough getting older without everyone making a fuss."

"You don't want anyone to know?" Sherry said.

"I always knew you were bright." Cora patted Sherry on the cheek, opened the front door.

"Where are you going?"

"Out for a cigarette. Since you won't let me smoke in here."

Sherry sniffed the air. "You've *been* smoking in here."

"Well, you weren't home."

Cora wrenched the cigarettes out of her purse and went on out. Sherry closed the door behind her. Cora frowned, fished in her purse for her lighter, lit up a smoke. She wished she'd had more notice of Sherry coming home. That was the problem with the office in the back of the house. You didn't always hear the car.

Cora managed to take another drag before Sherry burst out the front door.

"Aunt Cora! You're on-line."

"So?"

"You can't walk off and leave the computer on-line. It ties up the phone."

"You expecting a call?"

"And when did you learn to use the computer anyway? I thought you barely knew how to turn it on."

"You *left* it on."

"But you can't smoke in the office. Do you know what it smells like?"

"Do you know what you *sound* like? My head's spinning. Pick a topic and go with it."

"Oh, get in here." Sherry pointed to the cigarette. "I mean, put that out and get in here."

Cora ground the cigarette out with her heel, followed Sherry meekly through the house, into the study. Cora placed the butt in the china saucer on the desk.

Sherry ignored the makeshift ashtray, pointed to the computer. "Do you know how many screens you have open?"

"No. How would I?"

"Well, for one thing you could count the little icons down here at the bottom. That will tell you how many programs you've shrunk."

"If you say so."

"What do you mean, if I say so? You opened and shrunk them." Sherry looked at her aunt in amazement. "Cora. You actually know what you're doing."

"Well, let's not get carried away."

"That's excellent advice, Cora. Coming from a woman doing seven things at once."

"Seven?"

"Well, let's see." Sherry began expanding and shrinking the icons at the bottom of the screen to see what they were. "You're on Amazon.com." Sherry shrunk the icon, opened another. "And on Barnes and Noble. And on the Advanced Book Exchange."

"I was comparing prices."

"And on the *As the World Turns* website."

"I missed an episode."

"How could you miss an episode?"

"I was on-line."

"No kidding. You're on eBay, where you appear to be bidding on a makeup kit."

"Right," Cora said. "I don't have a makeup kit. And you know how often I appear on television."

"And a hedge trimmer," Sherry said accusingly.

"Look how cheap it is."

"We don't have a hedge."

"What's your point?"

"You also appear to be in a chat room with someone named Ralph."

"Ralph is very nice."

"I'm glad you think so."

"Huh?" Cora leaned forward, peered at the message on the screen. Flushed slightly. "Well, maybe I misjudged Ralph. He certainly *seemed* nice."

"I'm sure he is. If you're particularly limber." Sherry

shook her head. "I was wondering why I was getting so much spam lately."

"So much what?"

"Junk e-mail's called spam, Cora. Even you should know that. You attract it by the places you go on the Internet. And the places the people you contact have gone. I would imagine your friend Ralph has been fairly active."

"Are you enjoying beating me up like this?" Cora demanded. "So what was it you wanted to tell me, before you got distracted playing Humiliate the Aunt?"

"Oh. Nothing. It just occurred to me, you've got way too much time on your hands."

The phone rang. Sherry Carter scooped it up.

"Sherry, hi. It's Becky Baldwin."

Sherry instantly tensed at the sound of her rival, even though she and Becky had basically buried the hatchet. Becky *was* Aaron Grant's high school sweetheart, and she wasn't about to let Sherry forget it. And Becky was stunningly beautiful and a lawyer, to boot, a woman whose career was often of interest to young reporter Grant.

"What's up, Becky?" Sherry tried to sound casual.

"Actually, I was calling Cora. Is she there?"

"Yeah. Just a minute." Sherry covered the phone, passed it to Cora. "Becky Baldwin for you."

"You're kidding. What does she want?"

"She didn't say."

Cora took the phone. "Yeah, Becky. What's up?"

"You want a job?"

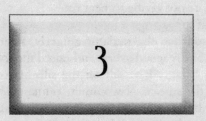

3

BECKY BALDWIN'S OFFICE DID not exactly inspire confidence. A one-room affair over the pizza parlor, it boasted an exposed radiator, cracked windows, and peeling paint. Judging from her office, it was hard to imagine the woman had any clients at all.

Becky, on the other hand, was as attractive as her office was drab. She had golden-blond hair, blue eyes, high cheekbones, long lashes, and perfectly understated makeup, which was imperceptible on the one hand, but managed on the other to dramatically highlight her exquisite eyebrows and lips. Her purple pants suit was at the same time attractive and trendy *and* nononsense and businesslike. Becky looked as if she'd be right at home in some high-powered Madison Avenue law office.

Becky sat at her battered metal desk. Cora sank down in the overstuffed client's chair, and yanked her cigarettes out of her purse. "All right. Shoot."

Becky pointed. "Out the window, if you please."

Cora groaned. "Oh, hell, I forgot." She heaved

herself from her chair, eyed the radiator under the window with suspicion. "Is that thing off? I burned myself the last time."

"They're not giving us heat yet."

"Is that so?"

Cora touched the radiator gingerly, ascertained it was cold. She reached over it and raised the frame window. She balanced herself on the sill, lit a cigarette, blew out the smoke. "I wouldn't wanna tell you your business, but frankly your salesmanship sucks. If I weren't bored out of my mind at the moment, I'd be out that door. But I'm here to tell ya, it's gonna take a pretty juicy case to keep me perched on this ledge."

"It's a good case."

"I don't want a good case. I want a rotten case with salacious details. Sex and scandal and murder and mayhem. Is that too much to ask?"

Becky smiled. "Actually, you're right on the money."

Cora blinked. "I beg your pardon?"

"Are you familiar with the case of Darryl Daigue?"

"No, why?"

"He was arrested for rape and murder."

"Now you're talkin'! And you're his lawyer?"

"No."

"No?"

"It's complicated."

"Then you'd better uncomplicate it, if you expect me to stick around."

"I've been retained by Darryl's sister."

"To act on his behalf?"

"That's right."

Cora snorted in disgust. "And you wonder why people hate lawyers. Talk about splitting hairs. I don't care if this creep hired you or the creep's sister hired you. As far as I'm concerned, you're the creep's lawyer." She frowned. "Unless he's hired someone else. Does he have another lawyer?"

"Not at the moment."

"Then you're his lawyer. 'Nuff said. Who'd he rape, and who'd he kill?"

"According to his sister, Darryl didn't kill anyone."

"Yeah, right. Who's he *supposed* to have raped and killed?"

"A girl named Anita Dryer."

"A girl? How old is this corpse?"

"Anita Dryer was only seventeen."

"I'm starting to like this less. Is there any chance your client didn't do it?"

"Like I say, he's not really my client."

"Yeah, yeah, fine. Any chance the perp whose sister hired you to be his mouthpiece did the dirty deed?"

"Yeah. A big one."

"Well, there's a refreshing admission from an attorney. A nice change from the usual stonewall. What's the matter, didn't they pay you enough?"

Becky's face hardened, belied her tender years. "Let's get one thing straight: I won't whitewash this guy if he did it. If he's as bad as they say, I don't want anything to do with it."

"What happened to innocent until proven guilty?"

"That doesn't apply in this case."

"Whoa! Somebody pushed *your* buttons!" Cora slipped down off the sill, took one last greedy drag, and flicked her cigarette out the window. "Let me be sure I got this straight. You want me to investigate this guy so you can make a decision as to whether you want to represent him?"

"I suppose you could say that."

Cora frowned. "I'm missing something here. Tell me, where did this murder take place?"

"Right here in town."

"Oh, really? Well, that's what's bothering me. How come I never heard of it?"

"Well, you're relatively new in town."

Cora blinked. "I beg your pardon?"

"This happened before you came."

"Is that right?" Cora cocked her head. "You mind telling me exactly when this rape and murder took place?"

"Twenty years ago."

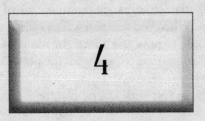

4

CORA FELTON YANKED THE pack out of her purse and lit
another cigarette.

Becky pointed.

"Don't out-the-window me. I'd just as soon walk
out the door. I don't like to be played."

"No one's playing you."

"Oh, no," Cora shot back sarcastically. "You call me
in here with a job. You say it's a murder case. You lead
me to believe it's a current murder case—and don't
bother telling me you didn't *say* it was a current murder case, I *know* you didn't *say* it was a current case, you
very carefully phrased things to avoid the truth."

"Cora—"

"Twenty years is a long time. I'd be surprised if this
case was still pending."

"No kidding."

"Just what *was* the disposition of the case?"

"Darryl Daigue was found guilty of murder. He
was sentenced to life in prison."

"Without possibility of parole?"

"That's right."

"And I assume he's behind bars now?"

"Yes, he is."

"Well, that changes the complexion of the case somewhat. When you said you weren't Mr. Daigue's attorney, I didn't know just how right you were. Before I go, would you care to tell me what the present situation actually is?"

"Just what you said. Darryl Daigue is serving a life sentence without possibility of parole. His sister has asked me to look into the situation to see if something might be done."

"With regard to what?"

"Parole, of course."

Cora snorted. "What exactly does *without possibility of parole* mean to you?"

"It means exactly that. However, if new information should arise . . ."

"What sort of information?"

"Indicating he might not have done it."

"You mean proving him innocent."

"At least casting some doubt on his guilt."

"You think there's any question?"

"I don't know. That's what I'd like to find out."

"Why?"

"What do you mean, why? Because his sister's hired me."

"To get dear old brother out of jail?"

"Yes."

Cora shook her head. "I don't like it. I don't have a brother, but if I did, and it came to getting him out of jail, I doubt if I'd have waited twenty years to try."

"You see why I'd like the story checked out?"

"I see why you *suspect* the story. Why you want it checked out is your business."

"Fair enough. Will you do it?"

"What do you want me to do?"

"Review the case. Talk to Darryl. Talk to the witnesses. See if his story holds up."

"Why can't you do that?"

"I could. But I don't want to obligate myself by taking the sister's money. On the other hand, I don't want to work without being paid."

"You and me both. If I do your dirty work, who's footing the bill?"

"I am. Unless you come up with something. Then I'll take the case, and pass the expenses on to the client."

"But that point shouldn't influence my judgment," Cora said sarcastically.

"Not at all. If you want to stick me with the tab, it's your call."

Cora's cigarette ash was the length of a pool cue. "Oh, hell!" She cupped her hand underneath it, hurried across the room. Miraculously, the ash held up. Cora flicked it out the window, tossed the butt out behind it, turned back to face Becky Baldwin. "What are the facts of the case? I'm not saying I'll take it, but you might as well fill me in."

Becky opened a file folder on her desk. "Darryl Daigue was a short-order cook. He worked at the diner on Route 9. Before they built the mall. Kids would come in for burgers and milk shakes. Nothing fancy. Just your simple diner food. According to the prosecution theory of the case, Darryl used to chat up the kids. He formed a relationship with Anita Dryer.

Got her to meet him on his dinner break. Met her at the old icehouse."

"What's that?"

"Just what it sounds like. A shaded wooden shack for storing blocks of ice. From back in the old days when there were iceboxes instead of refrigerators."

"Uh-huh." Cora managed to keep a straight face listening to Becky Baldwin tell *her* about the old days.

"Darryl got Anita to meet him there. He made a move on her. She resisted. He strangled her."

"Before or after he raped her?"

"He never actually raped her."

"I thought you said rape/murder."

"That's what he was originally charged with. Anita was found naked. The papers played it up. Then the medical examination showed she hadn't been raped."

"So what evidence was he convicted on?"

"Actually, damn thin. The medical examiner fixed the time of death to coincide with when Darryl got off work. Then there were witnesses who saw him talking to her in the diner. Big deal. It would be strange if there weren't. And one witness thought he saw the two of them heading in the direction of the icehouse."

"And that's it?"

"In terms of witnesses."

"What else was there?"

"Like I said, damn little. The autopsy indicated trace amounts of marijuana. That was admitted into evidence at the trial. Darryl Daigue had half an ounce of marijuana in his backpack. That wasn't."

"Wasn't what?"

"Admitted into evidence. Darryl's attorney got it suppressed on the grounds of an illegal search and seizure. The jury never knew about it. Assuming they didn't watch TV or read the papers. The jurors weren't sequestered."

"So you assume they knew about the grass?"

Becky shrugged. "Not my place to make that assumption. And God forbid the prosecution would ever leak something like that to the jury pool."

"Say they didn't. Is there any other bit of evidence you haven't told me about?"

Becky picked up a heavy sheaf of papers, flipped it in Cora's direction. "Here's the transcript. You can read it yourself if you like."

"What will I find?"

"Nothing. Absolutely nothing. No more than what I told you."

Cora frowned. "I don't understand."

"Join the club. Here's a man convicted two decades ago on the skimpiest of evidence. Suddenly a sister gets it in her head she'd like to see him freed. To the extent of being willing to spring for some dough."

"The retainer you haven't accepted?"

"That's right."

"I don't think you mentioned how much she offered."

"I don't think I did."

Cora scowled, frustrated.

"So will you do it?" Becky persevered. "Otherwise I'll just have to get someone else."

"And you'd have to pay *them*," Cora said archly.

"I'll pay *you*. I'll give you a two-hundred-dollar cash advance. Will you do it?"

Cora shook her head. "Nope."

"You're not interested?"

"I didn't say that. But I'm not taking any two-hundred-dollar cash advance. I'll do what you're doing. I'll look into it, see if I want to get involved."

"Fair enough," Becky said.

Cora peered at her searchingly. "You sure there's nothing you're holding back? You have no idea why this man's in jail?"

Becky shook her head. "I'm hoping you can tell me."

5

THE BRANDON STATE PENITENTIARY was in a wooded mesa in north-central Connecticut, a good hour and a half drive from Bakerhaven. It wasn't that far, but it was accessible only by a tangled series of back roads on which the speed limit ranged from twenty-five to fifty, with a tendency toward the former, and God forbid you should get behind a truck. Which is precisely what Cora did, and it was miles before she could get around it, and then only by zipping by in a no-passing zone that must have been so designated largely for Sunday drivers, because there was adequate visibility, and you didn't have to be Mario Andretti to pass a car there. Or whoever the hell the latest racing sensation was—Cora knew she was dating herself with Mario. At any rate, she shot by the truck, cursing mightily at the SUV that came speeding around the curve at her from the opposite direction. For a second she was young James Dean, playing chicken in *Rebel Without a Cause*. The terrified driver of the SUV hit the horn and the brakes. Cora floored it, managed to squeeze in front of the truck without actually running the SUV off the road. Cora grinned in satisfaction, gunned the Toyota around the curve.

Ahead the road forked. Cora grunted, snatched her directions off the passenger seat, and squinted at them while trying to keep one eye on the road. Cora had been pleased as punch when she'd found the directions on MapQuest and printed them out all by herself, but it was a pain in the fanny trying to actually read the damn thing. There were a whole slew of directions, numbered one through nineteen, such as "12: Bear right through intersection 3/4 mile," which didn't really do you much good because by the time you found number twelve and read all that, you'd probably *gone* three-quarters of a mile, if not farther, and Cora couldn't see why the directions didn't just say "Bear right at the Getty station," like a normal person would.

Eventually, Cora reached the prison, a massive compound in a clearing on a plateau nestled between two mountains. Departure from the prison, Cora noted, was discouraged by a smooth, twenty-foot-high stone wall, topped with barbed wire. There were no gun turrets. Apparently, the wall was sufficient. Or, Cora thought cynically, casting an eye on the MapQuest directions, the prison authorities counted on the fact that convicts breaking out would have no hope of finding their way.

Cora drove up to the front gate, a wrought-iron affair some two stories high, fitted snugly in the stone wall. Up close, Cora could see the barbed wire on top was actually razor wire. Scaling the wall would be a painful prospect indeed.

Next to the front gate was a sentry box. The guard on duty looked like a prisoner himself. His crew cut was as short as you could get without actually denuding your head. He had a scar on his cheek. He wore a gun on his belt. A rifle was propped up behind him in the box. The guard stepped out, but not to open the gate. Instead, he motioned for Cora to roll down her window.

"Park around the side," he told her. It was an order, not an invitation. "If you don't want people pawing through your purse, leave it in the car. Leave anything sharp in the car. If you're wearing a hat pin, take it off."

"I'm not wearing a hat," Cora said.

The guard never cracked a smile. "Any brooch, safety pin, or whathaveyou. It can be your lucky pin, it won't be so lucky when you have to surrender it."

"You're not exactly filling me with confidence," Cora said.

"That's not my job." The guard pointed. "Park over there. Don't leave your keys in your car. Roll up the windows, lock the doors."

"Aren't the prisoners inside?"

"Yes, they are, and that's where we wanna keep 'em."

Cora recognized that statement, though fundamentally true, to be blissfully illogical, and perhaps even a non sequitur. However, she didn't prolong the conversation, merely followed the road around the side of the compound to where another forty or fifty cars were parked. Cora locked hers and went to go into the prison.

Only there wasn't a door. A bare stone wall greeted her at the mouth of the parking lot. She was forced to retrace her path to the gate and the guard.

"Hmm. Didn't believe me about the purse," the guard observed.

"They're really going to search my purse?" Cora said.

"No, they'll just hold on to it. You got anything in it you want, you better get it out now."

Cora flushed, as she realized she had a gun in her purse. She considered going back to her car. It was a long way. "Just these." She pulled out her cigarettes and lighter. "They'll hold my purse at the desk?"

"They'll hold your cigarettes too. The visiting room is a no-smoke zone."

"Are you kidding me?"

"I wish I were."

The guard jerked a ring of keys off his belt. Cora waited for him to unlock the gate. He didn't, of course. The gate leading into the courtyard was for trucks. Instead he unlocked the normal-sized solid steel door to the left of it.

Cora went inside, found a bored-looking corrections officer sitting at a desk in what could have passed for a reception office. File cabinets lined the walls.

The corrections officer swung his feet down off the desk, and grunted, "Yeah?" He was a surly fellow, but compared to the guard, looked positively benign.

"I'm here to see Darryl Daigue."

"You his mother?"

"You want a fat lip?"

"No offense, lady. Who are you?"

"I'm a private investigator."

"Right. And I'm the Queen of Sheba." He handed her a clipboard with a form attached. "Fill this out. You plan to surrender that purse?"

"May I keep it with me?"

"No, you may not."

"Then why'd you ask?"

"To see if I had a fight on my hands. I take it I don't."

"Can I keep my cigarettes?"

"You can't smoke in there."

"You're smoking."

"I'm not in there."

"Can I smoke here?"

"You always this much trouble?"

"I'm a pussycat. One with a nicotine addiction. If I can't have one there, how's about I have one while I fill out your form?"

"And I won't have to pry your purse away from you with the Jaws of Life?"

"Deal."

Cora sat down, lit a cigarette, and started filling out the form. She had no trouble with NAME, ADDRESS, TELEPHONE #, and SEX, though for the last she was tempted to answer *Yes*.

The next blank was DATE OF BIRTH. Cora left that blank, moved on to NAME OF PRISONER, and filled in *Darryl Daigue*.

Next was RELATION TO PRISONER. Cora almost wrote *None,* but didn't want to make waves. Instead, she put *Private Investigator.*

On the bottom of the form it asked the question, DO YOU HAVE A CAR IN THE PARKING LOT? Assuming yes, it then asked MAKE, MODEL, YEAR, and LICENSE PLATE #. It then asked for DRIVER'S LICENSE #. Cora blithely made these numbers up.

Cora filled in the form leisurely, giving herself time to finish her cigarette. When she was done, she handed the clipboard back to the corrections officer at the desk.

He looked it over. "You left out birth date."

"Did I?" Cora smiled. "Well, it's next week. November 1."

"I'll send you a gift," the officer said dryly. "What year were you born?"

"Why?"

"I gotta fill out the form. When were you born?"

"That's a very impolite thing to ask a lady." When the officer said nothing, she added impatiently, "Oh, for goodness' sake, give me the form!" She snatched the clipboard, filled in the date, handed it back.

The corrections officer looked at the form, blinked. "Nineteen *seventy*?"

Cora leaned in confidentially and winked. "Promise you won't say anything. The girls think I'm twenty-five."

Cora wasn't sure, but she thought the corrections officer had a narrow escape from a smile. He picked up the phone, pressed the intercom button, and punched in a number. "I have a female visitor for one of the prisoners. Could you send the matron?"

"Matron?" Cora asked.

"She'll be right down."

The matron made Cora look like an anorexic fashion model. Weighing in at two hundred fifty pounds of solid muscle, and sporting a flat face and a broken nose, the woman might have gone a few rounds with George Foreman, or perhaps tried to steal his charcoal grill. She studied Cora as if sizing up a side of beef, then crooked a finger in her direction. "Come on, dearie."

Cora could think of few things one could say on network television she preferred less to be called than *dearie,* but she wasn't about to pick a fight. Instead, she managed her most proper "Harrumph!" and followed the woman down a corridor and into a small side room with a chair, a coatrack, and a bank of six metal gym lockers.

"Okay, dearie. Take off your shoes, jacket, and skirt."

Cora raised her eyebrows. "I beg your pardon?"

"No one brings anything into the visiting room we don't want brung. You got something for the prisoner, you give it to me. If they decide he should have it, they'll see that he gets it."

"I don't have anything for the prisoner."

"That makes it easier. Take your things off. You can use those coat hangers on the rack there."

"Suppose I don't want to?"

The matron shook her head. "That's a problem. You were a prisoner and gave me lip, I'd take 'em off for you. But you're just a visitor. You don't wanna co-operate, that's your call. I can't touch you. But then you can't see the prisoner. See how it works, dearie?"

"How extensive is this search?"

"I'm not gonna touch you. I'm gonna run a metal detector over you like they do at the airport. You got any reason why it should buzz, tell me now."

The search completed, Cora was led down another corridor, where another bored-looking guard at a desk pushed a button releasing a rather formidable-looking steel door.

"There you go. Go on in, make yourself comfort-able. The prisoner will be right in. You buzz the door when you want to come out."

Cora walked in and the door slammed behind her. She shuddered at the clunking of the huge locks and bolts.

The visiting room was not much larger than your average phone booth. In New York City, Cora thought cynically, it would rent for fifteen hundred a month as a studio apartment.

A single chair sat facing a plate-glass window. The window might have been a mirror. On the other side was a bare room with a chair and a door.

A phone hung on the wall next to the window. There was no dial, no buttons, no numbers of any kind. The telephone receiver was connected only to the phone on the other side.

The wall and window were totally solid. There was no slot, no door, no drawer, no bars, no open space of any kind, through which fingertips could be touched or a cigarette could be passed. What, Cora wondered, was that search all about? It occurred to her the matron was probably so grouchy because she knew she was performing a useless task.

After what seemed forever, but was probably not more than thirty minutes, the door on the other side of the window opened, and a guard ushered in Darryl Daigue.

And one mystery was solved.

6

DARRYL DAIGUE WAS A tall, thin man with stringy bald hair. Cora realized that wasn't quite right. He would have been bald, but for a few wisps of hair on top and a fringe around the ears. He had a hawk nose and heavy tortoise-shell glasses. He had chains on his wrists and chains on his feet. He jingled as he shuffled along. At least Cora assumed he jingled. With the thick pane of glass, she couldn't hear a thing.

The guard leading Darryl Daigue was the size of a small steam engine. He had a hand on Daigue's shoulder, guiding him to the chair. The guard sat the prisoner down, looked through the window, saw Cora, and rolled his eyes. He retreated to the door and stood with his back to it, arms folded, face impassive, as if he weren't there.

Before Darryl Daigue even opened his mouth Cora knew why the jury had found him guilty. Daigue *looked* guilty. His face seemed etched in a permanent sneer. It was a nasty face, the face of a man who could easily rape and kill an innocent girl. And it wasn't just the passage of twenty years' time, and hard time at that, prison time, the type of time to desensitize a man, burn out his soul, leave him a bitter, angry wreck. No, what Cora sensed was something inherent in his nature, some vibration Daigue gave off, the feeling that everything wasn't quite all right. Cora could sense it, and she realized the jury must have sensed it too. That was why he had been sentenced on such skimpy evidence, the admission of his marijuana stash notwithstanding.

There was something in his eyes, and not just the usual shifty eyes of a criminal. No, Darryl Daigue's eyes were steel-gray, steady as a rock, unblinking.

Uncaring.

Unfeeling.

He sat watching her, not moving a muscle, just staring at her like a cobra about to strike.

Cora repressed a shudder, picked up the phone.

After several seconds, he did so too.

"Darryl Daigue? I'm Cora Felton."

He didn't answer, just stared at her as if she were a creature from another planet.

"Are you Darryl Daigue?" Cora persisted.

"What do you want?" he demanded.

"I just want to talk to you."

"Why?"

"I'm a private investigator."

His guffaw was rude. Ugly.

Cora ignored it, said, "I'd like to get you out of here."

That got his interest. His dead eyes narrowed. "What, are you nuts? I'm here for life."

"Not necessarily."

"Yeah, necessarily. No possibility of parole."

"There is if I find new evidence."

"Fat chance of that."

"You mean there is no evidence?"

"After twenty years? You're mental, lady. You're a real head case."

Cora muttered a pithy expletive and slammed down the phone.

That got Darryl's attention. He waved his hands. She could see him mouthing the words, "Hey! Hey!"

Cora picked up the phone again. "Let's start over. A lawyer asked me to look into your case, see if there's any hope of you getting out. On the surface, your chances would appear slim. Since you happen to agree with that assessment, I see no reason to pursue this any further—"

"Wait a minute, wait a minute. A lawyer asked you to look into me?"

"That's right."

"Why?"

"That's between you and the lawyer."

"*What's* between me and the lawyer? I haven't *got* a lawyer. I didn't even have a lawyer at my trial."

"You had a public defender."

"Yeah, sure. He didn't know anything. The judge had to run his case for him."

"Oh, really? It was my understanding you were caught with marijuana and it was suppressed at trial."

He snorted. "So the jurors never heard about it. And if you believe that one, lady . . ."

"I'm not saying the jurors never heard about it. I'm saying the lawyer you keep putting down got it suppressed."

"Well, excuse me, lady. Like I should be the guy's

cheerleader. My lawyer got me a life sentence. Gee, a regular Perry Mason."

"You want my help or not?"

"What, if I bad-mouth my lawyer you'll walk out on me? That seems a little harsh."

"I don't give a damn what you say about your lawyer. The question is whether you want to cooperate with *me*."

Daigue thought that over. Cora could practically see the wheels turning in his brain.

"Okay."

"Fine," Cora said. "Tell me about it."

He blinked. "Huh?"

"Your case. Tell me about your case. Why are you in jail?"

"Oh, for Christ's sake!"

"I know what the prosecution says you did. Tell me what you really did."

"I didn't do anything."

"No wonder you got convicted."

"Huh?"

"The flat denial is less than persuasive." Cora was pleased with that statement. She thought she sounded like Sherry. "Tell me what happened." As he opened his mouth, Cora put up her hand. "And don't say nothing happened. Something did happen. A young girl wound up dead. Your contention is you didn't do it?"

"Of course I didn't do it."

"You must not have had a good alibi."

"I had a good alibi. I just didn't have a good lawyer."

"What was your alibi?"

"I was working."

"At the diner?"

"That's right."

"You were a short-order cook."

"Sometimes."

"What do you mean by that?"

"Sometimes I cooked. Sometimes I worked the counter."

"Is this important?"

"The cops figured it was."

"Why?"

"If I didn't work the counter, I wouldn't know the girl."

"You met her working the counter?"

"I knew who she was."

"You talked to her?"

"Of course I talked to her. I took her order."

"You took her order that day?"

"Whenever."

"Whenever what?"

"Whenever I worked the counter."

It was like pulling teeth. Cora took a breath. "According to the transcript, you were cooking that day. You wouldn't have taken Anita Dryer's order. So if you talked to her, it would have been about something else."

"But I didn't talk to her."

"That's not what Ray Tucker says."

He grimaced. "That dweeb!"

"According to Ray, you came to the window between the kitchen and the counter, and you talked to Anita through there."

He shook his head. "That is so unfair."

"Why?"

"That's the pickup window. Where the waitresses

get the food. There's a little bell on the counter. You put the plate on the counter, and you look out, and if the waitress isn't looking your way, you ring the bell. I look out that window every time I put an order up."

"Ray says you talked to Anita, and that she asked you when you got off."

"Sure he did."

"You didn't do that?"

"No."

"Then why'd Ray say so?"

"You figure it out."

"You mean *he* killed her?"

"That wimp? He wouldn't have the guts."

"Then what do you mean?"

Daigue shrugged. "He's lying, he's exaggerating, he's making it up. He's trying to be a big man. He was on TV, you know, same as me. He liked being on TV."

The prospect of getting Darryl Daigue out of jail was seeming less and less attractive. "What time did you get off work?"

"Ten."

Cora, who'd already formed the next question, stopped with her mouth open. "And— Did you say *ten*?"

"That's right. Ten o'clock. Way after the murder."

"But the transcript says you got off work at eight."

"The transcript is wrong."

"How can that be?"

"I told you. I had a lousy lawyer."

"But everyone testified you got off at eight."

"Yeah? Who's everyone? The boss said I got off at

eight. The boss wasn't there. The cook who relieved me said I got off at eight, 'cause that's when he relieved me. And Ray said I got off at eight 'cause everyone else says that, and Ray wants to be a big star on TV. Only he wasn't there at eight, he just claims he heard me say it to the girl."

"But if the cook relieved you at eight . . ."

"Doesn't mean I left. I left the kitchen, yeah, but I worked the counter from eight to ten."

Cora felt a tingling on the back of her neck. "What are you talking about?"

"What do you think I'm talking about? I'm talking about the fact I didn't do it. I *couldn't* have done it. I didn't get off work till ten."

"But you couldn't have worked eight till ten. Someone would have known."

"Someone did."

"Who?"

"Ricky."

"Who's Ricky?"

"Ricky Gleason. The kid I worked the counter for."

Cora's mouth fell open. "Wait a minute. Are you saying Ricky Gleason was the counter boy and you took his shift?"

Darryl Daigue looked disgusted, as if she were an idiot for being so dense. "Not his shift. How could I take his shift? I'm cooking in the kitchen. Just the last two hours. From eight till ten."

"Ricky Gleason was working the counter while you were cooking. When you got off at eight you relieved him and he left?"

"Now you got it. Finally. I was beginning to think I was talking to the wall."

Cora looked at him incredulously. "But if that's true, why didn't Ricky come forward at the trial?"

" 'Cause he didn't want anyone to know where he'd been." His scowl was scathing. "I gotta spell it out for you, lady? Ricky went out to meet Anita Dryer."

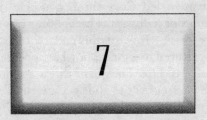

7

CORA FELTON WAS COLLECTING her drawstring purse from the corrections officer at the front desk when a dapper little man in a blue suit and a gray knit tie came bustling up. He had a face like a cherub and he was beaming all over it.

"Miss Felton, how are you? I just heard you were here. I certainly hope you've been extended every courtesy."

That was not exactly how Cora would have described the experience. "Absolutely," she said. "I believe the matron even apologized before she mauled me."

The little man looked shocked. "Oh, my goodness."

"I'm kidding," Cora said. "Everything's hunky-dory. I will not be filing suit."

"I'm certainly glad to hear it. Oh, excuse me. I'm Warden Prufrock. Perhaps we could have a few words before you go? It might facilitate things. In the event you decide to come back."

The last seemed almost a question. Cora ignored it, said, "Sure. Let's do that."

"Fine. If you'd just follow me."

The warden led Cora through a side door and down a series of hallways. The lighting was dim, the walls bare brick. Toward the end of their journey Prufrock gestured to a guard in what appeared to be a bulletproof glass box. The guard threw a switch, causing a gate of iron bars to slide on a well-oiled track. Cora followed the warden in, repressed a shudder at the clang of the bars closing behind her.

They reached a massive steel door. The warden unlocked it, and ushered her into a small but homey office: oak desk, overstuffed chairs, red drapes, and a portable bar.

The warden motioned to a chair and asked, "Drink?"

Cora grimaced. "I'm on the wagon."

Prufrock looked disappointed, probably figuring under those circumstances he couldn't have one himself. "Do you smoke?"

"Is the Pope Polish?"

"Excellent." He opened a humidor on his desk, took out a cigar. "I suppose you prefer cigarettes."

"You suppose wrong," Cora replied. "Chuck one of those things over here, and let's fire it up."

The warden smiled, extended her a cigar, then came around the desk to light it. He lit his own, sat back in his desk chair, puffed contentedly.

Cora blew a smoke ring. "What do you want, Prufrock?"

He frowned. She wasn't sure if it was the question, or the realization she was better at smoke rings.

"I've been warden here for ten years. In that time,

things have gone pretty well. Not that these are model citizens. Occasionally they kill each other. Occasionally they riot. So far no one's gotten out, no one's killed a guard. Not on my watch."

The warden seemed damned proud. Cora couldn't help marveling how modest some achievements were. "I wasn't thinking of organizing a prison break," she told him.

"Ah, but that's not quite true now, is it, Miss Felton? You're here to see a prisoner. You have no relationship to him whatsoever. One might wonder why."

"Would you be the one who might be wondering?"

"Miss Felton. You are not exactly unknown. You have a famous crossword-puzzle column. You appear on TV."

"You were hoping for an autograph?"

"I was hoping for some cooperation. I find it hard to believe you are considering writing a crossword puzzle around the exploits of Darryl Daigue. On the other hand, you have something of a reputation for delving into crime. You fancy yourself an amateur detective."

"Oh? Who told you that?"

"No one had to tell me that, Miss Felton. It's in the papers. On TV. Your exploits are not exactly unknown."

Cora leaned forward, knocked the ash off her cigar into the crystal ashtray on his desk. "What's your point?"

"Let's be blunt, Miss Felton. In case you were thinking of clearing Darryl Daigue, you're making a huge mistake."

"And why would that be?"

"Because he's guilty, of course. Guilty as sin."

Cora smiled. "How would you know that, Warden? He was here when you got here."

"Yes, he was. And he'll be here when I leave. He's a bad one, Darryl Daigue. Hell, you met him. Can't you tell?"

"So he's not Mr. Congeniality. That doesn't make him guilty."

"No, but other things do."

"What other things?"

"Twelve jurors, for one. In case you've forgotten."

"Juries aren't infallible."

"No, and they're not always wrong, either." The warden tried a smoke ring. It wasn't as good as Cora's but it was probably sufficient to save face. "I'm not up to sparring with a wordsmith. Straight out, what's your interest in Darryl Daigue?"

"A lawyer asked me to look into it."

"What lawyer might that be?"

"I can't tell you that."

"Why not?"

"Not my place. Lawyer wants to tell you, that's the lawyer's business."

"I could always find out."

"Good. Then I'm off the hook."

The warden frowned. "I'm not sure I'm getting through to you, Miss Felton. Let me try again. You seem like a good sort. I would hate to see you getting mixed up with a bad sort."

"Why?"

His frown deepened. "What do you mean, why?"

Cora smiled. "What difference could it possibly make? You tell me Darryl Daigue is as guilty as sin. He's in for life without possibility of parole, and you tell me there's absolutely nothing I can do to help him. So why should you care if I try?"

He frowned, chewed his cigar. "You're a celebrity. What you do is news. **PUZZLE LADY REOPENS DAIGUE CASE.** Pretty nasty headline. I would hate to read that."

"Yet you insist it would do no good."

"Technically, yes. On the other hand, the case is twenty years old. It would be hard to prove it again. Not that we'd have to do that. The burden of proof would be on you. But just let the press get wind of it, and some bleeding-heart liberals will fall all over themselves sticking up for Darryl Daigue. The same people, by the way, who would be championing the victim in the case if he were *out* of jail. You see what I mean?"

"You got a tough job, Warden."

"You plan to make it tougher?"

"Not if I can help it. I'm not looking for publicity. If I can fly under the radar, it's fine by me."

The warden wasn't mollified. "So you intend to continue with this?"

"I have no idea. I'm just getting started. I have little to go on, one way or another."

"Damn."

"You said yourself, what can it hurt?" Cora stood up. "Thanks for the cigar." She stubbed it out in the ashtray.

The warden came around his desk. "I wish you'd reconsider. Before you go ahead, there's something you should know. Even if you were able to prove Darryl innocent—which you can't—he's probably caused enough mischief here to keep him locked up for the rest of his life."

"That's hardly fair, Warden. Throw an innocent man in jail, and then fault him for not liking it."

"Darryl isn't innocent."

Cora smiled. "Your hypothetical, not mine, Warden." She patted him on the cheek. "But set your mind at rest. If Daigue's guilty, I have no intention of setting him free."

8

CORA FELTON FROWNED AS Becky Baldwin ordered a tossed salad. Becky was young and thin, but was still ordering rabbit food. The fact Becky Baldwin was so glamorously slim *because* she watched her diet never occurred to Cora. She hesitated only a moment before ordering a double bacon cheeseburger with fried onion rings, then, in a fit of remorse, topped it off with a Diet Coke.

Becky and Cora were lunching in the Wicker Basket, a popular, homey Bakerhaven restaurant. It boasted red-and-white-checkered tablecloths. In all the times she had been there, Cora had yet to see a wicker basket.

"So," Becky said, "why are we meeting here?"

"You're buying me lunch. In lieu of paying my fee."

Becky's face showed disappointment. "You mean you struck out?"

That set Cora's teeth on edge. "I did not 'strike out.' I have more than you asked for. Whether you wish to continue is up to you. But I do not have the smoking gun that proves the man innocent. And it is quite possible I may never get it."

Cora described her meeting with Darryl Daigue.

Becky showed interest. "He has an alibi for the time of the murder?"

"So he says. Unfortunately, he's the only one saying so. You have his unsubstantiated word, which ain't worth squat."

"Even so. This wasn't in the transcript. This wasn't brought up at trial. And it should have been. His lawyer should have hit on it. It's an alternate theory that accounts for the facts of the case."

"That it is."

"So, what's the deal? Didn't he tell his lawyer?"

"He claims he did."

"Do you believe him?"

"What's the difference?"

Becky frowned. "What's the difference? If his lawyer withheld that, it would be malpractice. It would be grounds for a new trial."

"So ask his lawyer!"

"Yes, that would be so easy, wouldn't it?" Becky nibbled at her salad. "Public defenders tend to fall into two categories, Cora. Lawyers at the beginning of their careers, and those at the end. Darryl Daigue's lawyer was seventy-two at the time of the trial. Do you know how old he is now?"

"Dead?"

"Good guess. But if Darryl makes the claim, and no one contradicts it, we might have something."

"I suppose." Cora didn't sound convinced.

"What's wrong with that? The lawyer suppressed something. I could get a new trial."

"The lawyer didn't suppress anything. He just didn't put Darryl Daigue on the stand."

"Which effectively suppressed Darryl's testimony."

"Yeah, yeah, I hear you," Cora muttered. "The thing is, a lawyer is supposed to look out for his client's best interests."

"So?"

"You haven't met Darryl Daigue. Believe me, putting him on the stand would not be in his best interests."

"He projects that badly?"

"He's a creep. He's a horror show. He's thoroughly unlikable."

"So? That's something else to argue. How could the decedent possibly have been interested in such a man?"

"You're rather young, aren't you?"

Becky frowned. "What?"

"You never noticed some girls find bad boys exciting? A lot more than you'd think." Cora raised her eyebrows, cocked her head. "It seems to me I remember a certain sophisticated lawyer lady riding around on a motorcycle with a young man who turned out to be a major creep."

Becky flushed, said coolly, "You were telling me what you've got."

"Which isn't much. The guy claims he didn't do it. What a shock. What a stunner. Caught me flat-footed. And you fault his lawyer for not thinking of it."

"Anytime you're through having fun."

Cora took out her cigarettes, fired one up, looked around. "Hey, can I get an ashtray?"

The waitress hurried over. "I'm sorry. There's no smoking in the Wicker Basket."

Cora's mouth fell open. "Since when?"

"Since New York passed the law."

"This is Connecticut."

"We try to keep up with the City."

"Not with *this*. This is not *progress*. This is *repression*."

"I'm sorry. You'll have to put that out."

"How? There's no ashtray."

"You could take it outside."

"Oh, for God's sake." Cora stuck her cigarette in her glass of water, handed it to her. "Never mind the ashtray. Bring me a glass of water."

Suppressing a smile, the waitress bore away the glass.

"You gotta watch yourself," Becky told Cora. "By tomorrow the story of the prima donna Puzzle Lady will be all over town."

"Ah, the price of fame," Cora murmured sardonically.

"So, before we were so rudely interrupted, you were telling me where we stand."

"Actually, I was telling you Darryl Daigue is unlikely to be innocent. Even if he is, it would be very hard to prove. If not impossible. And even if you could, he's such an unattractive son of a bitch it would be very hard to work up any enthusiasm for getting him released."

"Then you would advise me against taking his case?"

"Ah . . ."

"See?" Becky exclaimed. "There *is* something."

"Well, that's the thing. The way I see it, there's only one real incentive for taking the case."

"What's that?"

"The warden doesn't want you to."

Cora told about the meeting in Warden Prufrock's office.

Becky listened with interest. "He did everything he could to talk you out of digging into Darryl's case?"

"He sure did. He was also very interested to know who hired me."

"Did you tell him?"

"No way. I told him I was working for an attorney. He wanted to know who. I told him I would relay that message, in case the attorney wanted to get in touch."

"Did he like that answer?"

"Not at all. He did his best to impress upon me that Darryl Daigue had been such a naughty boy in jail, he was bound to stay there even if I proved he was an altar boy. He assured me I was wasting my time."

"Why would he care?"

"He said he was afraid of the media hype of a Free Darryl Daigue movement."

"That's silly. I'm surprised he even talked to you."

"Me too. Except . . ."

"Except what?"

Cora looked sheepish. "I had to surrender my purse when I went in to see him."

"So?"

"I had a gun in it."

"Oh, for pity's sake. Why on earth did you take a gun?"

"I didn't *take* a gun. I *have* a gun. I always have a gun. I don't think about it. It never occurred to me it would make any difference. Frankly, I don't think it did."

"But the warden treated you like Typhoid Mary?"

"How does a young girl like you know about Typhoid Mary?"

"I have a law degree. It requires some basic education."

"Anyway, the warden warns us off the case. The question is, are we going to go?"

"What's your opinion?"

"My opinion is, you should see the perp yourself. Because I can't really convey the essence of his personality through mere description. You have to decide for yourself if you want to function as his attorney."

"I'd be his sister's attorney."

"Small distinction. But perhaps enough to help you sleep at night." Cora shoved the last bit of burger in her mouth, pushed back her chair. "Come on," she mumbled. "Get me out of this smoke-free hell."

9

Cora got back to the house to find Sherry Carter at the computer creating a crossword for the Puzzle Lady column.

"How'd it go?" Sherry asked.

Cora shrugged. "Becky's gonna think it over, let me know."

"What'd you tell her?"

"Same thing I told you last night. Which isn't much, when you come right down to it. She really ought to see the guy herself."

"Think she will?"

"I would, if I were her. Of course, there's a lot of things I'd do if I were her."

"Aunt Cora."

"Nothing wrong with men, dearie." Cora shuddered at the realization she'd used the same form of address as the prison matron. "Actually, there's a lot wrong with particular men. I mean in general. My second husband—"

"You were saying about the case," Sherry prompted.

The idea of Cora envisioning herself as Becky Baldwin was uncomfortable, to say the least.

"I was saying the case is only a case if Becky calls it a case. Meanwhile, I'm off duty. You going to be long? I wanna check my e-mail."

"I'll check it for you."

"You're not gonna let me check my own e-mail?"

"You can read it. I'm just going to retrieve it."

Sherry shrank Crossword Compiler to an icon, clicked on Cora's mailbox. Cora's e-mail server filled the screen.

"You have six messages," Sherry announced. "And it looks like most of them are spam."

"I get a lot of it. A surprising number of them seem to think I'm inadequately endowed."

"It's a computer-generated mailing. Don't take it personally."

"I don't want to be embarrassed in the athletic-club locker room."

"Oh, you'll get over it," Sherry assured her.

"You mind if I check my e-mail that isn't about sexual fulfillment?"

"There's only two. And they look like fan letters. They both came from your website."

"How can you tell that?"

"They came to *puzzlelady*. Your personal e-mail is *coraf*."

"Live and learn. So you gonna let me read my fan mail?"

Sherry smiled. "I don't know. Who writes the Puzzle Lady column anyway?"

"Well, it's my damn mailbox," Cora groused.

Sherry clicked on the first heading, retrieving the body of the e-mail. It read:

Dear Puzzle Lady,
*Love your column. Keep up the good work. When
are you going to update your website?*

"You haven't updated my website?" Cora said.
"Shame on you."

"Don't look at me. It's your fan."

"Oh, now it's *my* fan? What happened to 'Who
writes the Puzzle Lady column?' That message is
clearly yours. The other is probably mine. Scoot over
and let me see."

Sherry got up from the chair. "I've never seen you
so eager to get on the computer."

"I'm not eager to get on the computer. I just like to
read my own mail."

Cora sat down, moved the mouse, and retrieved
the e-mail.

The message was brief.

Dear Cora,
Best wishes.
Nancy

"Why do all my fans turn out to be women?" Cora
grumbled.

"Maybe it's *my* fan," Sherry said.

"Who could tell? It's not much of a message."

"There's an attachment."

Sherry pointed. At the far right of the screen, separated from the message by a vertical straight line, was a
tiny icon.

"Aw, hell," Cora said. "I'm not good with attach-
ments."

"Nothing to it. Just click on it."

PARTY FAVOR
by Nancy Salomon

ACROSS

1 Illegal act (foiled by the birthday gal)
6 Spill the beans
10 Enthusiastic, and then some
14 Butler's lady
15 "Othello" fellow
16 Writing on the wall
17 The birthday gal
19 Egg on
20 Sailors' assents
21 Souped-up Jaguar
22 Niece of the birthday gal
24 Has a bite
26 Cooks in a 47-Down, perhaps
27 Final transport
30 Simon Templar
31 Mil. training program
32 Early Peruvian
34 O.K. Corral name
38 The birthday gal's crime-solving cohort
42 Put-on
43 Fable feature
44 Denver-to-Detroit dir.
45 Just for laughs
48 Distress call
50 Feeds a crowd
52 Bore for ore
53 Constructor sending best wishes to the birthday gal

54 Delta rival: Abbr.
55 Not fatty
59 Naysayer
60 The birthday gal's alter ego
63 Write-off
64 In the thick of
65 Southwest desert risers
66 Single-named New Age singer
67 "The Right Stuff" org.
68 "I'm all ears"

DOWN

1 Caesar's sidekick
2 "Hello, sailor!"
3 Cut back
4 Miscalculator's aid
5 The "so few" of 1940: Abbr.
6 Defrauds
7 After the bell
8 Many moons ___
9 Japanese miniature tree
10 Enterprising one
11 Love, Italian-style
12 P, N, R, e.g.
13 Pop artist Warhol
18 Reach out

23 Barbarian
25 "Get real!"
26 Relatively rational
27 Mystery author Edward
28 Sound on the rebound
29 Gobi's locale
30 Permanent place?
33 "The Stranger" novelist
35 Impersonated
36 Sofer of soaps
37 The hunted
39 Emigrant's document
40 Skater Dorothy
41 Fed head Greenspan
46 Born abroad
47 Cooking utensil
49 Disney dog Old ___
50 Maker of cameras and copiers
51 Pretentious
52 Miata maker
53 In good shape
54 Israeli submachine guns
56 "Piece of cake!"
57 Rodin sculpture at the Met
58 Big Board inits.
61 Emma's portrayer in "The Avengers"
62 CPR expert

"Right. And then it tells me my message is in some sort of program I don't know how to open. And by the time I figure it out I've burned the toast."

"What toast?"

"Just an example."

"Is that why the kitchen was full of smoke yesterday?"

"I have no idea how that happened."

Sherry ignored her protest, said, "Come on. I'll walk you through it. Go ahead. Click on the icon."

Reluctantly, Cora moved the mouse and clicked.

"See," Cora said. "What did I tell you. Crossword Compiler Six."

"No problem."

"Are you telling me we have it?"

"Yes, we have it. We not only have it, it's open. It's the program the Puzzle Lady writes her column in."

"Oh."

"Click on that little icon there."

Cora moved the mouse. Clicked.

A crossword puzzle filled the screen.

"Ah, hell," Cora groaned. "It's a goddamned puzzle."

"Oh, my God!" Sherry exclaimed. "Look who that is."

"Who?"

"Nancy Salomon."

"Who's Nancy Salomon?"

"A constructor."

"Do you know her?"

"Not personally. I know her puzzles. She's a famous constructor. Contributes to the Sunday *New York Times*."

"Well, bully for her. If she thinks I'm gonna solve this, she's got another think coming. Why's she sending it to me?"

"Maybe she says in the puzzle."

"Yeah, and maybe it gives the secret location of the missing weapons of mass destruction. I don't care, I'm still not solving the damn thing."

"You expect me to solve it for you?"

"I don't think I could stop you. Not if it's from this famous Nancy Salmon."

"Salomon."

"Whatever. You wanna tell me what it says, fine. If you don't, I'll probably live."

The phone rang.

Sherry scooped it up. "Hello? Hi, Becky. Yeah, just a sec." She passed the phone to Cora. "Some lawyer for you."

Cora gave Sherry a look, took the phone, said, "Yeah? What's up, Becky?"

"I'm taking the case."

10

IT WAS A SLOW crime day in Bakerhaven. Cora found Chief Harper relaxing with a mug of coffee and a copy of the *Bakerhaven Gazette*. Had she not knocked on his office door, she'd also have found him with his feet up on his desk.

The chief was less than pleased when he heard what she wanted. "Darryl Daigue, huh? Now there's a thankless task."

"You remember the case?"

"Who could forget it? Son of a bitch kills a sweet young girl. Hell, not much older than my Clara is now." He shuddered at the thought. "I hope the bastard rots in hell. He did it, Cora. I'll bet my life on it. I was on the force back then."

"You weren't in charge."

"No," Harper conceded. "I had Dan Finley's job. Young, eager rookie. Well, maybe not quite *that* young. Anyway, I was on the case. In on the arrest. Read him his Miranda. Testified at the trial."

"I read the transcript."

"Then you know. The guy has absolutely no redeeming factors. I hope he rots in hell."

"Suppose he didn't do it?"

"He did it, Cora. Trust me, he did it. You know how it is? Sometimes you have doubts. That time I had none. I sat in on the trial. I heard the testimony."

"You sat in on the trial?"

"Every day. I wanted to see that son of a bitch go down."

"Was there a party when he did?"

Chief Harper started to answer, then noticed Cora's look. "Oh, don't give me attitude. I don't deserve attitude."

"Since when did *attitude* become bad? I can remember when people had *good* attitude."

"Please lay off the linguistics."

Cora smiled. Sherry was always after her to talk more like the Puzzle Lady. Chalk up one in the plus column. "Come on, Chief. You wanna give me a little help here? We all concede Darryl Daigue is a rotten person. The question is, what if he didn't kill the girl?"

"But he did. Come on, Cora. You read the transcript."

"What about the counter boy?"

"What about him?"

"Why didn't he testify?"

"Why should he? He didn't have anything to do with it."

"Says who?"

"What do you mean, says who? No one says any different."

"Darryl Daigue does. Darryl says he relieved the

counter boy, and the counter boy went off with Anita Dryer."

Chief Harper wasn't impressed. "Oh, that's what he says now?"

"What do you mean *now*?"

"As I recall, he used to blame it on the witness. What's-his-name. It's been so long."

"Ray Tucker?"

"That's it. Ray Tucker. Good for you. Of course, you just read the transcript."

"And you didn't. Like you say, Chief, it's been twenty years. Isn't there a chance your memory's a trifle hazy?"

"Of course there is. I can't remember the name of every witness. I'm not even sure who was on the jury. But there's one thing I do know. There was no doubt in my mind we had the right man."

"Even though you had no evidence." As Chief Harper opened his mouth to protest, Cora added, "And I'm not talking about the pot that got suppressed. I know all about that. You also didn't have a rape kit, did you? 'Cause it turned out she wasn't raped. That charge was dropped before trial."

"It's not uncommon. The prosecution will often dump a charge it thinks it'll have trouble proving."

"Doesn't it hurt their case, there being no evidence of rape?"

"Not at all. In fact, a lot of these sex crimes escalate to murder for just that reason. The perpetrator lashes out in frustration when he's unable to perform."

"Yes, the prosecutor made that point in his closing argument. Several times, as I recall."

"It's certainly a valid argument."

"It's making the best of it. If there was evidence

she'd been raped, the prosecution would be harping on that. There's none, so they turn it around and pretend the *absence* of evidence is damning."

"What's wrong with that?"

"A little unfair, don't you think? If she's raped, it proves he did it, if she's not raped, it proves he did it? What would prove he *didn't* do it?"

"Nothing. But that's not so strange, because he did."

The phone rang. Harper scooped it up, said, "Police." He listened a few moments, said, "All right, put me down for two," and hung up. "The PTA's raffling off a turkey," he explained.

"A live turkey?"

"Good lord, I hope not. Clara would just get attached to him, and we'd wind up with a pet instead of a meal."

"So, help me out here, Chief. Who can I talk to about Darryl Daigue?"

"Damned if I know. It's been a long time. His lawyer's dead. The judge is dead. Prosecutor left town. You can hunt up whatever jurors are left, but they're not gonna help you much. They all voted guilty."

"Doesn't mean they were all sold. Sometimes one strong juror can sway the tide."

"I suppose." Chief Harper said it with a complete lack of enthusiasm.

"Whatever happened to Ricky Gleason?"

"Who's that?"

"Counter boy Darryl says he took over for."

Harper shrugged. "You got me."

"You remember him at all?"

"Can't say as I do. He didn't testify in the trial. Didn't figure in the case at all, as far as I know. I'm not even sure what he looked like."

"He have parents in town?"

"I'm sure he did at one time. Probably dead or moved away, or I'd have heard of 'em."

Cora sighed, got to her feet. "You're a big help."

"Actually, I am. I'm giving you some good advice, Cora. I'm telling you to leave this alone."

Cora nodded grimly. "Join the club."

11

SHERRY WAS COOKING DINNER when Cora got home. A marvelous cook, Sherry loved spending time in the roomy kitchen, whipping up delicacies. When Cora came in, Sherry was at the butcher-block table, massacring onions for the pot roast.

"I solved your puzzle," Sherry told her.

Cora Felton dropped her purse on the kitchen table, flopped into a chair, and groaned. "Don't tell me. It's a secret message, warning me off the Daigue case."

Sherry's mouth fell open. "What makes you say that?"

Cora stared at her. "You mean it is?"

"Not at all. I'm just wondering where you got the idea."

"Oh, everyone's telling me to lay off the case. I'm starting to get a complex."

"Then this isn't as bad news as I thought."

"Bad news?"

"It's *not* bad news," Sherry said. "It's just how you're going to take it."

PARTY FAVOR

by Nancy Salomon

ACROSS

1 Illegal act (foiled by the birthday gal)
6 Spill the beans
10 Enthusiastic, and then some
14 Butler's lady
15 "Othello" fellow
16 Writing on the wall
17 The birthday gal
19 Egg on
20 Sailors' assents
21 Souped-up Jaguar
22 Niece of the birthday gal
24 Has a bite
26 Cooks in a 47-Down, perhaps
27 Final transport
30 Simon Templar
31 Mil. training program
32 Early Peruvian
34 O.K. Corral name
38 The birthday gal's crime-solving cohort
42 Put-on
43 Fable feature
44 Denver-to-Detroit dir.
45 Just for laughs
48 Distress call
50 Feeds a crowd
52 Bore for ore
53 Constructor sending best wishes to the birthday gal

54 Delta rival: Abbr.
55 Not fatty
59 Naysayer
60 The birthday gal's alter ego
63 Write-off
64 In the thick of
65 Southwest desert risers
66 Single-named New Age singer
67 "The Right Stuff" org.
68 "I'm all ears"

DOWN

1 Caesar's sidekick
2 "Hello, sailor!"
3 Cut back
4 Miscalculator's aid
5 The "so few" of 1940: Abbr.
6 Defrauds
7 After the bell
8 Many moons ___
9 Japanese miniature tree
10 Enterprising one
11 Love, Italian-style
12 P, N, R, e.g.
13 Pop artist Warhol
18 Reach out

23 Barbarian
25 "Get real!"
26 Relatively rational
27 Mystery author Edward
28 Sound on the rebound
29 Gobi's locale
30 Permanent place?
33 "The Stranger" novelist
35 Impersonated
36 Sofer of soaps
37 The hunted
39 Emigrant's document
40 Skater Dorothy
41 Fed head Greenspan
46 Born abroad
47 Cooking utensil
49 Disney dog Old ___
50 Maker of cameras and copiers
51 Pretentious
52 Miata maker
53 In good shape
54 Israeli submachine guns
56 "Piece of cake!"
57 Rodin sculpture at the Met
58 Big Board inits.
61 Emma's portrayer in "The
   Avengers"
62 CPR expert

"What do you mean by that?" Cora said suspiciously.

"Oh, for goodness' sake. Just take a look at it."

"Where is it? On the computer?"

"No, I printed it out. It's right there on the kitchen table."

There were some pages next to Cora's purse. She snatched them up.

On the top was the filled-in crossword puzzle grid.

"Yeah. So?"

"Look at the long clues."

"Clues?"

"Solutions. The three long entries going across."

Cora looked. Her eyes widened. "*Cora Felton!* What the hell is this? Oh, my God! *Chief Dale Harper? Puzzle Lady?*"

"Look at clue 17."

"*The birthday gal. Cora Felton.* Oh, no!"

"Oh, yes. It's a birthday card crossword puzzle."

"But I don't even *know* this Nancy what's-her-name."

"No, but someone else does. Look at 53 Across."

Cora read, "*Constructor sending best wishes to the birthday gal. Harvey.* Son of a bitch!"

"He meant it nicely."

"Nicely, hell. *Nicely* isn't a crossword puzzle. *Nicely* is a gold necklace. *Nicely* is a ruby ring."

"Cora, what does it hurt? I solved the puzzle for you. You can read it, you can thank Harvey for it, and we're done with it."

"I have to *thank* him for this?"

"You can hit him with it, if you'd rather." Sherry dropped the onions in the pan. "So how'd it go with Harper?"

"It didn't."

"What do you mean?"

"I told you. He warned me off the case. He was totally negative. Told me nothing that would help." Cora grimaced. "Except . . ."

"Except what?"

"It's a small thing. So small you'd miss it. Except there aren't any large things. But when you got nothing, you're desperate, and you're grasping at straws."

"What are you talking about?"

"Chief Harper sat in on the trial. He told me so himself. He was interested, he sat in on the whole bloody thing."

"So?"

"He was also a witness."

"Yeah? So?" Sherry's eyes widened. "You mean he shouldn't have been allowed to?"

"Bingo. He should have been under the rule. If somebody's gonna testify, he shouldn't have been allowed to hear anybody else's testimony."

"Is that the law?"

"It's the law if the judge says it's the law."

"And in this case?"

"I don't know. I'd have to look at the transcript again."

"What do you think?"

"I don't recall anything like that."

"Then it wouldn't matter?"

"Not at all. It's just like the rape-kit nonevidence."

"What do you mean?"

"Rape kit showed no sign of rape. Prosecution turned that around, and argued that rape often escalates to murder when the rapist fails to perform."

"And this time?"

"If the judge didn't put the witnesses under the rule, it's probably because the defense didn't ask for it. In which case, Becky could argue that Darryl Daigue had incompetent representation."

"What's wrong with that?"

"Nothing, except the prosecutor would be mad as hell. And Chief Harper would be right in the middle of a firestorm just for innocently mentioning he happened to sit in on the trial."

Sherry added tomato sauce to the sauteed onions, sprinkled in herbs, stirred it around. "So what are you telling me, Cora? This whole thing is bad news, you wish it had never happened?"

Cora shrugged. "No big deal. Most cases are like that."

"I know. But this one in particular—would you rather bail out?"

"I wouldn't leave Becky high and dry. That wouldn't be fair."

"No, but if you could get her to drop it."

"If I don't find out anything, I'll sure as hell try."

"Uh-huh."

"Unfortunately, I have this tidbit about Chief Harper. So I gotta come up with something else."

"Such as?"

"This counter boy. Ricky Gleason. The one who went off with the victim. According to Darryl Daigue."

"So what have you got on Gleason?"

"Nothing. No one remembers Ricky. He didn't testify at the trial. He wasn't important. No one even remembers his name."

"Are you sure he existed?"

"Of course he existed."

"How do you know?"

"Because *somebody* waited on the counter while Darryl Daigue was cooking burgers. And when Darryl Daigue was done, that somebody either stayed on the counter while Darryl went off with the girl, or went off with the girl while Darryl stayed on the counter. Ricky Gleason may be unimportant and unmemorable, but Ricky Gleason sure as hell exists."

"Did you Google him?"

"What?"

"Did you Google Ricky Gleason?"

Cora glared at her niece. "What, are we back in high school? No, I didn't *google* Ricky Gleason. I don't know what that *is,* but I sure as hell didn't do it."

"I thought you were becoming computer literate. Google is an Internet search engine. You type in the name *Ricky Gleason,* push *Search,* and see how many hits you get."

"Hits?"

"It's easier just to show you."

Sherry turned the heat down to simmer, led Cora into the office, and sat down at the computer. "You wanna check your mail first?"

"I can check my own mail," Cora said irritably. "I'm a big girl now."

"And you've never Googled? Well, don't worry. Everyone's nervous their first time."

"You lookin' for a fat lip?"

"Not at all. I'm just trying to help my innocent aunt. First you open your Internet provider." Sherry clicked on an icon. "I like Internet Explorer because the Google window's open on the home page."

"Please tell me you didn't just say 'Google window.' "

"There you go. Just type *Ricky Gleason* right in the window and click on *Search Internet.*"

Sherry did so. A page of listings appeared.

"Hey, we got a hit," Cora said.

"Yes, we did. Actually, we got twelve thousand seven hundred and three hits. These are just the first ten."

"You're kidding!"

"Not at all. See? There's the number right there." Sherry pointed to the screen:

Results 1–10 of about 12,703. Search took 0.25 seconds.

"Of course, these aren't the files, just the headers. You have to open the files."

"You expect me to sit here and open thirteen thousand files?"

"That would be a little time-consuming," Sherry said. "Why don't we narrow our search?"

"How?"

Sherry typed in *Bakerhaven, Connecticut* after *Ricky Gleason,* and hit ENTER.

"Hey!" Cora warned. "You didn't hit *Search Internet*!"

"I hit *Enter.* Same thing."

"And you wonder why I can't learn computer!"

Sherry peered at the screen. "Well, that narrowed it down a bit."

"How many hits do we have now?"

"One."

Sherry stood up, smiled, motioned to the chair. "Sit down and read your account of Mr. Ricky Gleason, of Bakerhaven, Connecticut."

Cora sat down and looked.

Highlighted in blue on the screen were the words *DANBURY REGION ROUNDUP.*

Below, in black, were the words . . . *Ricky Gleason of Danbury, Connecticut . . . Bakerhaven, Connecticut . . .*

Below was a website address.

"Click on it," Sherry said.

"Click on what?"

"Anything you can." As Cora gave her a look, Sherry amended. "Anyplace your arrow turns into a hand you can click. Try the big blue headline."

Cora did, clicked.

A new page filled the screen with a heading for the Danbury paper. Underneath was the whole article.

Cora scanned it quickly for the part she wanted. Sucked in her breath.

Ricky Gleason of Danbury, Connecticut, was killed instantly yesterday morning when his car went out of control and slammed into a tree. Gleason, 43, was born and raised in Bakerhaven, Connecticut. Mr. Gleason left no next of kin.

12

Sᴇʀɢᴇᴀɴᴛ Wᴀʟᴘᴏʟᴇ, ᴏғ ᴛʜᴇ Danbury police, was beaming. "The Puzzle Lady. Ain't that something! You're the Puzzle Lady."

"Pleased to meetya," Cora murmured, demurely.

It was clear that Sergeant Walpole was the one who was pleased. A hefty man with a bulldog jaw, and a gut that spilled out over his belt, the good sergeant clearly hadn't had so much fun since the last police barbecue. "Wait'll I tell my kids the Puzzle Lady was in my station. You know, they eat your cereal."

"Is that right?" Cora said. She'd never eaten it herself. She wondered if the damn stuff was nutritious. "So, Sergeant, I was hoping you could help me out."

"You get a speeding ticket? I can't imagine that, nice lady like you. The thing is, if I fix it for you, it'd cause a stink, you bein' famous and all. First thing you know, some investigative reporter trying to make a name for himself digs it up, and then there's hell to pay."

"I need help with a traffic accident."

Sergeant Walpole looked astonished. "You had a traffic accident?"

"No. Ricky Gleason. Few months back. Car went out of control, hit a tree."

"I remember that. Smashed all to hell. Him, and the car." He glanced at her. "You're not related, are you?"

"No."

"Well, the guy was a mess, that's for sure. Must have been doin' ninety. There was a curve, a warning sign. He missed 'em both. Only thing he didn't miss was the tree."

"Seat belt on?"

"Oh, yeah. Held him right in place. So the tree mashed him flat. Must have been spectacular to see. Not that anyone did. Caught the tree dead-on. Front of the car stopped. Back of the car kept going. Flipped up. Top hit the tree. Mashed in the top of the car and the top of his head."

"You see the wreck?"

" 'Course I saw the wreck. Anytime there's loss of life, I get the call."

"So what do you do?"

"Do?" The sergeant seemed nonplussed by the question. "I take charge. See that everything's done right."

"Such as?"

"Determine the cause of the accident. This one was a no-brainer. Literally. Guy's brain was mashed in. Piece of cake. Guy just lost control. At that speed that's not surprising."

"How did you determine the speed of the car?"

"Skid marks, for one. Alcohol level for another. You figure a guy that drunk ain't gonna be goin' slow. Except for his reflexes."

"How do you know Ricky was drunk?"

"Another no-brainer. Car smelled like a brewery."

"You take his blood level?"

"I'm sure the doc did."

"You don't know what it was?"

"Not my job."

"Would it be in the report?"

"Are you asking me to pull his file?"

"Is that something you could do?"

Sergeant Walpole picked up a thick rubber band from his desk, began stretching it around his fingers. "Could you tell me again why you're interested in this?"

"I didn't tell you the first time."

"Is that right? No, I don't believe you did. Just why are you interested, Miss . . . ah, Puzzle Lady?"

"It's Felton. Cora Felton. Gleason was a witness in a case I was looking into. I wanted to talk to him about it. If I can't talk to him about it, I wanna know why."

"What's the case?"

"Not important. Particularly in view of what you just told me."

Walpole's eyes narrowed. "You were thinking maybe someone didn't *want* Gleason to talk?"

Cora smiled. "An absurd notion, I know. I'd just like to rule it out."

"Well, you certainly can. The guy got buzzed and missed a turn. He's a poster boy for one of those don't-drink-and-drive groups."

"So you got no objection to pulling his file?"

"Not at all. But I gotta tell you, the only way it's gonna help you is if you're getting paid by the hour."

Sergeant Walpole went into the outer office, came back with a manila file, plopped it on the desk. "Here you go. Knock yourself out. But I tell you, you're wasting your time."

Cora flipped open the file. There was an accident report, filed by the officer on the scene, describing what happened, including one of those little line drawings of a street with every conceivable intersection, turn, curve, or type of highway. On the diagram the officer had dutifully drawn a little block car with a triangle front, and arrows showing the direction. The direction was easy. He also had to draw the tree.

For DESCRIPTION OF ACCIDENT the officer had written: *Car going east on Red Oak Road. Driver speeding. Skidded on turn. Lost control. Hit tree.*

"No mention of alcohol," Cora said.

"No reason for it. He wasn't arresting the guy."

"Wasn't alcohol a contributing cause to the accident?"

"Oh, sure. It's in there. That's just the preliminary report."

Cora flipped a few pages to the medical examiner's findings: *Severe trauma, head and chest. Ribs crushed, lungs punctured. Heart compromised. Veins and arteries severed. Spinal cord severed between C3 and C4. Skull fractured, brain crushed.*

Cora looked up. "Was there anything this guy *didn't* die of?"

"Trust me, it wasn't pretty."

"Blood alcohol point one two five," Cora read.

"That's legally drunk. Unfortunately, not too drunk to drive a car."

Cora turned the page over, frowned. "Is this an autopsy?"

"It's the medical examiner's findings."

"Yeah, I know. But what does it entail? According

to this, he looked at the guy and drew blood. Which he checked for alcohol. Weren't any other tests performed?"

Sergeant Walpole was beginning to be *less* than pleased at having the renowned Puzzle Lady in his police station. "What more do you want? A drunk drives his car off the road. What should we be checking for? Traces of cyanide?"

"Cyanide works much too quickly. He could never have driven the car."

"I was kidding."

"I know. Could I see the crime scene?"

"It's not a *crime* scene. It's a *motor vehicle* accident."

"Drunk driving's a crime, isn't it?"

Sergeant Walpole started to retort, then smiled and shrugged. "Damned if it ain't."

13

IT WAS A NASTY curve, a hard right at the bottom of a steep hill. If you went into it too fast, the car would skid sideways, cross the oncoming lane, mount the shoulder, and smash into the guard posts lining the curve. If the car were going way too fast, it would *take out* the guard posts lining the curve.

Gleason's blue Chevy had taken out four. The guard posts had been replaced, but they were easy to spot, as the wood was newer and lighter in color.

Behind the guard posts just a few feet off the road was Ricky Gleason's tree. The mighty oak still sported a gash in its trunk, but otherwise stood proud and tall.

"Okay," Sergeant Walpole said. "We're here. What does it tell you?"

The turn showed Cora absolutely nothing, but she was damned if she was going to admit that to Sergeant Walpole. "Was the road wet or dry?" she asked.

"Dry, as I recall."

"You recall right. At least, according to the officer's accident report."

"Then why the hell'd you ask?"

"Reports aren't always accurate," Cora replied breezily. "Let's try a little experiment, shall we?"

"Experiment?"

"You mind standing over there by the guardrails and letting me know if anything's coming?"

Cora's red Toyota was parked behind Walpole's unmarked cruiser. She hopped in, drove to the top of the hill, turned the car around.

At the bottom of the hill, Sergeant Walpole stood watching with some exasperation.

Cora stuck her head out the window, shouted, "All clear?"

Walpole hesitated a moment, probably deciding whether to help her or arrest her. Then he sighed, crossed the road, peered around the curve. It must have been clear, because he raised his hand, waved to her to come ahead.

Cora floored it.

The tires squealed in protest as Cora peeled out, leaving rubber, and hurtled down the hill.

The astonished look on Sergeant Walpole's face gave way to one of sheer terror. Suddenly he was stumbling up the road, away from the newly replaced guard posts, as the madwoman in the Toyota sped right toward them.

Cora hit the curve, downshifted, let up on the gas, and spun the wheel. The Toyota shuddered, swerved to the left. Dry leaves spun out from under the wheels. Then the tires caught, screeched, held. In a flash she rocketed around the turn and onto a straightaway.

Cora hit the brakes, slowed the car, made use of a private driveway to turn around. She drove back to where Sergeant Walpole stood waiting on the high side of the curve. The officer was sweating profusely. He looked like he'd lost a good ten pounds.

"What the hell were you doing?" he demanded.

"I told you. A little experiment," Cora answered placidly. "The theory is, the guy drove too fast and went off the road. I took the corner at seventy, and made it just fine. I skidded a little bit, but I didn't come near going off the road. I never even crossed the center line."

"You're sober," Sergeant Walpole pointed out. He exhaled heavily. "At least I thought you were."

"Hey, I'm a little old lady and I made the turn. You're telling me a forty-three-year-old man can't handle it? He's gotta be pretty impaired."

"He was."

"Point one two five?"

"That's legally drunk."

"Maybe so, but it's not a world record. I seem to remember people driving a lot worse than point one two five."

The people she seemed to recall were all Cora Felton, who had been stopped for speeding several times in her less sober days. On those occasions the Breathalyzer had indeed registered far more than point one two five. The fact Cora was unable to recall any of these incidents with any degree of accuracy was not at all surprising.

"What's your point?" Sergeant Walpole said peevishly. His nerves were rather frayed, and he'd had just about enough of the nationally famous Puzzle Lady.

"I'm saying Ricky wasn't that drunk. I'm saying he could have made the turn. I'm saying there's gotta be some contributing factor to the accident."

"You mean like someone ran him off the road?"

"All I'm saying is, you got a traffic accident that isn't accounted for by the facts in the file. The medical examiner's report is damn skimpy. Makes you wonder if something was missed."

"I assure you, nothing was missed."

"I'd rather hear it from the horse's mouth, Sergeant. Do you suppose I could talk to the doc?"

"I'm sure he'll be delighted," Sergeant Walpole said dryly.

They drove back to the police station, and Walpole called the medical examiner. He listened a moment, said, "Oh, is that right? . . . I see. When? . . . Okay, thanks." He hung up the phone.

"I'm not going to like this, am I?" Cora asked.

"I'm afraid the doctor's not in his office."

"How come?"

"He's in jail."

"What?"

Walpole grinned. "Dr. Jenkins is also the prison doctor. One day a week he's up at the penitentiary treating the inmates."

"Oh." Cora cocked her head. "By any chance, would that be Brandon State Penitentiary?"

"Yeah. Why do you ask?"

"Just a hunch," Cora said sweetly.

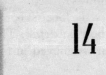

14

CORA FELTON LURCHED TO a stop at the top of the driveway, got out, and slammed the door. She stomped up to the house, barged in, yelled, "I'm back," over her shoulder as she clomped into the kitchen.

Cora flung her purse on the table, and threw open the cupboard over the sink. It was empty, except for a couple of disposable roasting pans.

Cora scowled, slammed the door, tried the cupboard next to the refrigerator. She was greeted by boxes of cold cereal. Cora muttered an appreciation of the product that probably would have cost her her TV commercial.

She banged the doors shut, bellowed, "Sherry!"

A faint "Yeah?" wafted from down the hall.

Cora stomped into the office where her niece sat typing. "Damn it, Sherry! Where's the booze?"

Sherry looked up from the computer. "I beg your pardon?"

"Don't play coy with me. You threw out my liquor!"

"You quit drinking."

"That's right," Cora said. "*I* stopped drinking. *I* did. *Me*. I'm not in a twelve-step program. I didn't join AA. I just *didn't* drink. But I didn't clean up the house. I didn't throw out my booze."

"It's bad to have around—"

"No!" Cora interrupted. "See? There's the problem. *You're* telling *me* how to drink. That. Doesn't. Work. Remember when we moved in together? Remember the first rule?"

"I don't tell you what to drink."

"That's right. You don't tell me what to drink. If I wanna drink, that's my business. If I don't wanna drink, that's my business too. But you don't make that decision, I do. And you don't throw out my booze, I do. If I don't, it stays. See the problem?"

"Aunt Cora—"

"Don't placate me. Do you see the problem?"

"Yes, I do. Aunt Cora, why are you so angry?"

"You took my booze."

"Before that. What made you angry enough to take a drink?"

"This goddamn case." Cora took out her cigarettes, lit one up.

"You're smoking in the office."

"You wanna confiscate my cigarettes too?"

"Never mind. You were saying . . ."

"I wasn't *saying* anything."

"No, you were telling me why you were mad. Something about the case." Sherry peered at her closely. "Cora, are you telling me you don't want this case? You wish it would go away?"

"Cases don't just go away."

"No, but you can get out of them. No one says you have to do this."

"I promised Becky."

"Becky wouldn't mind."

"Now you're talking for Becky Baldwin?"

"I forgot. You're angry enough to argue anything. Okay, so tell me. What exactly is wrong with the case?"

Cora told Sherry about Ricky Gleason's "accident."

"So?" Sherry said. "What's wrong with that?"

"Guy wasn't drunk enough to wreck his car. He was barely drunk enough to slur his words."

Sherry could see what had put Cora in mind of having a drink. "Some people hold it better than others."

"Granted. But it takes a snootful to drive into a tree."

"I think you're making too much of this guy."

"Me? You're the one who Googled him to death."

"It was a traffic accident. Months ago."

"Quite a coincidence, don't you think?"

"It's been twenty years. People die."

"Yeah, but he died before I could find out what he knows."

"Come on, Cora. You got it all backwards. If someone killed Ricky Gleason to keep you from finding out what he knows, they did it months before you started looking."

"Interesting point," Cora mused. "That makes me wonder."

"Wonder what?"

"When all this started." Cora motioned to the computer. "Lemme check my mail?"

"Sure," Sherry said, happy to have her calmed down. She slid out of the seat, let Cora take her place.

Cora opened her e-mail server. Six messages came in.

"Hmm. Salami. Salami. Salami." Cora hit DELETE.

"Spam," Sherry corrected, gently. "Who's Rocky?" she asked, looking over Cora's shoulder.

"None of your damn business. You gonna let me read my mail or not?" Cora clicked down. "What the hell is this?"

"What?" Sherry looked. "Oh, my God! Manny Nosowsky!"

"You know him?"

"I feel like I know him. He posts all the time on Cruciverb-L."

"You mean he's a crossword person?"

"You gotta learn to say that less like you swallowed a bucket of nails."

"Oh, hell," Cora said, opening the e-mail. "Here it is. 'Cheers from Manny.' And there's an attachment."

"Click on it."

"Do I have to?"

"Only if you wanna know what it is."

Cora clicked on the attachment. It opened a puzzle in Crossword Compiler.

"Oh, look at that," Sherry said.

"What?"

"It's a seventeen by seventeen."

"Oh, for Christ's sake. You mean it's bigger?"

"It certainly is."

"Aw, hell."

"What do you care? It's not like *you* were gonna solve it."

"No, but I gotta read the damn thing. Harvey will probably grill me on what it says."

"Boy, talk about lazy."

"Lazy, hell. How'd you like people to make a fuss about your birthday?"

The sound of tires in the driveway announced the

arrival of Aaron Grant. Sherry and Cora met the young reporter at the front door.

"Hi, girls," Aaron said. "What's up?"

"Girls?" Cora said. "My, my, how tactful."

"Tactful in your case," Sherry said. "In my case, it's politically incorrect."

"Yeah, talking's a minefield these days." Aaron headed for the kitchen. "You got anything to drink?"

Cora shot a look at Sherry. "Funny you should ask."

"Lemonade or iced tea?" Sherry said.

"Iced tea would hit the spot." Aaron jerked the refrigerator open, took out the pitcher of iced tea, poured himself a glass. He sat down at the table, took a sip. "Ah, that's good. Hear you got a murder, Cora."

"Oh, you hear that, do you?" Cora picked up the pitcher. "Guess I'm reduced to iced tea too."

Aaron shot Sherry an inquiring glance. She pretended not to notice. "Yeah," he said. "I hear you're doing some work for Becky Baldwin."

"You're not writing it up, are you?"

"Good lord, no. I don't even know what it's all about."

"If I tell you, are you going to write it up?"

"Not if you don't want me to."

"Remember the Darryl Daigue murder case?"

"That what you're working on?"

"Remember it?"

"I'm not that old. I know about it, of course."

"How'd you like to get back in my good graces?"

"I didn't know I was in your bad ones."

"You're not. How'd you like to win a few points for Sherry?"

Aaron raised his eyebrows inquiringly.

"I dumped her booze," Sherry translated.

A PUZZLING SITUATION
by Manny Nosowsky

ACROSS

1 Nostalgic yet fashionable
6 Computer game gobbler
12 Green land?
16 Neptune's domain
17 Actor Peter of "Becket"
18 Where the auction is on-line
19 Soundtrack of the Puzzle Lady's favorite sci-fi movie
22 Freebie
23 Steinbeck migrants
24 Call for a dealer?
25 "Give it ___" ("Check it out")
27 They go up and down
30 Grammarian's shtick
33 Hole in the ground
36 ___ Xing (street sign)
37 Blubber
40 Like the Puzzle Lady
44 ___ tai cocktail
45 Areas
46 "Uh-uh!"
47 Grammy winner Morissette
49 Popular gas-guzzler
50 Jayhawker
52 Fill the bill?
53 Firehouse fleet

55 Make a lap
56 What the Puzzle Lady hopes you'll do
60 Inspirational talk: Abbr.
61 Emulate Chief Dale Harper
62 Doubling prefix?
63 ___ fit (tantrum, Southern-style)
64 Allen or Frome
66 Bank claim
68 Confidence games
71 Gobbled up
74 "Night" author Wiesel
78 What we have to say to the Puzzle Lady
82 "I'd hate to break up ___"
83 Gromyko or Sakharov
84 New currency
85 Like buildup on a floor
86 Injury
87 Lost one's balance?

DOWN

1 College military unit: Abbr.
2 Say again
3 Be rife (with)
4 "Elephant Walk" climax
5 Married or single?
6 "Th-th-that's all, folks" speaker
7 Yours, en français
8 Join the party
9 Unlike a rolling stone?
10 Space bar neighbor
11 PBS benefactor
12 Clark's exploration partner
13 Blind as ___
14 Close, in hide-and-seek
15 NASDAQ rival

20 In favor of
21 Old Valerie Harper sitcom
26 Country singer Gibbs
28 Major work
29 Nonetheless
30 Reveals, on Halloween
31 Shipping route
32 Fly guy
34 "___ Fair" (Don Cornell song)
35 Premeditation, say
37 Obeys the periodontist
38 Helpers from abroad
39 Itsy
41 Director Craven
42 For all to see
43 Larry King employer
48 In mint condition
50 Barbie's beau
51 "Steady ___ goes"
53 Napoleon's isle
54 Sealed shut with a hammer
57 On pins and needles
58 "Well, ___-di-dah!"
59 Seder container
64 Running on fumes
65 Teased teenagers
67 One-million link?
68 "Pygmalion" playwright
69 "Mi ___ es su..."
70 High point
72 Longfellow's "The Bell of ___"
73 The other Van Gogh
75 Tales of the tribe
76 Multivitamin supplement
77 Sun spot?
79 ___ Harbour, FL
80 It makes Paul a girl?
81 Ouija board reply

"I thought you weren't drinking, Cora."
"Oh, now *you're* starting with me?"
"Not at all. What was it you wanted?"

"I was wondering if the *Gazette* had any papers in the morgue with articles on the Darryl Daigue case."

"Probably would, if they hadn't converted to microfilm. It's on file in the library. Jimmy Potter will dig it out for you if you want."

"What do you know of the case?"

Aaron shrugged. "No more than anybody else. He raped and killed a girl, was found guilty, went up for life."

Cora grimaced, shook her head. "See, now that's the thing."

"What?"

"He didn't rape her. He was charged with raping her, but the charge was dropped when the medical examination showed she wasn't raped."

"Is that right?"

"Yes, it is. You see my problem? You just know what everybody knows." Cora shook her head. "And everybody knows *wrong*."

15

DR. JENKINS WAS YOUNGER than Cora had expected, with straw-colored hair that had a habit of slipping down into his sky-blue eyes. Rather inconvenient in examining patients, but damned effective in arousing the passions of the opposite sex. Cora had to keep reminding herself that the good doctor was married, on the one hand, and considerably her junior, on the other. Though the latter would not necessarily have deterred her, if she felt inclined.

Nor the former, for that matter.

"I'm sorry to bother you, Doctor," Cora purred, disingenuously. "If I could just have a few moments of your time."

"Sergeant Walpole said you had some questions about Mr. Gleason."

"You performed the autopsy?"

"I examined the body, yes."

"I was interested in your medical report."

"Really? I don't recall anything special about it."

"That's what interested me. There *wasn't* anything

special about it. That would help me determine what caused the accident."

"Clearly a case of drunk driving."

"That seems the only explanation. But the man wasn't particularly drunk."

"He was legally drunk, as I recall."

"Yes, which makes things nice and tidy. Still, one wonders why the man would drive into a large tree."

"I assure you, I don't know."

"But that's your job, isn't it? As medical examiner? To determine the cause of death? Isn't that what you look for in your autopsy?"

"I assure you we have the cause of death. There was never any question of any other."

"You ruled out other causes in your autopsy?"

Dr. Jenkins frowned. "What would you like me to rule out? The man died of multiple contusions and lacerations. His lungs were punctured. His skull was mashed in. The cause of death was traumatic injuries."

"How can you tell?"

He stared at her. "How could I tell? Good God, how could I *not*? I assure you, Miss Felton, not that I'd wish it upon you, but *you* could have looked at the man and told what killed him."

"I'm not sure I could, and I'm not sure you could, either."

"I beg your pardon?"

"What you've described for me, Doctor, are injuries *sufficient* to have caused death. Whether or not they *did* is another matter. Did you learn anything from your autopsy—anything at all—that would prove these injuries were not sustained postmortem?"

Dr. Jenkins scowled. "Sergeant Walpole said you might be trouble."

"Did he, now? I fail to see the trouble in telling what you know."

"I have no trouble telling what I know. You just don't seem to want to hear it."

"I'm still waiting to hear it. I asked you if your autopsy proved the injuries weren't sustained after death."

"My examination did not show anything one way or another. But there's no reason why it should."

"Really, Doctor? I thought there were several methods of determining exactly that. Isn't there a huge difference between a heart that is pumping blood and one that isn't? Can't you tell if a punctured lung was still breathing air? Wouldn't that show in your autopsy?"

Dr. Jenkins took a breath. "In my examination of the body—"

"Come on, Doc," Cora cut in. "Just between you and me, I've referred to your autopsy several times. While you've never contradicted me, you've always carefully used the word *examination*. So I'm wondering, did you actually perform an *autopsy* on Gleason's body?"

"Miss Felton—"

"That's a bad start to a yes-or-no question. Kinda makes me think the answer is no."

"There's no call to autopsy an accident victim."

"How about a murder victim?"

"Gleason was not a murder victim."

"How do you know?"

Dr. Jenkins exhaled in exasperation. "Because I work within the bounds of reason. And the guidelines of the law. If there was any reason to suspect foul play, I would look into it. But there wasn't."

"So you didn't," Cora said. "Kind of a catch-22 situation."

The doctor glowered at her.

"I mean, you'll do an autopsy if you suspect foul play, but you'll never know if there's foul play unless you do an autopsy."

"I'm familiar with Joseph Heller," Dr. Jenkins snapped. "It's not that way at all. If the police have reason to suspect something's wrong, I of course look into it. If *I* have reason to suspect something's wrong, I look into it. If there is no reason in the *world* to suspect something's wrong, I *don't* look into it."

Cora took a manila folder out of her purse, extracted a piece of paper.

Dr. Jenkins's eyes widened. "That's my medical report! Where did you get it?"

"Sergeant Walpole gave me a copy to get rid of me." Cora turned it over. "I notice you checked for alcohol, got the reading point one two five. You also checked for heroin, marijuana, and cocaine. And found none. Why did you check for those drugs?"

"One might have been a contributing factor to the accident."

"You didn't think the alcohol sufficient?"

"The alcohol was a sufficient cause. It might not have been the only cause."

"Now you're talking," Cora said. "Did you check for chloral hydrate?"

"What?"

"Chloral hydrate. A Mickey Finn. Did you check for that?"

"Certainly not. Why would I check for that?"

"Well, if someone slipped the guy a Mickey, it would certainly be a contributing cause to his hugging a tree to death."

"There was no reason to suspect any such thing."

"There was no reason to suspect he took cocaine either, but you checked for that."

"Miss Felton—"

"Would chloral hydrate have shown up in an autopsy?"

"Only if it was there."

"Let's find out, shall we? Why don't you perform that test now?"

"That would be a neat trick. The accident was months ago. The body's buried."

"Can't you exhume it?"

"Not without a court order."

The phone rang.

Dr. Jenkins frowned, picked it up. "I'm busy, Margie. I said not to ring. . . . Well, tell her to wait. I'm in the middle of—" He broke off, said soothingly, "Oh, hi. Of *course* you don't have to wait. Tell Margie to put you in an examining room, I'll be right with you."

The doctor hung up the phone. "I have patients to see. I'm sorry I can't help you. But, trust me, Ricky Gleason's death was an accident."

"Uh-huh. You were saying something about a court order?"

"You'll never get one."

"Why not?"

"You haven't a shred of evidence." Dr. Jenkins shrugged the sexy hair out of his bedroom eyes and grinned. "I'm afraid you're back to your catch-22 situation. You can't get permission to exhume the body without the very evidence you're hoping to find by exhuming it."

16

Cora stomped out of the doctor's office in what was rapidly becoming her usual foul mood. Goddamned doctor. Good looks or no, the son of a bitch needed his ears pinned back. Of all the smug, incompetent morons. It was getting so they'd let anybody into medical school these days. Cora wondered what percent of his class the doctor was in. After all, *someone* had to be in the bottom five, didn't they?

Cora's Toyota was at a parking meter across the street. She'd put a quarter in the meter for fifteen minutes, reluctantly added another. Now she was glad she did. Dr. Jenkins had kept her waiting a good quarter's worth before he'd seen her, which was one of the reasons she'd been so aggressive in her questions. She'd be lucky if the meter hadn't run out.

Evidently it had, because a traffic patrol car was pulled up next to it.

Cora set a new record for the thirty-yard dash, a feat of broken-field running punctuated by the unmistakable blare of the horn of a Mack Truck.

The meter maid had pad in hand. Cora knew she shouldn't call her a meter maid, but if the woman had begun writing, that would seem a compliment compared to certain other modes of address.

Cora was in luck. The woman smiled, said, "Just in time," and immediately transformed herself from a lowly meter maid into a stalwart, highly respected officer of the law.

Cora unlocked the door and got in, flopped her purse down on the passenger seat, and dug for a smoke. Her cigarette pack was empty. The elation of not getting a ticket vanished in an instant. Of all the times to run out of cigarettes. Just when she really needed one. She crumpled up the pack, looked around.

A few stores down the street was a newsstand. Cora got out of the car, started for it. Stopped. In front of the newsstand the meter maid was ticketing a car. If Cora walked right by her, the woman would see she didn't drive off. Would she back up, check the meter?

Feeling like a damn fool, Cora went back and dropped a quarter in the meter. But she really resented it. Not to mention the meter maid, who was no longer her friend. When she came out of the newsstand clutching the cigarettes and discovered the woman had not gone back to check her meter, Cora felt like telling her she wasn't doing her job.

Cora climbed into her car, rolled down the window, and lit up a smoke. There were still eleven minutes on the meter. Cora had half a mind to wait them out. She lingered for a few drags, and even took time to check her makeup in the rearview mirror. Satisfied, she started the engine and pulled out of the space.

Down the block behind her, a black sedan, idling next to a fireplug, pulled out and drove down the block.

Cora signaled for a right turn.

The car sped up. Halfway down the block it met the meter maid/traffic officer, ticketing another car. Oncoming traffic prevented the sedan from going around.

As Cora turned the corner, the black sedan shot across the center line, straight at an oncoming cab. The taxi driver slammed on his brakes and hit the horn as the black sedan swerved back into its lane, just ahead of the traffic patrol car.

The horn made Cora turn her head. In the split second before she rounded the corner, she could see the black sedan righting itself as it sped down the block.

Cora's first thought was, *I'm being tailed.*

Her second thought was, *I watch too many movies.*

Nonetheless, Cora slowed up, kept an eye on the rearview mirror to see if the black car turned the corner.

It did, skidding as it came, beating the light by an eyelash.

Cora slowed down to get a better look.

Oddly enough, the black sedan, having all but killed itself to make the corner, seemed suddenly to have lost all sense of urgency. It slowed, as if considering parking spots on the block. Since there were none, and since it had zoomed by the perfectly good spot Cora had just left, this seemed a hollow ruse.

Cora slowed some more, tried to make out the driver, but the sun glinting off the tinted windshield spoiled her view. And the driver of the car kept hanging back.

Of course, Cora rationalized, this was probably all in her mind. The person tailing her was probably some housewife taking her toy poodle to the groomer.

On the other hand, it might not be.

Cora pulled up to the corner, put her directional

signal on left. In her mirror, the black sedan also signaled left.

The light at the corner had been green for some time. Just before Cora got there it turned yellow. Now all she had to do was snap a quick left, and the black sedan would never make it.

Cora didn't do that. She slowed in the left-hand lane, came to a complete stop, let the light turn red.

Waited for the black sedan to pull up behind her, so she could check out the driver.

The black sedan had a change of heart. Its left-turn signal abruptly changed to a right. The car pulled up to a fireplug halfway down the block.

The woman-with-dog theory was beginning to look like a long shot.

Cora waited through what seemed like an interminable series of lights. Finally catching a green, she hung a quick left, sped down the block, and made a right, leaving the black sedan in the dust. It hadn't made the left yet, wouldn't know where she'd gone.

Gotcha! Cora thought. She hunched over the wheel, Gene Hackman in *The French Connection,* Steve McQueen in *Bullitt*. Ignoring the light at the next corner, she skidded into a right and floored it, weaving in and out of traffic. She reached the next corner, ran her second straight red light, and hung her third straight right turn.

Now she was back on the street where she'd started, heading for the corner where she'd turned left, only from the opposite direction. She reached it, and hung her fourth right, completing the square.

Sure enough, halfway down the block, the black sedan was crawling along, trying to figure out where the hell she'd gone.

Cora couldn't resist. She drove down the street, crept up behind the black sedan.

It was a Chevy with Connecticut plates. Cora pulled up closer. She hit the brake, fumbled in her purse for a notebook, wrote the license-plate number down.

Then she pulled up alongside the car. In the front seat was a fortyish blonde, with teased hair and too much makeup, chattering away on her cell phone. The woman was off in her own little world, probably not even aware she was driving a car.

Poking out the backseat window was the unmistakable nose of a toy poodle. That brought Cora up short. Her sarcastic prediction had come remarkably true.

Cora snorted in disgust. Of course it had. This wasn't the only black sedan in the world. The one following her wouldn't have parked in the middle of the block. It would have sped to the corner to see if she turned off on either street.

Cora did that now, looked both directions, saw nothing. Had the sedan been smart enough to follow the turns she made? Was it in back of her now?

No, the only black sedan behind her was dog-lady, planning her life. The black sedan, arriving at the corner too late and seeing nothing, would continue through the light to the next, and the next, looking up each side street.

Cora did the same. To no avail.

The black sedan had vanished.

17

CHIEF HARPER TOOK A sip of coffee. His smile was ironic. "You want me to run a license plate?"

"That's right."

"Because you *think* you were being followed?"

"Yes, I do."

"Only the plate you want me to run *isn't* the plate of the car you think was following you?"

"No, that car got away."

"Since you can't run the license plate of the car it *was,* you'd like to run the license plate of the car it *wasn't.*"

"On the off chance I'm wrong."

"Off chance? How could you possibly go wrong, bringing me a story like this?"

"I admit it's shaky."

"Shaky? Miss Felton, I can come up with a better conspiracy theory just going to the post office. You think the cop's in on it. You think the doctor's covering up. You think the car that isn't following you might be following you."

"That's hardly a fair assessment of what I said."

"You're right. A fair assessment of what you said would be, *What a load of crap*. Really, Cora, this isn't like you." Chief Harper stopped, bit his lip. He realized what he'd just said was too close to the bone. Cora really wasn't acting herself, hadn't been since her last intended trip to the altar had ended tragically. "What would be the point of running this plate?"

"Well, it would be good practice for you. You'll know how to do it when I find the real car."

"I know how to run a license plate."

"Good. Then you'll have no trouble running this one. Tell me, Chief, what do you think of Sergeant Walpole?"

"I don't know a *thing* about Sergeant Walpole. I've never *heard* of Sergeant Walpole. Which doesn't mean he doesn't exist. The number of times we've had to cooperate with the Danbury police you can count on the fingers of one hand."

"Aw, hell."

"You're making too much of this, Cora. I don't want to see you going out on a limb and getting hurt."

"Least of my worries."

Cora went out the front door of the police station, stomped up the steps of the Bakerhaven Library.

The librarian, Edith Potter, had her hair styled in a trendy flip cut, chestnut with blond highlights.

"Hey, nice haircut, Edith," Cora said.

The librarian smiled. "Reckless extravagance, twice a year. The rest of the time it grows out and I put it in a little bun like a stereotypical librarian."

"How does Hal like it?"

"Depends what's on TV. If it's the NFL, Hal doesn't even notice."

Cora chuckled, said, "Is Jimmy around?"

Edith's face showed concern. "What's Jimmy done now?"

"Nothing. Aaron said he'd look stuff up for me."

Edith smiled. "Yes. He's good at that."

Jimmy Potter was working upstairs in the stacks. A gawky boy of college age, the librarian's son had always been a little slow, but he was very eager to please, and liked to be asked.

Jimmy was thrilled to help the Puzzle Lady. "Sure, Miss Felton. What do you need?"

"Can you find newspaper articles from about twenty years ago?"

"Sure. That's how it's filed, by date."

"I'm looking for the Darryl Daigue trial. You know about the Darryl Daigue trial, Jimmy?"

"Sure. Killed that girl."

"Well, I need to find newspaper articles about the murder and the trial. Can you help me find those?"

"Did my mom say to do it?"

The question surprised Cora. She thought Jimmy would be eager to help. "I asked her if you could."

"Good deal," Jimmy said. "That means I can print out things. If Mom doesn't say so, I can't print out things. Then you gotta look through the viewer, or I gotta write it down."

"Your mom knows about it," Cora assured him. "Can you find the articles all right?"

"Sure can."

Jimmy plunged out of the stacks, whirled around a spiral staircase to the ground floor, and darted through a doorway.

Cora followed at a more leisurely pace. By the time she reached the ground floor, Jimmy was back with the first article.

"You can sit in the reading room, Miss Felton. I'll bring you the rest. Printing out is good."

Jimmy darted out again.

Cora dumped her drawstring purse on the large wooden table that dominated the reading room, and sat in one of the dozen chairs that surrounded it. There were only two other people in the room, a man reading the paper, and a woman with a reference book. Cora sniffed at the prominently displayed NO SMOKING sign on the wall, then turned her attention to the printout.

CO-ED KILLED was the headline. It appeared to have run the width of the front page. Jimmy Potter had shrunk it down so it fit on an ordinary piece of copy paper. Unfortunately, that shrunk the text to a size Cora could have read only with a microscope. She harumphed loudly enough to incur a baleful glare from the man with the paper, then discovered a second page under the first. She pulled it out, saw that Jimmy had also printed out an enlargement of the column without the headline.

The body of Anita Dryer, 17, of Bakerhaven, was discovered late last night in the icehouse in Kingman Grove, after her failure to return home from school prompted her parents to call the authorities. An initial police search failed to find the girl, who remained missing until her body was stumbled upon accidentally by two high school students.

Cora raised her eyebrows. How about that. Something already. Cora knew the two high school students from the trial transcripts. According to their testimony, they'd joined the police search and found Anita's body. A contradiction. Of course, one easily explained. The young couple had gone to the icehouse to make out. Either they or their parents hadn't wanted them to testify to that fact. "Joined the police search" was a useful euphemism. Still, it was a fact at variance.

Cora wondered how many others there might be.

There were no more in the initial article, but Cora had barely finished it when Jimmy Potter bounced in with a stack of papers. "There's more, there's more!" he whispered, and bounced out again.

Cora sat and read it all. For the most part, it was stuff she already knew. There was no mention anywhere of the recently deceased then counter-boy Ricky Gleason. If Darryl Daigue had told his lawyer, his lawyer certainly hadn't passed it on. The counter boy was to all intents and purposes the man who wasn't there.

Jimmy kept the printouts coming. Cora sat there for hours, sifting through the articles, but came up empty.

At last Jimmy came back with nothing in his hands.

"That's it?" Cora said.

Jimmy heard the disappointment in her voice. His face fell. "Didn't find what you wanted?"

"No, no, you did well," Cora assured him. "I just wish there was more."

"There's one more article, but I can't print it out."

"Why's that, Jimmy?"

" 'Cause it's not what you wanted. The trial or the murder. It's not one of those."

"What is it, Jimmy?"

"It's just a whachamacallit. Not news, just a meet-the-townsfolk. They did one on me, once," he said proudly. "Working in the library. With a picture and everything."

"A human-interest story?"

"That's what they said." Jimmy laughed. "Which is kind of stupid. Like the other stories interest *animals*?"

"They did a human-interest story on Anita Dryer?"

Jimmy shook his head. "No. On Darryl Daigue."

"Oh. I'd like to see that, Jimmy."

"I'm not sure Mom wants me to print it out. 'Cause it's not about the *murder*."

"It's okay. I'll go with you."

Jimmy led Cora through a door off the reference room into a long, narrow room lined with what at first glance appeared to be library card-catalog files, but proved to hold tiny canisters of microfilm. He pointed out a desk at the far wall with a computer and scanner on it. "We're transferring the microfilm to computer. Then we burn it on CD-ROM."

"You can do that?"

"Sure can. But that's just getting started. Most everything you want you gotta see like this." Jimmy pointed to a desk where a viewer was threaded up with microfilm. "That's the article there, Miss Felton. Look through this hole here. You see these knobs? You turn this one if the picture's fuzzy. And this one makes it go up and down."

Cora peered into the viewer. The picture was indeed fuzzy. She turned the knob to bring it into focus.

WHO IS DARRYL DAIGUE? was the headline.

Cora could see why Jimmy didn't think the article would pass muster. The murder trial was referred to only to identify who Darryl Daigue was. The article itself concerned Daigue's life in Bakerhaven, and focused on his job at the diner. Several of his coworkers were mentioned. Maddeningly, none of them were Ricky Gleason.

Cora read with disappointment to the bottom of the column.

The last sentence read:

Darryl Daigue's girlfriend, Cindy Tambourine, declined to be interviewed.

Cora's mouth stretched into a grin. She practically purred. "Thanks, Jimmy. Good job!"

Cora beat it out of the library, hustled across the street.

Chief Harper grimaced as she came in. "Twice in one day? Cora, you're working too hard on a hopeless case."

"Maybe, maybe not," Cora said. "You run that license plate for me?"

"Yes, I did. And I don't want you to think it sets any precedents. I didn't do it because I think there's anything to it. I didn't do it because I think it's a valuable lead. I didn't do it because I think it has anything to do with Darryl Daigue. I did it largely so you would leave me alone. The fact you're back already is not encouraging. It makes me think maybe I wasn't negative enough. Is there any way I can impress upon you how worthless I think the information I am about to give you is?"

"I don't know, Chief. That would depend largely on whether the license plate you ran happens to be registered to a Ms. Cindy Tambourine."

Chief Harper's mouth fell open. "How in the *world* did you figure that?"

Cora shrugged, smiled modestly. "Just a lucky guess."

"Not that lucky," Chief Harper told her dryly. "According to the Department of Motor Vehicles, that car is registered to a Miss Valerie Thompkins, of Danbury, Connecticut. Ms. Thompkins is a widow—her maiden name is Thompkins, by the way, her married name was Fleckstein—and she has no connection with either Anita Dryer or Darryl Daigue whatsoever."

18

"CAN YOU GOOGLE ME some people?"

Sherry looked up from the pumpkin she was carving. She'd taken the top off and was scooping out the seeds with her hands. "Cora, I'm kind of in the middle of something."

"You're making a jack-o'-lantern?"

"Tomorrow's Halloween."

"Already?" Cora said. "Gee, time flies when you're having fun."

"Where have you been?"

"The library, mostly. And if that isn't a place to drive you wild! You can't eat, you can't drink, you can't smoke. You can't talk. Damn lucky there's stuff to read. A person could go batty there."

"You want me to Google someone you met in the library?"

"Someone I read about in the library. And someone I didn't."

"Cora, didn't I show you how to Google?"

"Yeah, you did. If I knew which icon to click I could probably do it."

"Just keep clicking till you hit it."

"Oh, no. I'm not opening your programs. I can't close 'em. Some of them are fine. But some of them say, 'Would you like to save so-and-so?' And I don't wanna delete your program by saying no. But if I say yes, it asks me to do something else stupid, like slip in a disk. Or enter some password. Or promise it my firstborn child, not that that's gonna happen, knock on wood. I had a stressful day, I don't need some computer talking back to me too."

"Who do you want to Google?"

"One of them's Cindy Tambourine. She was Darryl Daigue's girlfriend."

"Who's the other?"

Cora dug out her notepad. "Valerie Thompkins."

"What's her connection to the case?"

"She doesn't have one."

"Oh?"

"I don't want to talk about it," Cora said irritably.

"Okay." Sherry picked up a big spoon, began scraping the bottom of the pumpkin.

After a few moments Cora said, "Someone might have followed me today."

"'Might have'?" Sherry said, spooning out seeds.

Cora told Sherry about the black sedan.

"You traced the wrong license plate, and now you'd like to Google it?"

"Just because Chief Harper says it's wrong doesn't mean it's wrong. What does he know?"

"Yeah, he's just the chief of police," Sherry said.

"You know what I mean. Just because Harper can't find a connection doesn't mean there isn't one."

"Uh-huh. But you personally think it's the wrong car?"

"More than likely."

"So why don't you find the right one?"

"How?"

"Go back to Danbury, see if it starts following you again. Where did it pick you up?"

"First time I noticed it was when I came out of the doctor's."

"Who knew you were going in?"

"The doctor. The cop. The doctor's receptionist. The woman with the poodle. The one I wanna Google. Good God, did I really say that? I wanna Google the woman with the poodle."

"And how would the woman with the poodle know you were calling on the doctor?"

"How would *anyone* know I was calling on the doctor? Why would anyone *care* if I was calling on the doctor, unless they happened to kill what's-his-name. Ricky Gleason. Who wasn't mentioned in the newspapers, or the transcript, or by anybody else, for that matter. With the possible exception of Darryl Daigue, who claims it could have cleared him, but didn't manage to pass it on to either the police or his attorney."

"Well, when you put it that way."

"How else can I put it? You got a case that doesn't add up from any angle. You got a sister who'd like to free her big brother, who can't be freed, and who only came up with this idea after twenty years of not giving a good goddamn. You got a prisoner with the brains of a tree slug, only slightly less appetizing, whose chance of redemption is even lower than that of the Red Sox winning the World Series."

"Hey, you're not in New York anymore. I'd watch that talk around here."

"I have, in short, the least promising case I can imagine. And yet when I start poking into it, what do I find? My lead suspect died under suspicious circumstances, and the fact I'm looking into it raises someone's hackles."

"So you wanna Google them. Or at least Google the leads you got. Tell me, what is the optimum result you'd like from this Internet adventure?"

Cora tried to see if her niece's eyes were twinkling, but Sherry was busy scraping the pumpkin. "I'd love it if Valerie What's-her-face and Cindy Gotsagoo were one and the same person. That would teach Chief Harper to be so damn smug."

"Oh, so *that's* what this is all about."

"No, it isn't. But I'd like *something* to make sense."

"All right." Sherry put the pumpkin aside, washed her hands in the sink. "Come on, let's Google."

They went into the office and Sherry sat at the computer.

"We didn't get any more puzzles?" Cora said apprehensively.

"No, but I solved the last one. You wanna see?"

"Not really. What is it?"

"Another birthday card. You really need to thank Harvey."

"I really need to rap Harvey upside the head. Did I *ask* him for these cards?"

"He doesn't know you're illiterate, Cora. He thinks it's fun."

"Can't I just tell him, Sherry? The guy's a real pain."

"Sure, if you think he can keep a secret. If you don't

think he'll put it around the whole crossword puzzle community."

"Of course he will. He's worse than an old maid." Cora raised her finger. "I didn't say that. Don't quote me. There is nothing wrong with people who choose not to marry. I think they're nuts, but that's just me."

"Well, here's Manny's puzzle." Sherry called it up on the screen. "Take a look."

"Do I have to?"

"You need to know it if you run into Harvey."

"Yeah, I guess so." Cora leaned over, looked at the puzzle.

"Wonderful. Seventeen by seventeen. I can kid Harvey about having puzzle envy."

Sherry, reading over Cora's shoulder, said, "Your favorite sci-fi movie is *Star Wars*?"

"Huh?"

Sherry pointed. "Nineteen Across. 'Soundtrack of the Puzzle Lady's favorite sci-fi movie.' "

"I guess *Planet of the Apes* didn't fit the space."

"Cora—"

"So I like *Star Wars*. Is that a crime? The first *Star Wars* movie was good." Cora looked up from the computer. "Enough of this damn puzzle stuff. Can we Google?"

"Sure."

Sherry called up the program, plugged in *Valerie Thompkins,* and hit SEARCH.

"Well, you got two hits, Cora. Both from the *Danbury News-Times*. Valerie Thompkins to wed, and Valerie Thompkins widowed. The gentleman in question is a Marvin Fleckstein. Marvin appears to have been a used-car salesman. No, that's unfair. Actually,

A PUZZLING SITUATION
by Manny Nosowsky

R	E	T	R	O		P	A	C	M	A	N		L	A	W	N
O	C	E	A	N		O	T	O	O	L	E		E	B	A	Y
T	H	E	M	E	F	R	O	M	S	T	A	R	W	A	R	S
C	O	M	P		O	K	I	E	S			H	I	T	M	E
		A	T	R	Y			Y	O	Y	O	S				
U	S	A	G	E		P	I	T		P	E	D		F	A	T
N	E	V	E	R	W	I	T	H	O	U	T	A	C	L	U	E
M	A	I		R	E	G	I	O	N	S		N	O	P	E	
A	L	A	N	I	S		S	U	V		K	A	N	S	A	N
S	A	T	E		E	N	G	I	N	E	S		S	I	T	
K	N	O	W	A	L	L	T	H	E	A	N	S	W	E	R	S
S	E	R		N	A	B		T	W	I		H	I	S	S	Y
		E	T	H	A	N			L	I	E	N				
S	C	A	M	S		E	A	T	E	N		E	L	I	E	
H	A	P	P	Y	B	I	R	T	H	D	A	Y	C	O	R	A
A	S	E	T		A	N	D	R	E	I		E	U	R	O	S
W	A	X	Y		L	E	S	I	O	N		S	P	E	N	T

ACROSS

1 Nostalgic yet fashionable
6 Computer game gobbler
12 Green land?
16 Neptune's domain
17 Actor Peter of "Becket"
18 Where the auction is on-line
19 Soundtrack of the Puzzle Lady's favorite sci-fi movie
22 Freebie
23 Steinbeck migrants
24 Call for a dealer?
25 "Give it ___" ("Check it out")
27 They go up and down
30 Grammarian's shtick
33 Hole in the ground
36 ___ Xing (street sign)
37 Blubber
40 Like the Puzzle Lady
44 ___ tai cocktail
45 Areas
46 "Uh-uh!"
47 Grammy winner Morissette
49 Popular gas-guzzler
50 Jayhawker
52 Fill the bill?
53 Firehouse fleet

55 Make a lap
56 What the Puzzle Lady hopes you'll do
60 Inspirational talk: Abbr.
61 Emulate Chief Dale Harper
62 Doubling prefix?
63 ___ fit (tantrum, Southern-style)
64 Allen or Frome
66 Bank claim
68 Confidence games
71 Gobbled up
74 "Night" author Wiesel
78 What we have to say to the Puzzle Lady
82 "I'd hate to break up ___"
83 Gromyko or Sakharov
84 New currency
85 Like buildup on a floor
86 Injury
87 Lost one's balance?

DOWN

1 College military unit: Abbr.
2 Say again
3 Be rife (with)
4 "Elephant Walk" climax
5 Married or single?
6 "Th-th-that's all, folks" speaker
7 Yours, en français
8 Join the party
9 Unlike a rolling stone?
10 Space bar neighbor
11 PBS benefactor
12 Clark's exploration partner
13 Blind as ___
14 Close, in hide-and-seek
15 NASDAQ rival

20 In favor of
21 Old Valerie Harper sitcom
26 Country singer Gibbs
28 Major work
29 Nonetheless
30 Reveals, on Halloween
31 Shipping route
32 Fly guy
34 "___ Fair" (Don Cornell song)
35 Premeditation, say
37 Obeys the periodontist
38 Helpers from abroad
39 Itsy
41 Director Craven
42 For all to see
43 Larry King employer
48 In mint condition
50 Barbie's beau
51 "Steady ___ goes"
53 Napoleon's isle
54 Sealed shut with a hammer
57 On pins and needles
58 "Well, ___-di-dah!"
59 Seder container
64 Running on fumes
65 Teased teenagers
67 One-million link?
68 "Pygmalion" playwright
69 "Mi ___ es su..."
70 High point
72 Longfellow's "The Bell of ___"
73 The other Van Gogh
75 Tales of the tribe
76 Multivitamin supplement
77 Sun spot?
79 ___ Harbour, FL
80 It makes Paul a girl?
81 Ouija board reply

he was a dealership owner. Probably made a pretty penny. Probably what Valerie's living on now."

"Try the girlfriend."

"Okay. Cindy Tambourine." Sherry did a search. "Absolutely nothing."

"What?"

"No hits at all."

"How can that be? She was in the *Gazette*."

"Yeah, twenty years ago. I hate to break it to you, Cora, but twenty-year-old Bakerhaven papers aren't going to be on-line."

"So the woman just ceased to exist. I wonder what happened to her."

"Why don't you ask your client?"

"My client?"

"I don't mean your client. I mean the killer."

"Do you have to call him 'the killer'?"

"A jury did."

"Yeah." Cora pointed to the computer. "Google him."

"What?"

"Darryl Daigue. Google Darryl Daigue. I want to see if there's anything at all."

"There should be."

"Oh, yeah? If twenty-year-old papers aren't on-line, they missed the trial."

"Well, let's give it a try." Sherry typed in *Darryl Daigue*, hit ENTER. "There you are. A hundred and seventeen hits."

"A hundred and seventeen?"

"They won't all be what you want. You'll get stuff like, 'Hoop star Darryl Dawkins performed charitable work for the Daigue Foundation.'"

"How the hell do you know about Darryl Dawkins? You don't like basketball, and you're not old enough."

"I do crossword puzzles, Cora. I know everybody. Let's see. Here's a book called *Lifer* by A. E. Greenhouse, based on the author's interviews with several life prisoners, including Darryl Daigue."

Cora snorted. "Having interviewed Darryl Daigue, I wouldn't expect much."

"Here's an article on sex crimes, by a Lester Moffat. Sort of unfair, since the sex charge was dropped. I wonder if Lester mentions that."

"I don't care if he does or not. Darryl Daigue shouldn't be in the article. How old is it?"

"Just last year."

"And they're still calling it a sex crime? That is so unfair."

"Then you'll love this one."

"What is it?"

"Article is called 'Death Row.' "

"Death Row? Darryl Daigue isn't on Death Row."

"Yeah, that seems to be the point of the article. How the system keeps the scum of the earth like Darryl Daigue alive for years at a considerable expense to the state, while the man has no hope of redemption, no possibility of parole, no future prospects outside of a ten-by-ten cell, so why not give the gentleman the lethal injection he so richly deserves?"

"Yeah, that would be just great until a DNA test showed he was innocent."

"It's not going to happen. Anita Dryer wasn't raped."

"Talk about unfair," Cora said. "The guy gets blamed for raping the girl, but he didn't, so DNA can't set him free."

"Yeah," Sherry said. "If only he hadn't killed her. That's probably where he made his big mistake."

"Nasty girl. Okay, smarty-pants. What was Darryl Dawkins's nickname?"

"Chocolate Thunder. Want the computer?"

"Please."

Cora sat down, scrolled through the articles. Which were, in Cora's humble estimation, depressing, inaccurate, and annoyingly uninformative. Only one in four was actually about Darryl Daigue. Of the ones that were, most contained no more information than the ones that weren't.

On a whim, Cora Googled *Brandon Prison*. It seemed to Cora the machine hiccupped slightly, and yet the search took only one point seven seconds, and yielded twelve thousand six hundred and twenty-two articles.

Cora scrolled through the first page of listings. The heading **WARDEN PLAYS HARDBALL** caught her eye. Cora clicked on it, was greeted by a picture of the little man who had ushered her into his office, given her a cigar, and blown a slightly inferior smoke ring.

Cora skimmed the article. The gist of it was that in light of a prison riot, Warden Prufrock had cut prisoner exercise time to free up prison staff for guard duty.

Cora wondered if Darryl Daigue had been involved in the riot. She deleted *Brandon Prison,* typed in *Warden Prufrock*. That yielded three hundred fifty-six hits. Cora scrolled through, looking for Darryl Daigue. She wondered if there was a subsearch, to search these three hundred fifty-six articles for him. If so, it wasn't readily apparent.

Cora continued to scroll through the headings, hoping for a hint. The name Darryl Daigue didn't appear, but a theme began to emerge. Evidently "Warden Plays Hardball" was not an isolated article. Other headlines were **WARDEN GETS TOUGH, WAR-**

DEN CRACKS DOWN, WARDEN DRAWS LINE, WARDEN STANDS FIRM. There was even an article with the headline **IRON MAN.** Cora couldn't help smiling at the thought of the warden described that way.

Halfway down page ten Cora found something new. **WARDEN COMMENDS PAROLE BOARD.** The article began,

> *Warden Prufrock issued a vote of thanks and hearty well done as the parole board wrapped up hearing cases today. In response to detractors who characterize the board as a rubber-stamp organization that routinely approves the parole of any prisoner who has met the minimum requirements of time served . . .*

Cora clicked on the heading to bring up the article. The article continued,

> *The current board has only a fifty-three percent approval rate, proving that each case had been judged on an individual basis.*

Cora wasn't reading the article.

Cora was staring at the picture that accompanied it.

The picture was captioned "Parole board gets high marks."

The caption then identified the five men and women in the picture.

Four of them Cora had never seen before.

The fifth was Dr. Jenkins.

19

WARDEN PRUFROCK WAS SURPRISED to see Cora again. "Miss Felton, I can't understand what you're doing here."

"Working for Darryl Daigue."

"But you asked for me."

"Yes, I did."

"Why?"

"I like your office. It's much cozier than that visiting room. No Plexiglas. No telephone. And you gave me a cigar."

No cigar seemed forthcoming this time. Warden Prufrock sat behind his desk, his fingers laced together, a frown on his lips.

"Miss Felton, I have no time to play games. I'm a very busy man."

"I know. I Googled you."

"I beg your pardon?"

"Please, Warden Prufrock. You have a computer on your desk. Surely you Google."

"You mean an Internet search?"

"Now we're talking the same language. I'm not sure if it's Mac or PC, but we're talking it. Anyway, I did a Google search and read up on you, and there was one article in particular I wanted to ask you about."

"Which article was that?"

"The parole board. You commended them. Which, I guess, is commendable. Anyway, I thought it was a nice gesture. You thanking the board publicly and all. I was wondering if you happened to know them."

"What?"

"The parole board. I wonder if you know any of them. Personally, I mean."

"Now see here—"

"Oh, bad tactic, Warden. Don't you ever question any prisoners? An evasion is a dead tip-off. It doesn't deflect the question. It merely makes for more questions. So I take it you know the board. Personally, I mean."

"Miss Felton, I don't care if it's an evasion or not, I don't know what the hell you're talking about. I don't even know which parole board you mean."

"Oh, well, is your computer on? I'll find it for you. Google your name, and I'll show you the article."

"I have no intention of Googling my name. Miss Felton, I don't owe you anything. But I must say, you are one of the most amazing women I have ever met. You come in here and adopt the position I owe you an explanation. When the reverse is true. Miss Felton, what are you trying to prove?"

"Actually, I'm trying to *disprove* something."

"What?"

"Do you happen to know Dr. Jenkins?"

"He's on the parole board, why?"

"Do you know him personally?"

Warden Prufrock threw up his hands. "I don't know how to answer that. I know him because he's on the parole board. I know him because he's sometimes tended to a prisoner. I don't play golf with him, if that's what you mean."

"Or have him for dinner?"

"Miss Felton, I'm married. I don't invite young men for dinner. I don't know what you're getting at, but whatever it is, you're wrong."

"Fine. I'm sorry to bother you. Answer me one more question and I'll leave."

"What's that?"

"Did Dr. Jenkins ever consider Darryl Daigue for parole?"

Warden Prufrock's mouth fell open. "What the hell!"

"Did he?"

"I have no idea."

"Well, that's mighty strange, Warden. Darryl Daigue is serving a life sentence without possibility of parole. And you can't tell me for sure that the parole board never heard Darryl's case?"

"You don't understand."

"I certainly don't. Just what does *without possibility of parole* mean?"

"Exactly that."

"Then why would Darryl Daigue *ever* go before the parole board?"

"Just because a prisoner has no hope of parole doesn't mean his behavior with regard to parole wouldn't be evaluated. The parole board might assess the prisoner with no intention of letting him out."

"Was that done in this case?"

"I would have to check my records."

"Could you do that?"

"Not right now. Things are not filed in that manner. Did such-and-such a parole officer evaluate such-and-such a prisoner. I'm going to have to look up the prisoner's records, cross-check them with the records of the board. I'm not even sure how to go about it."

"Perhaps I could help you."

"No, you couldn't!" Warden Prufrock realized he'd spoken a little too harshly, softened it with a smile. "Miss Felton, I don't think you're aware of the responsibilities of running a prison. A warden is under a microscope. If an investigative reporter wants a story, I will be portrayed in the worst light possible. If the people don't like what they read, I can be replaced."

"You're worried about your job?"

"Not at all. I am concerned with doing it right. Look here, you're an intelligent woman. Suppose you read in the paper that I had allowed a private citizen with no standing whatsoever to come in here and browse through the prisoners' records with free access to the prison files? What would you think of that?"

"Why would that bother me?"

"Suppose your husband was in jail."

Cora smiled and nodded. "Warden, you've finally come up with something I can relate to. I've had a number of husbands I can imagine in jail."

20

DARRYL DAIGUE LOOKED WORSE. Cora found that hard to fathom. The first time she'd seen him he'd looked an absolute fright. But now there was a bruise over his left eye and a scab on his chin. He limped as the guard ushered him into the visiting room, sat him in the chair.

"What happened to you?" Cora asked him, once he'd picked up the phone.

Darryl snuffled. His lips twisted into a sneer. "Cut myself shaving."

It occurred to Cora that the prevarication was probably true. Darryl had a faint nick on his right cheek that could have come from a razor blade. Still, it was only a half-truth. The whole truth was, he'd cut himself shaving *and* been beaten within an inch of his life.

Cora didn't press the point. "I have bad news. Ricky Gleason's dead."

Daigue frowned. "Ricky Gleason?"

"The counter boy. The one whose shift you took.

The one who went off with Anita Dryer. *That* Ricky Gleason."

"Oh? He's dead?"

"That's right. He can't confirm your story anymore."

Daigue's grin was diabolical. "He can't deny it, either."

"Look here, did you know he was dead?"

"No, why should I?"

"Aren't you curious how he died?"

"What difference does it make?"

Cora waited.

Daigue said, "Yeah, sure. How'd he die?"

"Car accident."

"Tough luck."

"A couple of months ago. Got drunk, drove off the road."

"Shouldn't drink and drive."

"That's sound advice. You ever have a parole hearing?"

"I don't get parole."

"I know. I was wondering if you get hearings."

"Sometimes people talk to me."

"You mean a group of people? In a special room?"

"I don't know how special. They sit down. I sit down. The guard stands up. They ask questions."

"What kind of questions?"

"Dumb questions. Am I sorry? Do I repent my crime? Do I apologize to the victim? Victim's dead, for Christ's sake."

"What did you say?"

"What do you think I said? I didn't do nothing. I should be sorry I didn't do nothing?"

"What did they say?"

"Who cares? They got no power over me."

"Uh-huh. I'd like to run a few names by you."

"Why?"

"Why not?"

"Good answer. Shoot." Darryl Daigue began to pick his nose.

"Ricky Gleason."

"I gave you that name. He was the counter boy. He killed Anita."

"How come you didn't tell your attorney that?"

"I did."

"How come he didn't use it?"

"He's stupid."

"Uh-huh," Cora said. "Cindy Tambourine."

Darryl frowned. "What about her?"

"Who is she?"

"A girl."

"I could've figured that. Anything special about this girl?"

"Had big knockers."

"That wasn't exactly what I meant. What was your relationship with this girl?"

"Oh, here comes the moral lecture."

"Cindy was your girlfriend?"

"Yeah? So?"

"What happened to her?"

"What happened to her? How the hell should I know? I'm in jail, for Christ's sake."

"She ever visit you in jail?"

"No."

"You're pretty sure about that one."

"No one visits me in jail. Except you. Why don't you leave me alone, lady?"

"Got a couple more names to run by you."

"Jesus Christ!"

"That wasn't one of them."

"What are you, a comedian? We're done talking."

"Dr. Jenkins."

Darryl Daigue had started to hang up the phone. He brought it back to his ear. "Who'd you say?"

"Dr. Jenkins. You know him?"

"Yes, I know him. He's the doc. Little weasel."

"You don't like him?"

"I'm in pain. I want Percodan. He gives me aspirin with codeine. Aspirin with codeine, for Christ's sake. You can practically get it over the counter."

"So Dr. Jenkins is tough on drugs?"

"Goddamned Nancy Reagan. Now, the old doc, he was okay."

"What happened to him?"

"Got old, I guess. Or died. First thing I know, this young punk's in here reading the riot act, cutting off the supply."

"Tell me something. This Dr. Jenkins. He ever on your parole board?"

"How the hell should I know?"

"Well, if you were there and he was there . . ."

"Like I give a good goddamn. You done, lady? I got a really busy day ahead of me."

"One more name."

"Who?"

"Valerie Thompkins."

"Never heard of her."

"Marvin Fleckstein?"

"You said *one*."

"Humor me. You heard of Fleckstein?"

"No." Darryl curled his lip insolently. "Can I go now?"

"I don't see why not." Before he could hang up, Cora added, "If you don't mind a word of advice?"

Darryl Daigue stared at her as if she were some loathsome bug he was about to squash. "What's that?"

"Be real careful shaving."

21

Dr. Jenkins walked into his waiting room to find seven patients perched uncomfortably on and about a couch made for two, and Cora Felton seated alone on a couch for three. The good doctor leaned over, had a brief whispered discussion with his receptionist, then straightened and said through gritted teeth, "Miss Felton?"

Cora gathered up her drawstring purse, and followed the doctor into his office.

Dr. Jenkins closed the door slightly harder than necessary, then turned to glare. "Miss Felton. My receptionist told you I was very busy and couldn't see you."

"Yes, she did."

"Whereupon you raised your voice and said it was an emergency, you were afraid you might have SARS."

"Actually, I feel much better now," Cora said.

"I'm sure my other patients will be glad to hear it. I don't know why you're doing this to me, but would you please stop? This is not a game. This is my profession. Those people are my patients."

"Yes, but they're not your only patients, are they?"

"What do you mean?"

"You put in one day a week at the penitentiary."

"Yes, I do. So what?"

"You didn't mention it to me before."

"I'm terribly sorry," the doctor said sarcastically. "I didn't realize we were discussing my general practice."

"No, we were discussing Ricky Gleason's automobile accident. I'm wondering if you were working at the penitentiary the day that happened."

Dr. Jenkins was genuinely surprised. "What in the world has that got to do with anything?"

"I don't know. It's a long day. A long drive. Maybe you weren't home yet when the call came in. Maybe you were late getting to the scene."

"That has no bearing on the situation whatsoever."

"Why?"

"The EMTs are often first on the scene."

"Was that true in Ricky Gleason's case?"

"I would imagine so."

"Can't you do a little better than that, Doctor? Jog your memory. Did you have no preconceived notions when you examined the body? Or did someone say, 'The dead guy's over there'?"

"As I recall, I was told on the phone it was a fatality. I fail to see what this has to do with me working at the prison."

"I just wondered if it was the same day."

"I don't remember."

"Could you check it for me, Doc? I'd really like to know."

"Oh, for goodness' sake. Do you have the date of the accident?"

"Yes, I do. It was ten-thirty on the evening of August 12."

Dr. Jenkins consulted his desk calendar, flipped back two months. Shook his head. "August 12 was a Tuesday. I'm at the prison Wednesday afternoons."

"You ever swap a day?"

"No, I'm always there on Wednesday."

"What if there's an emergency?"

"It sometimes happens. I don't think it did."

"Could you make sure?"

Dr. Jenkins scowled, picked up the phone, pressed the intercom button. "Margie, could you check the appointment book for August 12? This past August. Did I keep my appointments on that day?" He listened, said, "Uh-huh. Thanks," and hung up the phone. "I had seven appointments after lunch. One canceled, I kept the rest. I did not go near the prison."

"Uh-huh. And what day are your parole hearings?"

Dr. Jenkins winced. Clearly he hadn't seen the question coming. Though why it should bother him, Cora had no idea.

She pressed her advantage. "Is that on a particular day, or just when they call you?"

"What's that got to do with anything? What's any of this got to do with anything? Why am I even talking to you?"

"You're trying to cure me of SARS."

Dr. Jenkins took a breath. "Miss Felton—"

"I'm a pain in the fanny, Doc. And I don't go away. Trust me, you're much better off just having a little chat. Now, with regard to your parole hearings, is that a regular thing?"

"No. It meets whenever it's called."

"Is that often?"

"Not very. Brandon is a maximum-security prison. Prisoners aren't paroled often."

"But some of them have hearings."

"Some do. But as parole is unlikely, there's no particular urgency." Dr. Jenkins made a face. "Don't quote me on that. That wasn't really what I meant to say."

"Don't sweat it, Doc. The older you get, the harder it is to be a liberal. You'll find out. Anyway, have you had a parole hearing lately?"

"I would say it's been a good six months."

"Do you recall who you heard?"

"Good lord, no. Probably five to ten cases. Frankly, they all become a blur."

"I'll try not to quote you on that either, Doc. Would you happen to remember if Darryl Daigue was among them?"

"Darryl Daigue? The sex killer?"

"Actually, he didn't have sex."

"What?"

"He's in for murder. The rape was dismissed."

"Yes, I remember him. We were supposed to examine him, see if there was anything extraordinary that would lead to a reevaluation of his sentence. Of course, there wasn't."

"Uh-huh. Then his file would be stamped 'Parole Denied'?"

"Of course."

"Are any of the other inmates in Mr. Daigue's position?"

"What do you mean?"

"Hopeless cases. Men without a chance of parole."

"Of course. There always are."

"I see," Cora said.

Dr. Jenkins frowned. "What are you getting at?"

"Just trying to get the general picture. Now, you treated Darryl Daigue as his physician?"

"If you can call it that."

"What do you mean?"

"He's a malingerer. Just trying to get drugs."

"You give him any?"

"Just aspirin. I tell him it's aspirin with codeine. He grumbles, but he goes away."

"You give him any lately?"

"Last week. Why?"

"I wonder if he sold it."

"Why do you say that?"

"Just a hunch. All right, look, Doc, I may have to talk to you. That's my job. I don't wanna terrorize your patients, but I don't wanna be told to leave. I'll try to make it as seldom and as quick and as painless as possible. But if I need to see you, let me in. Okay?"

"Okay."

Cora and Dr. Jenkins shook hands.

Cora went out to the waiting room. A cute little blond number, not as young as she would have liked to think she was, but probably not as old as Cora cattily classified her, was at the reception desk. The woman clearly had money and liked to show it. Her simple, understated necklace glittered with small diamonds. Her matching earrings were flawless. Her hair gave the impression she never actually combed it herself, but stopped by the beauty parlor every morning for a tune-up.

The woman was giving the receptionist a hard time. Cora wasn't surprised. In fact, Cora would have been surprised if she weren't.

"I didn't *ask* you what his schedule was like, I just told you to fit me in. Oh, *there* you are," she said as the doctor appeared in the doorway. "I was trying to impress upon your *girl* that you *must* give me a minute, but she *really* doesn't get it."

The woman flashed venomous eyes at the receptionist, and sailed past the doctor into his office.

Cora went out through the waiting room and was only slightly amused to see that the patients were still avoiding her couch. In fact, she barely noticed. Her mind was fixed on the features of the woman who'd just been at the reception desk.

The woman seemed very familiar. It occurred to Cora she was most likely the same woman who had been so pushy on Cora's first visit to the doctor's office. But Cora hadn't seen that woman. Dr. Jenkins had talked to her on the phone.

Cora had seen the woman's face before, but she couldn't remember where. She was just getting into her car when it hit her.

The woman was in the picture of the parole board with Dr. Jenkins.

22

CHIEF HARPER FROWNED AS Cora walked in. "What is it now? You got another license plate for me to trace?"

"That's right," Cora said.

He looked dismayed. "I was kidding."

"Many a true word is spoken in jest. I forget who said that. Or why. The guy was probably joking. Doesn't matter. Here's the plate. Can you run it down?"

"Cora, this is becoming a bad habit."

"Not at all. This is a brand-new Mercedes. The woman lives in a ritzy part of town in a house big enough to have servants. Not that I think she does, just that she could."

"Was this woman following you?"

"I don't think so."

"Oh. Then it's just like the other license-plate number you wanted traced. I take it you still haven't found the car that was following you, which is why you'd like to trace another one that wasn't?"

"That's right, Chief. Can you do it?"

Harper shook his head. "I didn't know what a bad precedent I was setting. I mean, when I think of the number of cars in this state that *aren't* following you. You could easily bring me a new one every day. Hell, I bet I could spot a couple just by looking out the window."

"I'm interested in this particular one, Chief."

"You mind telling me why?"

"I'm not sure I'm up to the ridicule."

"I'm not sure I'm up to tracing the plate."

"She's on the parole board that heard Darryl Daigue's case."

"Really? Then I bet you could get her name without my help."

"I'd still like to know who registered the flashy car she's driving."

"Uh-huh. If I do this, you promise you won't be in here with another plate tomorrow?"

"I can't do that."

"You what?" Harper said incredulously.

"What if I get a solid lead, something that screams for attention. You gonna let an innocent man rot in jail 'cause you forced me into some ridiculous promise? That would be one of the most gross travesties of justice in the history of law enforcement."

"Can you promise not to bring me one as trivial as this?"

"I'd say that's a given, Chief. Can you *imagine* one more trivial than this?" Cora grinned, and ducked out the door.

The aroma of fresh-brewed coffee from Cushman's Bake Shop reminded Cora she'd missed lunch. A pastry would hit the spot.

Cora went into the bake shop, where Harvey Beerbaum had just been waited on.

"Well, well, if it isn't the instigator himself. Tell me, Harvey, are you about done?"

Harvey Beerbaum was all wide-eyed innocence. "Why, Cora, whatever do you mean?"

"You know damn well what I mean— Good afternoon, Mrs. Cushman; I'll have a coffee and a cranberry scone— You know exactly what I mean, Harvey. You happen to have a strange idea of confetti. Do-it-yourself birthday cards from some of the brighter lights in the crossword-puzzle community."

"Oh, really," Harvey said, all innocence. "I take it you have a birthday coming up?"

Cora took her coffee to the condiment counter, dumped in milk and sugar. "You gotta work on your innocent act, Harvey. You'd make a bad thief."

"I beg your pardon?"

"Just how many more puzzle cards can I count on?"

"How many have you received?"

"Two."

"Well, that hardly seems like a sufficient quantity. If, as you suspect, this was organized in some way, you would most certainly anticipate more than two."

"Yes," Cora said. "The question was, how *many* more than two?"

"That really depends on who chooses to play. If you send out invitations to a party, you don't expect everyone to come."

Cora's eyes narrowed. "A party?"

"Just an example." Harvey took the top off his coffee, added more milk. It was nearly white.

"Have a little coffee with your milk," Cora told him.

"Oh, dear, it is rather light, isn't it?" Harvey snapped the top back on, took a sip. "Who were your cards from?"

"Nancy Salomon and Manny Nosowsky." Knowing she'd be asked, Cora had been careful to memorize the names.

"Pretty impressive people."

"Yeah," Cora said. "Well, guess what? Nancy gave you up."

Harvey frowned. "I beg your pardon?"

"Fifty-three Across: *Constructor sending best wishes to the birthday gal.* Answer: *Harvey.*"

"Oh."

"And Manny just happened to know I like *Star Wars.* Where do you suppose he heard that?"

"I might have mentioned something to a couple of constructors."

"How many, Harvey?"

"I don't know. Half a dozen, maybe. Which doesn't mean they're all going to play. As you said yourself."

"I see."

"Happy birthday, Cora."

"It's not my birthday yet."

"No, of course not. Silly of me. But I couldn't ask them *on* your birthday. Then you'd never get them in time. So, better early than late, right?"

"Better for who?"

Cora stomped out of Cushman's Bake Shop and back to the police station.

Chief Harper looked up from his desk in weary resignation. "Back so soon? Please tell me you're here for the license plate, you haven't come up with something else."

"Well, actually . . ."

Harper's face fell. "Are you kidding me?"

"Yes, I am. You trace the plate?"

"Yes, I did. It's the woman's car, all right. At least I assume it's her car. It's registered to a woman."

"You didn't check that out?" As he looked up sharply, she added, "That was another joke, Chief. I'm grateful for the information you're giving me. I'll vet it myself."

"Well, for starters, the address on the registration is the same one you gave me, so the car belongs to the house."

"I don't suppose the woman's one of the names I gave you. You'd be slightly less sarcastic."

"Oh, I think I'd still manage," Chief Harper retorted. "The woman is Miss Ida Blaine. Just to show I'm a nice guy, I ran her driver's license. Blond hair, blue eyes, five foot four, a hundred and fifteen pounds. Married. Would you like her shoe size?"

"You're in rare form today, Chief."

"It's seldom I get to do such valuable work. Anyway, there's your info. Hope it helps."

Cora grimaced. "In this damn case, nothing helps."

23

SHERRY WAS ON THE couch watching TV when Cora came in. "You in a good mood?"

Cora frowned. "Why do you ask?"

"You have another card."

"Aw, hell!"

"No, no, you'll like this one."

"Wanna bet?"

"Trust me, you'll get a kick out of it."

"What makes you think so?"

Sherry handed it to Cora. "I printed it out for you. Here, take a look."

Cora looked it over. "Oh, hell. It's a whachamacallit."

"An acrostic."

"Right. I *hate* them."

"You'll like this one. Look who wrote it."

"Emily Cox and Henry Rathvon? Who the hell are they?"

"Cora!" Sherry was shocked. "*Everyone* knows who Emily and Henry are. They do the acrostics for the Sunday *Times*. They have one in every other week."

ACROSTIC
by Emily Cox and Henry Rathvon

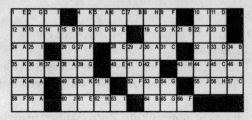

A. Joyful lack of seriousness

$\overline{38}\ \overline{5}\ \overline{30}\ \overline{24}\ \overline{59}\ \overline{48}$

B. Not sufficiently alert to danger

$\overline{21}\ \overline{34}\ \overline{46}\ \overline{64}\ \overline{7}\ \overline{15}$

C. Howler on the North American plains

$\overline{6}\ \overline{57}\ \overline{19}\ \overline{45}\ \overline{13}\ \overline{31}$

D. Hardly thinking clearly (3 wds.)

$\overline{53}\ \overline{17}\ \overline{41}\ \overline{11}\ \overline{33}\ \overline{23}$

E. The opposite of staccato

$\overline{28}\ \overline{40}\ \overline{18}\ \overline{49}\ \overline{1}\ \overline{61}$

F. Set free; release, as information (2 wds)

$\overline{52}\ \overline{66}\ \overline{9}\ \overline{27}\ \overline{58}\ \overline{42}$

G. Fourscore

$\overline{54}\ \overline{16}\ \overline{65}\ \overline{2}\ \overline{26}\ \overline{39}$

H. Given a smack on the cheek, perhaps

$\overline{56}\ \overline{62}\ \overline{36}\ \overline{43}\ \overline{8}\ \overline{51}$

I. On leave, like a sailor

$\overline{14}\ \overline{25}\ \overline{32}\ \overline{10}\ \overline{63}\ \overline{3}$

J. Repetitive recitation or listing

$\overline{44}\ \overline{29}\ \overline{37}\ \overline{55}\ \overline{22}\ \overline{60}$

K. Tutorial unit

$\overline{47}\ \overline{35}\ \overline{12}\ \overline{4}\ \overline{20}\ \overline{50}$

"Well, bully for them. You wanna solve this, feel free. I'm not in the mood."

Cora flipped the puzzle onto the coffee table, and sank down on the couch.

The doorbell rang.

Sherry and Cora looked at each other.

"Expecting someone?" Cora asked.

"No. You?"

"Are you kidding?"

Cora got up and opened the door.

Zorro, the Incredible Hulk, and Freddy Krueger stood in the doorway. "Trick or treat!"

"Oh, dear!" Cora called over her shoulder, "Sherry? We got anything?"

"What?"

"It's trick-or-treaters. What have we got?"

"Oh, hell!"

"Great." Cora shook her head, smiled apologetically. "Kids. We've been busy. We didn't even know it was Halloween."

"You've got a pumpkin," Zorro said accusingly.

"Huh?"

The Hulk pointed to the lighted jack-o'-lantern. "In your window. If you didn't know it was Halloween, how come you got a pumpkin?"

Cora wasn't about to be cross-examined by superheroes. "Sorry. Come back next year."

Cora closed the door and went back to the living room. "Well, I ticked off the Incredible Hulk. What else can go wrong?"

"Another bad day?" Sherry asked Cora.

"Are there any other kind?"

"What's your problem now?"

"You know that nice picture you got me, of the doc on the parole board?"

"Yeah. So?"

"Well, it has to mean something. But it doesn't. The good doctor's shocked as hell when I bring it up, but doesn't flinch at Darryl Daigue. Though he *does* seem to be having a bit of a fling with a married woman on the board. Unfortunately, *she's* not connected to the case in any other way."

"Uh-huh. And remind me, the doctor is important because . . . ?"

"He signed the death certificate on Ricky Gleason, ruling it an accidental death."

"Right." Sherry shook her head. "Cora, if this is a conspiracy, it's pretty deep. Considering the principal's already in jail for life."

"Was *presumably* in jail for life. Until his sister started trying to get him out. Suddenly, a whole bunch of things happen. How they make sense, I have no idea. But somehow they're interrelated."

"Or coincidence."

Cora grimaced. "I hate coincidence. You give me a mystery novel based on coincidence, I'll throw the damn thing across the room. No, there's a connection here. I just can't see it."

"Well," Sherry said. "Sometimes it helps to clear your mind by thinking of something else."

"Like what?"

Sherry pointed to the puzzle.

"You go ahead if you want. I'm going to Google Ida Blaine."

Cora was back within minutes.

"Well?" Sherry asked.

"Ida Blaine is married to Mr. Quentin Hawes. Evidently Ida doesn't like the name Hawes, because she isn't using it. Evidently she doesn't like Quentin, because she doesn't seem to be using him much, either."

"Aunt Cora."

"Well, don't blame me, dear. I'm not the one playing doctor. All I'm saying is, if she didn't marry him for love, she must have had *some* reason."

"Is he on the parole board?"

Cora's eyes widened. "Oh, for goodness' sake."

"What?"

"I didn't run him. Just her. The wedding announcement lists him as an industrialist."

Cora hurried back to the office.

Sherry filled in a few more entries before Cora came crashing down the hall. "Guess what?"

"He's on the parole board too?"

"No. Her husband, to the best I can determine, has no connection to anyone else whatsoever."

"Oh."

"Yeah. Thank God for that. This case is becoming like a snake that's eating its own tail. Pretty soon it will consume itself and disappear."

"That sounds rather unpromising. So what do you plan to do?"

"I don't know. I'm beginning to think I'm on the wrong track." Cora sighed, slumped down on the couch. "Maybe I should give it up."

The living room window exploded.

24

Sam Brogan popped his gum and surveyed the living room. "You cleaned up?"

"We swept up the glass," Cora told him. "Otherwise you'd be walking in it."

"Then you didn't consider this a crime scene?"

Cora's eyes narrowed. "I beg your pardon?"

"If this was a crime scene, you wouldn't have cleaned up. You know better than that."

"Thanks for your assessment. Listen, Sam, you think we could speed this along?"

Sam chewed his gum. "I'd sure like to. Just havin' trouble understanding the situation. The fact is, you called the police."

"Yes," Cora said. "Otherwise you wouldn't be here."

Sam scratched his head. "Well, that's my problem. Obviously you thought a crime had been committed or you wouldn't have called the police. Then, before I could get here, you clean up all the evidence."

Cora sighed. "Sam, take my word for it. Someone

threw a rock through our window. It shattered the glass. Glass went all over the living room. We cleaned it up. But I would think you still have enough evidence to go on. You got the shattered window. You got the rock."

"Where's the rock?"

"On the coffee table."

"That where it landed?"

"No, that's where I put it."

"You handled the rock?"

"Why? You thinking of fingerprinting it?"

"You think I should?"

"Sam, what the hell are you doing?"

"I'm trying to figure out why you called the police."

Cora's face was getting redder and redder. A vein was beginning to stand out on her forehead. "I called the police because it didn't occur to me they might send you."

Sam nodded judiciously, as if that were a reasonable answer, instead of a personal slur. "I see what you mean. I'm not trying to give you a hard time. Just trying to understand. 'Cause that's my job. At least part of it. You get a call, you go out, ask some questions, figure out why. Sometimes it's easy. Guy robs a convenience store, shot the clerk." Sam scratched his head. "Actually, don't think we've had one of those around here. 'Least not while I was on the job. But that's just a fer instance. Point is, most calls are pretty damn easy to figure out. Even a cat up a tree. They called 'cause the cat won't come down. Actually, that's usually the firemen they call. But you get the idea. Now here, you call 'cause a rock come through your window. So I ask myself, Do you think it's a crime? Well, you don't, 'cause you clean up the glass. But you do, 'cause you call me. So it's kinda like a borderline crime, you know? Someone broke your window. Well, what do you want me to do about it? You don't want me to look at the glass, 'cause you cleaned that up. And you handled the stone. Just what do you want me to do?"

Cora seethed in silence.

"I gotta ask you," Sam said cheerfully, "is there anyone you could think of might wanna throw a stone?"

Sherry shifted position on the couch.

"Yes, Miss Carter? Something you want to say?"

"The trick-or-treaters."

"What trick-or-treaters?"

Cora waved it away. "Just some kids."

"You think they might have thrown the stone?"

"Of course not."

"But your niece brought it up. Why'd you bring it up, Miss Carter?"

"We weren't expecting them. We didn't have anything."

Sam frowned. "You turned away trick-or-treaters?"

"It was a shock to see them," Cora said. "We're somewhat out in the sticks."

"Maybe to a New Yorker," Sam observed. "So, they said 'trick or treat', and you didn't treat? How old were these kids?"

"Preteen."

"How preteen?"

"I don't know. Ten, eleven, twelve, I suppose."

"Could they have been thirteen or fourteen?"

"How the hell should I know? They were dressed as aliens."

"Uh-huh," Sam said. He picked up the pace of his gum chewing. "You see my problem?"

Cora sighed. "Oh, Sam, if ever there was a straight

line, you just lobbed that one right down the middle of the plate."

Sam again pressed on as if he hadn't heard the remark. "Someone broke your window. Not only is this a rather minor event, but you have a perfectly good explanation for it in these trick-or-treaters. Yet you call the police. Which I could understand if you called to *report* the trick-or-treaters, but, no, they're the last thing on your mind. If your niece hadn't mentioned it, I wouldn't even know."

"What are you getting at?" Cora snapped, irritably.

"I'm wondering who you think threw the rock. You don't think it's the trick-or-treaters. You must have your own candidate."

"Well, I don't."

Sam grimaced. "Then I can't see you callin' the cops. On the other hand, I hear from Chief Harper you been nosin' around on a case. I wonder if this might be related."

"I have no idea."

"Yeah, but you must suspect. You start pokin' around, someone doesn't like it, wants you to stop. Breakin' a window's a lot politer than killin' you."

"Sam, you're being even more damned irritating than usual. You mind telling me what's up?"

"I knew Anita Dryer. Wasn't on the force then. I'm not that old. Actually, wasn't much older than her. Think I was a senior when Anita started junior high. Or something like that. Anyway, I didn't know her well, but I knew her. Took it real hard when she got killed. Type of thing you don't forget. And now you're diggin' it up again. Trying to get that bastard free."

"I'm just looking, Sam. Facts aren't gonna change."

"Uh-huh. Well, then, I have to tell you." Sam popped his gum.

"What do you have to tell me, Sam?"

"If that's what's goin' on, I'm kinda on the side of whoever threw that rock."

25

There were still trick-or-treaters out when Cora hit Danbury. That bothered her. It was nearly eleven, for Christ's sake. What were their parents thinking? Cora had a good mind to stop the next gaggle of ghouls and send them straight home. She'd had enough with trick-or-treaters tonight. It occurred to her she was considering hassling teenagers because she had so little else practical to do. She was on, she realized, a fool's errand. And the only reason she was on it was because she couldn't bear to sit home doing nothing. Not with someone throwing fastballs through her window.

Cora's acquaintance with the Bible consisted largely of placing her hand on it when testifying in court, but she seemed to remember something about people without sin casting the first stone. Cora would have bet long odds tonight's stone-caster was not sinless.

Cora patted the purse on the seat beside her. She was comforted by the cold steel outline of her gun.

Cora pulled the Toyota to the side of the road, snapped on the overhead light. She surveyed the printout from MapQuest. Wondered if she'd missed the last turn. No, the directions said three stoplights. She knew she'd only gone through two.

Spider-Man and Batman approached the car and requested candy. Cora switched off the overhead light and peeled out, leaving the superheroes in the dust. She hung a right at the next light, and it was as if someone had suddenly pressed the wealth button. The street was better lit, the houses larger and farther apart. The lawns spacious, the hedges trimmed.

Cora spotted a brass number on a gatepost. It was 8. She wanted 12. Cora slowed, drove down the street.

The house had a horseshoe drive, accessible through two gaps in a tall hedge. It led to a sprawling two-story colonial. A Ferrari was parked out front. Cora pulled up behind it and got out. She went up to the front door and rang the bell. She waited, rang again.

The door was flung open by a woman in a blue flannel robe. Her hair was up in curlers. She had some sort of mud plaster on her face. She looked like a ghoul.

"Trick or treat," Cora said.

The ghoul gaped at her.

"Don't recognize me? I recognize you. Even with the war paint. You were in Dr. Jenkins's office this morning. According to vital statistics, he's not your husband."

The woman started to slam the door.

Cora blocked it with her shoulder. "Bad idea. I outweigh you. I could also wait till your husband gets home and talk to him, but that's not gonna do either one of us any good. What do you say we have a little chat?"

After a moment, the ghoul snarled, "Come in."

"Good decision." Cora pushed past her through the foyer and into an ostentatious living room hung with what appeared to be original art. The furniture was some period or other, most likely Louis Quatorze. A plasma TV was the only modern touch. It was tuned to the Home Shopping Network.

Cora snickered.

The woman grabbed the remote, switched the TV off.

"Home Shopping, eh?" Cora said. "The good thing about that mud pack is, I can't see you blush."

"What do you want?" the woman demanded.

"Anyone throw a stone through your window?"

"Huh?"

"Just wondering. You were in Dr. Jenkins's office this morning. And I was in Dr. Jenkins's office this morning. Someone threw a stone through my window. I was just wondering if someone threw a stone through yours."

"Who *are* you?" the woman shrilled.

Cora nodded. "You either don't know or that's a very good bluff. My name's Cora Felton. I'm a private investigator. I'm looking into the case of Darryl Daigue."

"Who?"

Cora grimaced. "That's the trouble with the mud pack. I really can't tell if you're lying. I wonder if I could wear one playing poker."

"Cut the comedy. You got something to say, say it."

"You're on the parole board."

"Yeah. So?"

"And Dr. Jenkins is on the parole board."

"What about it?"

"Anyone ever try to swing your vote?"

"Now, see here—"

"Don't get all indignant. I'm not accusing you of anything. It just occurred to me, you're married, and Dr. Jenkins is married, and some unscrupulous person who wanted to rig the parole board might take advantage of that."

"You're way off base."

"I'm glad to hear it."

"There is no way I could spring a prisoner unless I could sway the whole board. Believe me, that would never happen."

"You mean someone would veto you?"

"You're damn right they would. Parole is not a free pass. It's an *earned privilege*. And we take it damn seriously."

"And the name Darryl Daigue means nothing to you?"

She hesitated a moment. "I didn't say that. There is a prisoner named Darryl Daigue who's appeared before us. I don't remember the details. I do know he wasn't released. Believe me, that's all I know. Now will you get the hell out of here?"

"My pleasure."

Cora got in her car, drove out the other end of the horseshoe driveway.

A black sedan was parked across the street, its lights off.

Cora pulled out of the driveway and hung a left without a glance in the direction of the sedan. She drove to the first stoplight, hung a right. She drove a quarter mile to the next stoplight, hung a right. She drove two stoplights, hung a right. She drove one stoplight and hung a right onto the street where Ida Blaine lived.

Half a block away from the house, Cora cut her lights, pulled to the curb, and got out. She walked up next to the black sedan, rapped on the window.

A flat-faced man with a broken nose and cauliflower ears looked surprised as hell to see her.

"You throw a stone through my window?" Cora asked.

The squashed-in face gawked.

"Naw, I didn't think so. You got your job." Cora pointed to the house. "Just a hint. She's in pajamas and robe and she's *not* going out. If you're getting paid by the hour, don't let me rain on your parade. But I promise you, nothing's happening tonight."

Cora beamed at the discomfited private eye, and walked back to her car.

26

CHIEF HARPER WAS APOLOGETIC. "I spoke to Sam. There was no reason for him to take that attitude."

"Did I complain?" Cora asked.

"You don't have to complain. There's still no call for it."

"Am I in a Marx Brothers movie? Chief, I didn't complain about Sam. Who told you he gave me trouble?"

"Oh. Sam did. Said you reported a busted window. Looked like trick-or-treaters. Even your niece thought so. So he yanked your chain."

"That's his version?"

"Version?"

"Did Sam mention he was less than cooperative because I was investigating Darryl Daigue?"

"I believe he expressed his annoyance."

"Was that before or after you read him the riot act?"

"You're in a pretty bad mood this morning."

"Why shouldn't I be? I'm investigating a twenty-year-old murder case where nothing makes sense.

Everybody and his brother agrees the guy in jail did it, with the possible exception of the guy in jail. Nothing I can come up with seems to cast any doubt on the guy's guilt, but someone doesn't like me digging. Actually, *no one* likes me digging, but someone in particular, because of the rock. And, no, I don't think it was trick-or-treaters, in spite of what Sherry said. I think it's someone telling me to mind my own business."

"I didn't throw that rock."

"Oh, very funny, Chief. You're forgetting this *is* my business. Becky Baldwin hired me."

"Yes, as I recall she hired you to see if there was any chance of getting Darryl Daigue out of jail. Isn't the answer no?"

"It would be if so many people weren't pushing it."

"Ah. Reverse psychology. So whoever threw that rock had just the opposite effect."

"You got a problem with that?"

"No, I see your logic. It's just, none of this makes Darryl Daigue any less guilty."

Cora reached into her drawstring purse, flipped a folded piece of paper onto Chief Harper's desk.

He eyed it suspiciously. "What's that?"

"A license-plate number of a Danbury P.I. I'm not asking you to trace it, Chief. I just thought you should have it."

"You mind telling me why?"

"Not at all. The private dick would appear to have been hired by Quentin Hawes to keep an eye on his wayward wife, Ida Blaine. Who happens to be one of the parole board members who turned down the application of Darryl Daigue. And who appears to be a little too chummy with Dr. Jenkins, who just happens to be one of the other parole board members who turned down the appeal of Darryl Daigue. Who also happens to be Darryl Daigue's prison physician, not to mention the medical examiner who signed off on the one-car accident of Ricky Gleason, the counter boy Darryl Daigue claims not only could have given him an alibi, but was most likely the actual killer."

"You told me all this before."

"I like to recapitulate. It's so confusing, even I lose track."

"Uh-huh. And what's this guy having his wife shadowed got to do with anything?"

"Nothing. Except the P.I.'s car would appear to be a dark sedan."

"You think it's the car that was following you?"

"There's one thing that points to it."

"What's that?"

"Car picked me up at the doc's. At least, that's the first time I noticed it. And this lady was also at the doc's."

"Wait a minute. You said the husband put a tail on this woman 'cause she was involved with the doc."

"Yeah, but I could be wrong."

"No kidding."

"I mean, the reason. If the dick's not tailing her 'cause she's stepping out on hubby, it could be for the same reason he's tailing *me*."

Chief Harper struggled to digest that. "Cora, this is convoluted, even for you."

Cora sighed. "I know. The case is driving me batty. If that isn't bad enough, I have to put up with Harvey Beerbaum's birthday surprise."

Chief Harper choked on his coffee. "Birthday surprise?"

"Yeah, he's got all these famous people sending me

ACROSTIC

by Emily Cox and Henry Rathvon

THE SECRET OF STAYING YOUNG IS TO LIVE HONESTLY EAT SLOW LY AND LIE ABOUT YOUR AGE

A. Joyful lack of seriousness
L E V I T Y
38 5 30 24 59 48

B. Not sufficiently alert to danger
U N W A R Y
21 34 46 64 7 15

C. Howler on the North American plains
C O Y O T E
6 57 19 45 13 31

D. Hardly thinking clearly (3 wds.)
I N A F O G
53 17 41 11 33 23

E. The opposite of staccato
L E G A T O
28 40 18 49 1 61

F. Set free; release, as information (2 wds)
L E T O U T
52 66 9 27 58 42

G. Fourscore
E I G H T Y
54 16 65 2 26 39

H. Given a smack on the cheek, perhaps
B U S S E D
56 62 36 43 8 51

I. On leave, like a sailor
A S H O R E
14 25 32 10 63 3

J. Repetitive recitation or listing
L I T A N Y
44 29 37 35 22 60

K. Tutorial unit
L E S S O N
47 35 12 4 20 50

crossword puzzles. I mean, it's embarrassing. I don't even know these people and they're sending me Happy Birthday crossword puzzles. What am I supposed to do, send them crossword puzzle thank-you cards?"

"That's a charming idea."

"Says who? They either gotta be individual, which is a pain in the fanny, or I risk offending 'em by sending everybody the same one."

"It can't be that bad."

"Oh, yeah? Look at this."

Cora dug in her purse, came out with a folded page. She smoothed it out, showed it to the chief.

"Recognize this? It's an acrostic."

"Like the ones last Christmas?" Chief Harper asked.

"Don't remind me."

"I assume this one doesn't tell you you're going to die?"

"Not likely. Look who wrote it."

"Emily Cox and Henry Rathvon? Who are they?"

"I don't know them personally. They just happen to do the acrostics for the *New York Times* Sunday section. They have one in every other week. They're not just acrostics constructors. They're *the* acrostics constructors. Sherry went nuts when she saw their names."

"Your niece is a bit of a puzzle buff, isn't she?"

Cora's smile slipped only a second. "Well, she oughta be. With all the work she does on my puzzles. I couldn't get the column out without her."

"So what's the puzzle say?"

Cora smiled. It was a good time to repair her puzzle-making image by parroting what Sherry had just told her. "An acrostic is a quote. And the first letters of the clues give you the title and the author of the quote. In this case, Lucille Ball."

"You're kidding!"

"Not at all. It's a famous quote. Emily and Henry took it and made it into a puzzle."

"Really? What is it?"

" 'The secret of staying young is to live honestly, eat slowly, and lie about your age.' "

Chief Harper grinned and scratched his head. "Well, how do you feel about that?"

Cora shrugged. "Not the worst advice I've ever had."

27

STACY DAIGUE DIDN'T LOOK at all like her brother. She had high cheekbones, a Roman nose, shaggy auburn hair. It was only when Stacy talked that she resembled Darryl at all. Her lip curled slightly in that same unmistakable sneer.

"So what are you doing here?" she demanded.

Here was a truck-stop diner outside of New Haven, where Stacy Daigue was working the counter. Evidently, the job ran in the family, along with the facial expression. Stacy lived just down the road in a third-floor walk-up. Her landlady had guided Cora to the diner.

"I'm a private eye looking into your brother's case."

Stacy's face showed alarm. It was mid-afternoon, and the diner was hardly crowded, but there was a customer just a few stools away. "What's that, Miss? Coffee? Just a sec." Stacy grabbed a Pyrex pot off the hot plate, filled a cup, and slid it in front of Cora. "You wanna keep your voice down?" she muttered. "Why don't you look at the menu as if that's why you came?

Better still, why don't you *order* something off the menu. Eat it, and get the hell out of here. I got a job to do."

"And I don't wanna jeopardize it," Cora said. "But there's some things I need to know."

"Well, I'm the last person you should ask," Stacy retorted. " 'Cause I got zilch."

"You might think so, but you might be wrong. You might know things without knowing you know them."

The Daigue sneer was in full force. "Lady, you're insane. You gonna order or not?"

"I'll have a piece of apple pie. But, please, go on writing things as we talk."

"If I write things down, you're gonna pay for 'em."

"I think you're missing the point." Cora jerked her thumb. "Why don't you give that guy his check? Then you won't have to whisper."

Stacy totaled up the bill, slapped it on the counter, cut a piece of apple pie. "You want ice cream with the pie?"

"Doesn't everybody?"

"Vanilla?"

"Chocolate."

Stacy scooped the ice cream onto the plate, presented it to Cora. The man at the counter paid his check. Stacy swept up his tip, which was all coins, and afforded it a sneer. "Big spender," she scoffed, as the man went out the door.

"Talk to me. I tip well," Cora said.

"What do you want to know?"

"I've been looking into ways to get your brother out of jail. Frankly, it seems a lost cause."

"I could have told you that."

"Yeah, but you didn't. Anyway, that's how it looks to me. Now, the question is, does it look that way because he's guilty, or does it look that way because someone is going to great lengths to make it look that way?"

"Are you kidding me?"

"Not at all. Your brother claims a counter boy named Ricky Gleason murdered Anita Dryer while Darryl covered his shift. This is difficult to verify because Ricky Gleason died last summer."

"That's inconvenient."

Cora stared at her. "That's a rather awful understatement. Were you aware that Mr. Gleason was dead?"

"I don't even know the name."

"Your brother never mentioned him?"

"My brother mentioned many things. Some of them might have been true. After a while, you stop listening."

"You doubt your brother's word?"

"Who didn't?"

"You're not making this very easy."

"I'm not making anything. This is your show. What's your point?"

"My point is, there are a lot of discrepancies in your brother's case that bear looking into. I'm wondering if you could help me with any."

"You can stop wondering. I don't know anything at all. You looking for me to bail you out, you might as well give up."

Cora sighed. "You want to hear what I got?"

Stacy leaned on the counter, gave Cora her best Daigue sneer. "Go ahead. Make my day."

"The parole board recently heard your brother's case."

"Wait a minute. Darryl doesn't get parole."

"Right. But his case still gets reviewed. Why, I don't know, but it does. Anyway, two of the parole board members are Ida Blaine and Dr. Jenkins. Dr. Jenkins is also the doctor who signed the death certificate for Ricky Gleason and determined the cause of death to be accidental."

"Was it?"

"Hard to say. Ricky Gleason was in a one-car accident. He missed a turn he should have made, even with the amount of alcohol in his system."

Stacy frowned.

"Dr. Jenkins also happens to be your brother's doctor. The doc sees him at the prison. Prescribes your brother's medicine. Lately, he's been giving him aspirin tablets, telling him they're aspirin with codeine. This is probably hazardous to your brother's health."

"What do you mean?"

"Your brother's been getting beat up lately. I'd say it's a good bet he's been selling pills and someone's not happy they've been buying aspirin."

The scowl deepened into the familiar Daigue sneer. "You think this doctor's trying to kill Darryl?"

"Hard to say. I don't know if he's malicious or just plain stupid. But he happens to be having an affair with parole board member Ida Blaine. They're both married, by the way."

"I'm shocked."

"That's it in a nutshell. It doesn't seem like much, but everyone from the warden on down is trying to get me to drop the case."

"Why?"

"That's the question. You want me to try to find the answer?"

"I don't give a damn what you do."

"You wanna pay for it?"

"What, are you nuts?"

"Well, I don't wanna work for nothing. Becky Baldwin's taken this as far as she wants to go. She'd tell you herself, but you don't have an answering machine."

Stacy frowned. "What are you talking about?"

"Your lawyer. She couldn't reach you, so she sent me. Authorized me to give you this report. As far as she's concerned, the job is incomplete. But she's done all she feels she can without further authorization. Not to mention money. If you don't wanna tell me, just give Becky a call and tell her what you'd like to do."

"Are you mental or something? Give who a call?"

"Miss Rebecca Baldwin. The lawyer you hired to get your brother out of jail."

"Yeah, sure," Stacy said. The Daigue sneer was mocking. "Listen, lady: I never hired any damn lawyer."

28

CORA'S GAZE WAS WITHERING. "You never met her?"

"Not personally."

"You never met your client?"

"I talked to her on the phone."

"Oh, like telemarketing? I didn't know lawyers did that."

"She called me. She hired me."

"She says she didn't."

"I can't understand that."

"You and me both. Didn't it strike you as strange she didn't come in person?"

"She lives in New Haven. It's not that near."

"Tell me about it. So, she hired you over the phone. What'd she do, give you a credit-card number?"

"She sent me a check."

"A personal check?"

"No, money order."

"That figures. A personal check would have a name and address. Whereas a money order is blank.

You can fill in anything you want. I presume this money order purported to be signed by Stacy Daigue?"

"That's right."

"According to her, it wasn't. According to her, she wouldn't pay a nickle to get her brother out of jail. According to her, he probably did it."

"This is most unfortunate."

"Well, there's a brilliant analysis of the situation. You accepted a two-hundred-dollar cash retainer in the mail. On the basis of it, you hired me to do some work. Now, I admit, not everything I've done has been on your direct instructions. But going to New Haven was. Would you like to take a guess how much of that two-hundred-dollar retainer my bill is going to chew up?"

"There must be an explanation."

"Indeed, there must. Would you like to hire me to find it?"

"Cora!"

"I'm sorry. I understand. You were taken in. It's an unfortunate situation. We have to make the best of it. But the best is looking none too good. So what do you know about this woman?"

"Only what she told me. Which clearly wasn't true."

"How many times did you talk to her?"

"Just once."

"She never called back?"

"No."

"And you never called her?"

"I never got an answer. Which is why I sent you."

"Uh-huh," Cora said. "According to Stacy Daigue, she *has* an answering machine. How come you never got it?"

Cora would not have thought Becky Baldwin could look more embarrassed, but she did.

"What now?" Cora demanded.

"I called information, double-checked the number she gave me. One of the digits was wrong."

"You think you wrote it down wrong?"

"Not a chance."

"So," Cora said. "This woman gave you the wrong number so you wouldn't get through. But she changed only one digit, so if you realized it was wrong, you'd think it was just a typo."

"It would appear so."

"This woman looks a lot smarter than we do. You say you only spoke to her once. What did she sound like? Old? Young? Hip? Square? Urban? Rural? Any sort of accent? A lisp, maybe?"

Becky shook her head. "Nothing at all. It's been a while, and there was no reason for me to notice."

"So you didn't. Wonderful. What do you wanna do now?"

"I can't see doing any more work."

"Oh, *you* can't see doing any more work. What work have you done so far? Aside from hiring me. Have you even met Darryl Daigue?"

"I haven't gotten out there yet."

"You gonna go now?"

"Not under the circumstances."

"The circumstances aren't gonna change. Not if we're dropping the investigation."

"You wanna work for nothing?"

"I have so far," Cora said pointedly.

29

AARON GRANT'S HONDA WAS parked in the driveway, so Cora called out, "Hi, guys," as she came in the front door.

There was no answer.

Cora admired the plywood patch over the living room window, then went in the kitchen and poured herself an iced tea.

Moments later Aaron and Sherry joined her.

"Hi, Cora," Aaron said.

"Hi, Aaron." Cora's eyes twinkled. "You two been canoodling?"

"Canoodling?" Sherry said.

"Well, Aaron's hair is mussed," Cora pointed out, "and I can't believe he got up this morning and buttoned his shirt wrong. You're a button off, Aaron. Gives you a delightful lopsided effect, but probably wouldn't do to interview a congressman."

Aaron Grant grinned good-naturedly, and rebuttoned his shirt. "So what's new with Darryl Daigue?"

"Nothing. Becky's dropping the case."

"What?" Sherry exclaimed incredulously. "She can't do that."

"Why the hell not? Turns out she was never hired in the first place."

"What are you talking about?"

Cora gave Sherry and Aaron a rundown on the Stacy Daigue situation.

"She never hired you?" Aaron said. "How the hell does that make any sense?"

"It doesn't. And we're never gonna find out because no one's paying us to do it."

"So you're just gonna let it drop?"

"Becky's already dropped it."

"How could she do that?" Sherry said. "Maybe the sister *didn't* hire her, but *someone* put up the money."

"Right," Cora said. "And if they wanna put up some more, Becky will stick with the case. But two hundred bucks does not go a long way."

"Two hundred bucks?" Aaron said.

"Right."

"I didn't even know you could retain a lawyer for two hundred bucks."

"Well, it wasn't like she was gonna *do* anything. Just evaluate the case and see if there was reason to proceed. Only she didn't do that, she hired me."

"Okay, what's your evaluation of the case?"

"You can't print it in your paper."

"No, I don't suppose I can. So, are you gonna quit?"

"That depends."

"On what?"

"Whether people keep shadowing me and throwing rocks through my windows."

"It could be coincidence."

"Coincidence?"

"Don't get her started," Sherry warned. "You don't wanna hear a lecture on coincidence."

"Okay," Aaron said. "You got a private eye following a woman in Danbury on the parole board who's friendly with a doctor who's also on the parole board who happens to be Darryl Daigue's doc. Who also signed the death certificate on the guy Darryl Daigue says committed the crime?"

"That's right."

"This is the point at which you're letting the case drop?"

"The client is letting the case drop. Who, if you wanna interview her, doesn't know a damn thing more than you do."

Aaron frowned.

"Horribly unsatisfactory situation," Cora said. "I've been fired. I have no business poking around in this anymore. I have no status whatsoever. You, on the other hand, are an investigative reporter. You have the whole weight of the *Bakerhaven Gazette* behind you. You could probably ask anyone anything you want."

"Yeah, if there was a story in it."

"Hey, there's probably no story in it," Cora agreed pleasantly. "Mysterious strangers hiring attorneys in the names of real people and sending cash retainers in the mail. Yeah, doesn't sound like a story to me."

"Maybe Aaron could find out something that would get you hired again," Sherry suggested.

"That's not gonna take facts," Cora said. "That's gonna take money."

"Even a juicy fact?"

"I don't know. Bring me some juicy facts. The juicier the better." Cora refilled her iced tea. "Anything

A CLUE FOR THE PUZZLE LADY

ACROSS

2 Flock of crows
4 "Dial M for ___"
6 Knock off
8 Liquidate

DOWN

1 Scream bloody ___
3 Hit
5 Rub out
7 Theme of this puzzle

else happening? Not that I'd expect the two of you to notice."

"Yeah, you got a birthday card," Sherry said.

Cora groaned. "Not another one of Harvey's puzzle friends. Where is it, on the computer?"

"No, this is a real card. Came in the mail."

"A real card? You mean like paper? An envelope you rip open, and the whole bit?"

"Sure looks like it," Sherry said.

"Who's it from?"

"I didn't open it."

"Why not?"

"You think I read your mail?"

"You read my e-mail."

"I *pick up* your e-mail. That's entirely different."

"And you tell me what it says while I'm reading it. Like the postman in that Dylan Thomas play."

"*Under Milk Wood*?"

"That's the one. Whose wife steams open the mail so they can read it. You steam open my birthday card?"

"It was a great temptation, but we resisted."

"I guess you had better things to do." Cora held the card up to the light. "Hard to tell what it is."

"*You're* allowed to open it," Sherry pointed out.

"Oh, thank you. Don't mind if I do."

Cora tore open the envelope, took out the card.

It wasn't a card.

It was a piece of paper, folded into quarters.

Cora unfolded it.

It was a puzzle.

"Oh, Christ!" Cora said. "Another damn puzzle. Can't anybody spring for a Hallmark card anymore?"

"Let me see," Sherry said.

"It's not even a *good* puzzle," Cora griped. "Hardly any clues. Hardly any words. Like Harvey asked somebody who really didn't wanna do it, but couldn't say no."

Aaron Grant, looking over her shoulder, said, "Not only that, they're all the same length."

"What?"

A CLUE FOR THE PUZZLE LADY

ACROSS

2 Flock of crows
4 "Dial M for ___"
6 Knock off
8 Liquidate

DOWN

1 Scream bloody ___
3 Hit
5 Rub out
7 Theme of this puzzle

Aaron pointed. "The answers. They're all six letters long. So what are the clues?"

Cora read them off. " 'A flock of crows.' 'Dial M for blank.' 'Knock off.' Oh, my God!"

Cora's mouth fell open as the answer dawned on her.

30

"THIS IS RIDICULOUS," CORA grumbled, as Sherry pulled the Toyota out of the driveway.

"Ridiculous?" Sherry said. "You just got a death threat."

"It's not a death threat. It's just a stupid puzzle."

"It's *not* a puzzle," Sherry said. "There's no such thing as a puzzle where every answer is *murder*."

"Why not?"

"What do you mean, why not? It's too easy to solve, for one thing."

"Hey, when it comes to solving puzzles, I can use all the help I can get."

"Oh, stop it. You read three clues and said, 'Oh, my God, it's murder.' "

"Well, what else could it be?"

"Nothing. That's the whole point. It's a threat, and the chief should see it."

"He could see it tomorrow."

"Oh, like nothing happens at night? When did that rock come through the window?"

"You're taking this way too seriously."

"Cora, I don't know what you're mixed up in here, but this is sick."

"We could have just called him."

"No, he should see this."

"What, like he wouldn't believe us?"

"Of course he would. But it's hard to describe. 'Chief, we got a puzzle and every answer's *murder*.' 'What?'"

"We don't even know if he's there."

"He's there."

"This time of night?"

"It's not that late."

"We should have called."

"Yeah, well, we didn't. And we're almost there. So why don't you stop griping about it."

Sherry drove down the main street of town. There was a cruiser parked in front of the police station.

"See, I told you he's here."

Sherry pulled up next to the police car. Aaron pulled in alongside.

The door of the police station opened and Chief Harper came out. "Hi, what's up?" he asked.

"Cora got a threatening letter," Sherry told him.

"Well, I wanna take a look at that. Can you give me a moment? I gotta go see Edith Potter."

"What for?" Aaron asked.

"I don't know. Jimmy's probably in trouble, or something." Harper started across the street. "Come on. Bring your letter. What type of threat is it?"

"It's a puzzle," Cora said.

"Yes, I suppose it would be. And what does the puzzle threaten?"

"Murder."

Chief Harper stopped at the foot of the library steps. "I beg your pardon?"

"Show him," Sherry said.

Cora unfolded the puzzle and handed it over.

"There's no answers filled in," Chief Harper pointed out.

"No, but they're all murder," Cora told him. "Look at the clues."

Chief Harper read them over. "That is strange. Come on, we'll make a copy."

They went up the steps of the library and in the front door.

"SURPRISE!!!"

The one-hundred-and-fifty-plus people jammed into the library foyer, front desk area, reading room, computer alcove, and rare-book room, all shouted in unison. They wore party hats and carried noisemakers, which they blew with wild abandon.

It was hard to tell just how many people were there because the library was awash with streamers, banners, balloons, crepe paper, and confetti. A huge sign hung over the front desk: HAPPY BIRTHDAY, PUZZLE LADY!!!

Cora was astounded. She gawked at the crowd. Everyone, but everyone, was there. There was Iris Cooper, in a silver party hat, and was that, yes, Judge Hobbs in a purple pointed one. Cora almost wished she had a camera as the august jurist blew one of those rolled-up paper party favors that come shooting out like a sword. And there was Mrs. Cushman of Cushman's Bake Shop, and Officer Sam Brogan, and Judy Douglas Knauer, of Knauer Realty, and Dr. Nathan, dapper as ever in a red bow tie, with matching red party hat. And there was Jimmy Potter, obviously in no trouble, standing with Chief Harper's daughter, Clara.

Oh, was Chief Harper going to get it!

From out of the crowd came Harvey Beerbaum. His eyes were sparkling, his face was wreathed in smiles.

The library fell silent.

Harvey pranced up to Cora, took her by the hands.

Cora cocked her head. She growled: "Harvey Beerbaum, you are in *such* trouble!"

Everyone laughed and cheered.

Harvey gave Cora a big hug. "Pretty good, huh? Tell me, did you ever suspect this was going on? You didn't, did you? You know why? The puzzles. I fooled you with the puzzles. That was the master stroke. Like a magician, I directed your attention to one hand, while I appropriated the playing card with the other." He frowned. "Or whatever the saying is."

"Palmed the ace?" Cora prompted.

"That's the ticket. Anyway, did you have the faintest idea this was happening?"

"I'm here, aren't I?"

"You mean you came because you *knew*?"

"Fat chance, Harvey. I swear, I'm gonna get you for this."

Harvey laughed. The little wordsmith was like a kid in a candy store. "Come on! Come on!" he exhorted. "You have to see this!"

The crowd parted as Harvey led Cora past the main desk into the central hallway that connected the original frame library building with the modern addition. Two stories high, with a skylight, the hall had a spiral staircase leading to the upstairs stacks, with a balcony all along the side wall. Taped to the balcony rail, in huge letters, was the sign, HAPPY BIRTHDAY, CORA!

Centered under the sign, two four-by-eight-foot tables had been pushed together to form an eight-by-eight square.

On the tables was the largest cake Cora had ever seen. It was flat and square. It was frosted with black-and-white icing.

It was decorated in the shape of a crossword puzzle.

"See!" Harvey cried triumphantly. "Isn't it phenomenal! Everybody baked a square, and we conjoined them with frosting, and we constructed a puzzle cake. Isn't that the most lovely thing you've ever beheld?"

Cora barely heard him. She was fixated on the clump of birthday candles clustered in 22 and 23 Across. "What's with the candles, Harvey?"

"Oh. Well, you see, no one would tell me just which birthday this was you were having. Silly, don't you think? And I couldn't ask you, for fear of spoiling the surprise. So I put in twenty candles, just to have some." He smiled roguishly. "You *are* over twenty, aren't you?"

"What about that one?" Cora pointed to a lone candle in square 55.

Harvey smiled. "Why, Cora Felton! Surely the Puzzle Lady is familiar with that old saying."

"What old saying?"

"You're not? I'm amazed. 'And one to grow on.' The extra candle on the cake is to grow on. For instance, a six-year-old boy would have six candles on his cake, and one extra candle, to grow on. You really never heard of it?"

Cora had had it. It wasn't enough to be ambushed

by this surprise party, now she had to put up with being needled about her knowledge of linguistics?

"Harvey Beerbaum," Cora said severely. "At my age, which, by the way, is none of your damn business, I have done all the growing I intend to, thank you very much, and you can take your extra candle to grow on and stick it—"

Before Cora could tell Harvey a good location for the extra candle to grow on, a body tumbled over the rail of the balcony, and landed smack in the middle of the birthday cake puzzle, filling in 14 Down.

31

"Now, NOW," DR. NATHAN soothed. "You have to stay put."

"I'm fine," Cora Felton said irritably.

"You may think you're fine, but you've had a terrible shock. You fainted and fell on the corpse."

"Harvey Beerbaum fainted and *pushed* me into the corpse."

"I'm tending to Harvey too."

"What do you mean, *too*? He faints, you treat *me* for shock?"

"You're a woman."

"You want a fat lip?"

"Granted, you're a feisty woman. But you are a woman, and you're not as young as you used to be, Cora."

"What a sweet thing to tell a woman on her natal day. You ever consider going into the greeting-card business?"

"If you're trying to impress me with your sarcasm, it will do no good. You've had a traumatic shock."

"Would that traumatic shock be seeing a dead body?"

"Of course."

"Then why aren't you tending to him?"

"You noticed the body was male?"

"Yeah, Doc. The suit and tie sort of gave it away. Don't you have to determine the cause of death?"

"Already been done."

"Good for you, Doc. How'd you work so fast?"

"It wasn't that hard. His throat had been slit. That's what kept him from crying out."

"Well, that's interesting as all hell. How's Harvey?"

"I was just going to check on him." The doctor raised his voice. "Miss Carter. Mr. Grant."

Sherry and Aaron, who'd been waiting outside the door, hurried over.

"Would you mind keeping an eye on Miss Felton while I check on Mr. Beerbaum? I don't want her wandering off."

"Do I have your permission to use force?" Aaron Grant asked.

Cora started to rail at him, but noticed his eyes were twinkling.

Dr. Nathan grinned, and ducked out the door.

"Now, look here—" Cora began.

"No, you look here," Sherry told her. "The doctor said to keep an eye on you, and we intend to. In the first place, do you know where you are?"

"Give me a break," Cora snapped. "I'm in the little office where Jimmy Potter works. There's the typewriter he uses to type his file cards. I'll be throwing it at somebody in just a minute. Now peek out the door and tell me if the doc is watching."

"Aunt Cora, Dr. Nathan said to stay put."

"He's not a cop, he's a sawbones. What's he gonna do, throw pills at me?"

Cora pushed by Aaron, slipped out the door.

The library had cleared out. There were crime-scene ribbons on all the entrances to the area under the rail. The body, of course, was gone, but the smashed cake remained. It held the dead man's imprint. It was not a neat outline, like when a cartoon character goes through the wall, but it was clear enough to tell the tale. The man had fallen facedown, with his feet toward the top of the cake, and his head toward the bottom. The legs had been slightly splayed, and had straddled the twenty candles. The candles were still there, jutting up from the frosting.

The candle to grow on had been wiped out by a direct hit.

The man's head had been facing left. Cora could tell that largely from the bloodstain on the cake's white icing. That side of the outline was somewhat marred by the fact that she had toppled over the corpse.

On the other side of the outline, where the left arm would be, was a semicircle in the frosting, as if a child had been making snow angels.

The rest of the cake was untouched. It occurred to Cora if you ignored the fact it was a crossword puzzle, the cake didn't look all that bad. She idly stuck a finger in the frosting, put a sticky glob in her mouth. It tasted pretty good too.

"Aunt Cora!" Sherry exclaimed.

Cora ignored her, took another taste.

"Eating the crime scene?"

Cora looked up, saw Chief Harper hurrying toward her from the direction of the main desk. She smiled. "Now, how often do you get to say that?"

He cast a withering gaze at Aaron and Sherry. "I thought you were keeping an eye on her."

"We are, Chief," Sherry said brightly. "How's she look to you?"

Before the chief could retort, Cora said, "Wasn't his hand up?"

"What?"

"He fell with his hand up. Over his head." She pointed. "It looks like it got pulled down."

"Ah, yes." Chief Harper tugged at his collar, uncomfortably.

"What's the matter, Chief?" Cora demanded.

"Do you remember the sequence of events? The man fell, just missing you. Harvey looked, fainted, knocked you down."

"Exactly," Cora said. "*I* didn't faint. I remained in perfect possession of my faculties."

"Does your head hurt?"

"Why?"

"You banged heads with Harvey. The doctor was concerned."

"I'm fine. What about his arm?"

"Oh. Well, after you got knocked down . . ."

"Yeah?"

"He moved it."

Cora made a face. "He was *alive*?"

"Barely. And not long. Dr. Nathan was right here. Rushed to the body, did all he could. Which wasn't much. The guy had his throat cut. You don't live with your throat cut."

"You ID the body?"

"According to his driver's license, he's Peter Burnside, of Danbury, Connecticut."

"Huh," Cora grunted.

"Mean anything to you?"

"Never heard of him." Cora stuck her finger in the frosting, took another bite. "You know, I think the vanilla's better than the chocolate."

"Will you *please* stop that!"

"Can I smoke in here?"

"Of course not."

"Then I gotta eat." Cora dipped her finger.

Out of the corner of his eye, Chief Harper could see Aaron Grant scribbling gleefully in his notepad. "Cut it out, Aaron."

Cora licked her lips. "So, what are you doing, Chief? You got two hundred suspects locked up and you're taking them one at a time?"

"Nobody's locked up. Everybody's going home. Dan Finley's out there right now writing down license-plate numbers. But it's probably too late."

"How do you figure that?"

"Decedent's upstairs keeping an eye on things from the balcony. He got lucky there. See the ribbon across the spiral staircase? Edith Potter closed it off, didn't want anyone upstairs in the stacks. He's got the whole place to himself. The killer sneaks up behind him, slits his throat, pushes him over the rail. There's a back stairs and a back door. In the confusion, the killer sneaks out. Could have driven off while the body's still flopping around."

Sherry Carter made a face.

"Hey, you're grossing out my niece."

"Sorry, but that's a fact. Anyway, if the killer was long gone, Dan Finley's license numbers won't do us any good."

"You sent Dan out to get 'em when you saw the Danbury ID?"

"I sent Dan out when I didn't recognize the corpse's face. No way he was from around here. I figure someone must have followed him."

Dr. Nathan came out from attending Harvey Beerbaum, said, "Hey, what are you doing up?"

"Oh, is it past my bedtime?" Cora looked at her watch. "You gotta give me a little leeway, Doc. After all, it's my birthday."

Dan Finley came in with a legal pad. "Okay, I got your plates. Most are Connecticut. A few are New York. A few Massachusetts and Vermont. There's one from Texas. I'm not sure what that's all about."

"Okay," Harper said. "Run 'em through the computer, group 'em by town. I'd particularly like to know who's here from Danbury."

"All of 'em?" Dan Finley said.

"Well, start with Connecticut. If you find a New York plate from Danbury, we got trouble."

"I could help Dan run those plates," Cora offered.

"Oh, I'm sure Dan can handle it."

"Fine. I'll help you with the crime scene." Cora speared another gob of frosting.

"Stop that!" Harper turned to Sherry. "Can you get her out of here?"

"Dr. Nathan told me to stay," Cora announced truculently.

"And now I'm telling you to go," Dr. Nathan said. "Just don't drive. Sherry, you'll take her?"

"Sure, Doc. Wanna come along, Aaron?"

"It's news, Sherry. I've gotta stay."

"Me too," Cora said. "You run along, Sherry. Aaron and I will stay here."

"Nice try, Cora." Sherry took her aunt by the shoulders and nudged her toward the door.

"Traitor," Cora grumbled.

Cora risked a backward glance. Chief Harper and Dr. Nathan were studying the smashed birthday cake.

Cora turned back, to find Sherry had stopped to talk to Aaron Grant.

"Come on, come on!" Cora hissed. "Let's get the hell out of here before the son of a bitch changes his mind!"

32

"You mind telling me what we're doing?" Sherry said.

"We're going to Danbury," Cora informed her. "Didn't you always want to go to Danbury?"

"Not at eleven o'clock at night."

"Is it eleven? Time flies when you're sedated."

"Are you sure you're thinking straight?"

"Sherry. Sweetie. I could drink a pint of rum and still recite the Gettysburg Address. You think a mild tranquilizer's gonna faze me?"

"You know the Gettysburg Address?"

"That was just an example."

"That was just a *bad* example. Which is my whole point. You're not thinking straight. If you were, we wouldn't be driving to Danbury."

"Why not?"

"Why are you going behind Chief Harper's back?"

"I'm not."

"Did you tell him you were going?"

"No."

"Pray, elucidate, oh wordsmith, how this does not constitute going behind his back."

"Oh wordsmith? Low blow."

"Would you prefer *prevaricator*?"

"I'm not entirely sure what that means."

"It means you deceived Chief Harper about the fact you're rushing off to Danbury. And now you're trying to claim you didn't."

"No such thing. Chief Harper has a crime to solve. I don't want to distract him from his purpose."

"Not even close. I think you may have impaired judgment."

"Okay, how about Chief Harper has no jurisdiction in Danbury, so the first thing he'll do is contact the local police. Who may or may not be in collusion with Dr. What's-his-face regarding the suspicious traffic fatality of the late Mr. Gleason."

"Not bad. You've almost got me convinced."

"You think that's good logic?"

"No, but you said it well. Maybe you're not that impaired after all."

"I'm fine."

"You certainly are. You've managed to evade the question very nicely."

"What question?"

"Why are we going to Danbury?"

"Do you have to ask? To check out the victim, Peter Burnside."

"You're not breaking into a dead man's house!"

"Of course not. I'm breaking into his office."

"Aunt Cora—"

"Which is not nearly so bad."

"I'm glad to hear it. How do you know he has an office?"

"He's a private investigator. Of course he has an office."

"How do you know he's a private investigator?"

"How do I know anything? Why else would he be keeping tabs on the guy's wife who's having an affair with the doctor on Darryl Daigue's parole board?"

Sherry Carter stared at her aunt. "You recognized the corpse?"

"Watch the road."

"And you didn't tell Chief Harper?"

"The chief didn't ask me."

Sherry pulled the car up on the shoulder.

"What are you doing?" Cora demanded.

"Turning around."

"No, you're not."

"Yes, I am. Cora, you're withholding vital information from the police. There's no way you can justify this one."

"I'm not withholding a thing. I told Chief Harper all about this detective shadowing the guy's wife."

"You didn't say the detective was the dead man."

"Give me a break. I gave Harper the guy's license number. If he traced it, he knows the guy's name, and he knows he's the corpse. If he didn't, that's hardly my fault."

"Oh, for God's sake—"

"I've given him all the facts. The deductions are up to him. It's not my place to figure things out for the chief of police."

"Like that's ever stopped you before."

"Could we have this discussion while you're driving? I'd like to hit Danbury before dawn."

Sherry sighed and put the car in gear. "You know, if you could just apply the same mental agility to crossword puzzles."

"God forbid!"

33

STILL BICKERING, SHERRY AND Cora drove into Danbury. They stopped at the first pay phone and Cora called Information. "Can you give me the number for the Peter Burnside Detective Agency?"

"You mean Burnside Private Investigators?"

"That's right."

Information gave Cora the number.

"Is that on Hudson Street?" Cora asked.

"No. Three sixteen Main."

"Thanks."

Cora got back in the car. "It's three sixteen Main Street."

"You know where that is?"

"Sure. Right across from three fifteen. Come on. Can Main Street be hard to find?"

It wasn't. Ten minutes later Sherry pulled up in front of a four-story office building in the middle of the block. The street was dead. There were no bars or restaurants, no residential buildings. Only stores and offices, all closed for the night.

There were no parked cars, so theirs stood out. A cruising police car slowed to take a look.

"Cora," Sherry warned.

"Got it." Cora switched on the overhead light, fished a map out of the glove compartment.

The cop pulled alongside, rolled his window down. "You ladies need any help?"

Cora managed to knock her glasses sideways peering over the map. "We're looking for Route 7 South."

The officer nodded, pointed. "Go down here, left at the light. Three blocks up you'll see a sign."

"Thanks."

"What do we do now?" Sherry asked Cora out of the side of her mouth.

"I fold the map, and see if he drives off."

He didn't. The cop waited patiently while Cora folded the map, stuck it in the glove compartment, and turned off the overhead light.

"I'm afraid he's a gentleman. Okay, follow his directions. Left at the light, and see if he leaves us be."

The officer followed right along behind.

"Looks like we're taking 7 South," Cora said.

Sherry turned onto the highway.

"Good," Cora said. "He went on by."

"Can we go home now?"

"Silly girl. Take the next exit and loop around back."

Sherry got off Route 7, drove a few blocks until they hit Main. "From this direction we'll be right out front."

"If we get there at all," Cora said. "Here comes the cop."

"Uh-oh. What do I do now, roll down the window and ask him for Route 8? I doubt if that's gonna fly."

"Shut up and let me think."

The police car drove on by.

"It's not him!" Sherry said.

"Yeah. We're lucky this town's big enough to have two cops on duty. Even so, it's giving me the willies. Whaddya say we park down a side street?"

"Sure. Why not make this look as suspicious as possible?"

"Hey, we're breaking and entering. I wouldn't worry about *looking* suspicious."

Sherry drove by the office building, pulled the car into the next side street.

"Remember," Cora said as they got out. "We just walk up to the place as if we had every right to be there."

"Despite the fact it's midnight," Sherry said dryly.

"Is it midnight?"

"Five after."

"That's a relief. I hate getting arrested on my birthday."

The front door of the building had a lock, but it wasn't engaged. Cora pushed the door right open.

"Look at that, Sherry. I really must speak to these people about their security."

"Yeah, when they visit us in jail."

"No one's going to jail. Let's see now. Where's the directory? Ah, right next to the elevator, of course. Here we are. Burnside Private Investigators. Room two-oh-four. See if the elevator works. If it doesn't, it's just one flight."

Cora pushed the button. The elevator door slid open. "Well, that's easy."

"Yeah. You think it's a trap?"

"No, I think it's just easy."

The elevator rumbled up to two. A door at the far end of a corridor had BURNSIDE PRIVATE INVESTIGATORS stenciled on the frosted-glass window.

"Think this door's unlocked?" Sherry said.

"If it is, this guy's too dumb to live." At Sherry's look, Cora added, "Sorry, but that's a fact."

The door was locked.

"Now what?" Sherry said. "You wanna try the fire escape or break the frosted glass?"

"Tough choice." Cora fished in her drawstring purse, came out with her gun.

"I was kidding!" Sherry exclaimed.

"Relax. I'm not going to shoot my way in." Cora fumbled deeper in her purse, came out with a ring of keys. "Let's see if one of these works."

"You've got burglar's keys?"

"Of course not. There's only, what, six keys here. What are the odds one would fit?"

The third one did. The lock clicked back, and Cora swung the door open. "Shall we?"

"Aunt Cora! Where'd you get those keys?"

Cora smiled, her bright-eyed, trademark, Puzzle Lady smile. "Like it? I do. It was worth driving all the way here just to see your expression."

"Damn it, where'd you get them?"

"A good magician never reveals trade secrets."

"You're not a magician. You're about to be a dead aunt."

"That's a nasty image. Like something stepped on at a picnic." Cora grabbed Sherry by the arm, jerked her into the office, kicked the door shut, and switched on the light.

"Hey, someone will see."

"So? We're secretaries working late. If it never happened, why would they leave the outer door open?"

"Don't change the subject. Where did you get those keys?"

"Oh, these?" Cora held them up, smiled. "When Harvey fainted, he knocked me down on the corpse. I'd already recognized the guy."

"You picked a dead man's pocket?"

"I thought his keys might come in handy. I simply jammed them in my purse."

"You weren't really knocked out?"

"More like freaked out. Can you imagine having Harvey Beerbaum fall on you?"

Cora headed for the file cabinet, jerked open the top drawer.

"What are we looking for?" Sherry asked her.

"I'm looking for a file on the Blaine broad."

"Broad?"

"When you've broken into a private dick's office after midnight, the skirt he's tailing is a broad. Don't you read books? All right. Here we go. Ida Blaine. No file. Right. The husband's paying the bills, and he's got a different name. Okay, Quentin Hawes." Cora slammed the drawer, pulled out a lower one. "Here we go. Damn! No file for him, either."

"Maybe he just hired him."

"There still should be a file. Maybe it's on his desk."

The desk was a rickety metal affair with a pencil drawer, and two deeper drawers. It supported a telephone, and a metal in/out box. The out-box was empty. The in-box was full with what appeared to be bills.

The desk chair was the type with arms and wheels. Cora sat in it, spun it around, jerked the right top drawer open. Found nothing more interesting than a pint of rye. How cliché, Cora thought. And how inviting. It was a great temptation to have a drink on the dead man. There was something poetic about it. Of course, Sherry would absolutely freak. Cora told herself that was why she was passing it up.

Cora closed the top drawer, opened the bottom.

Ah, this was more like it. A rectangular account book. Cora reached in, pulled it out, saw immediately that it was not an account book, but a checkbook. A hard-bound ledger with three checks down each page.

Cora flipped the stubs over. To her astonishment, there was nothing written on them.

"There's no check records," Cora said irritably. She glanced up to see Sherry sitting at a small computer desk in the corner. "What are you doing?"

"Checking his business letters. Maybe he wrote his client."

"Good thinking. Say, would that have his bank records too?"

"Sure, he's got Quicken."

"Can you check his last deposit?"

"Not without a password."

"Damn. Can't you get in some other way? Isn't there a back door?"

"Oh, now you're a computer geek? Talking about back doors? Hang on, let me try something."

"What?"

"He's got a lot of notepads open. Let me check 'em." Sherry clicked on one. "Well, here's the combination to his safe."

"What safe?"

"Damned if I know. But it's 'L-24, R-48, L-15.' Sure there's not a safe somewhere?"

"Go ahead. I'll look."

Sherry clicked on another icon. "Here's a license-plate number. 'PUB 1403-NY.' " She tried another. "Here we go. 'Passwords. Q = CASH.' Bet you a nickle that's Quicken."

"No takers. Give it a try."

Sherry opened Quicken. When asked for the password, she typed in *cash*. "Ta-da!" she said, as the program opened. "Would you prefer checking or savings?"

"Start with checking."

Sherry moved the mouse.

There was a knock on the door.

Sherry sucked in her breath, glanced at Cora. "What do we do now?" she whispered.

Cora put her finger to her lips.

The knock was repeated, louder this time.

"Cora!" Sherry mouthed.

Cora kept her finger raised insistently.

The door clicked open.

"Hello? Anybody here?"

A head peered around the corner of the door. The man spotted them, walked into sight. He was a paunchy security guard, most likely a retired cop.

Cora took one look, trilled, "Oh, thank goodness, it's you! We were so scared. We didn't know what to expect this time of night."

The guard's eyes narrowed. "You work here?"

"We're working now. Is that a problem? It's never been a problem before."

"I've never *seen* you before."

"I've never seen you, either. Are you new?"

"No, I'm not. How did you get in?"

"I got the keys from Mr. Burnside." Cora frowned. "He didn't say there'd be a problem."

"No problem. Just making sure. That's my job."

"Well, it's reassuring to know you're out there. We'll feel a lot safer going home."

The guard stared at her, rubbed his chin. After an agonizing few moments, he said, "Good night," and went out, closing the door behind him.

Sherry's eyes were expressive. She mouthed, "Let's get out of here!"

Cora smiled, said out loud, "Let's go over those files, shall we?"

Sherry glanced at the door, sighed. "Sure thing." She called up the page. "Let's see. These are all checks. Rent. Utilities. Telephone. Cell phone." She looked up at Cora. "How did you miss stealing that?"

"Go on, go on," Cora told her.

"Car payments."

"Huh. Poor man didn't own his car outright. Now he never will."

"Ah. Here we are. Five-hundred-dollar deposit a couple of weeks ago. And that is the last deposit since . . . Let me see. Five-hundred-dollar deposit the month before that."

"Anything that isn't regular?"

"I'm looking. But I don't see anything."

"That's strange. If the guy hired Burnside to tail his wife, there ought to be a record of it."

"Well, if so, he didn't put it in checking."

"Try savings."

The savings account showed little activity and a balance of less than fifteen hundred dollars.

"Any other accounts?"

"That's it."

"I wonder where his safe is."

"Aunt Cora."

"Well, we've got the combination."

Cora glanced around the office. It was a dreary affair. The off-white walls were dirty and unadorned, with the exception of a calendar and a bulletin board. The calendar was on the month of July. Either Burnside was too lazy to change it, or he happened to like the scantily clad model depicted on it.

The bulletin board, hung on a wire, was about three-by-four feet and contained mostly business cards and the jack of diamonds, which, Cora recalled, was a hard card to play. The majority of business cards appeared to be for takeout food. There were a couple of letters, one about parking space, another about lease renewal. Evidently, Burnside had been killed in the nick of time. His rent was about to go up three hundred bucks a month.

Cora pulled the bulletin board away from the wall, peered behind it. Her expectations were low. It was way too obvious a place for a wall safe.

Cora blinked in amazement. Recessed in the wall was a round metal door with a combination lock.

"Sherry!" Cora hissed.

Sherry didn't answer. She was busy at the computer.

Cora couldn't reach the safe. She glanced around the office. Leaning against the far wall was a folding chair.

Cora started for the chair.

The door flew open and a cop with a gun burst in.

"All right, hold it right there!"

Cora stopped in mid-stride. She gawked at the officer, then grinned at the absurdity of it all. "You're telling me to *freeze*?"

The young cop sported a crew cut, a beer belly, and a steely gaze. He probably hadn't smiled since his last doughnut. "I'm telling you to hold it right there. Take your hand out of your purse, slow, so I can see it. You at the computer, keep your hands on the keyboard, that will be just fine. And you take your hand out of your purse real slowly."

Cora was surprised to find she had her hand in her purse. She was even more surprised to find she was holding her gun. Her husband Melvin had trained her well. Too bad he was such a son of a bitch.

Cora pulled her empty hand out of her purse.

The security guard peered around the side of the cop. "That's them. Never seen them before. Good thing I called."

"All right, lady, who are you?" the young cop demanded.

"I'm Cora Felton, this is my niece, Sherry Carter."

"You got any ID?"

"Yeah. You wanna see it?"

"Yes, I do."

Cora suppressed a smile that the young cop was making her dig into the same purse he just made her take her hand out of. She actually had to push her gun aside to get to her wallet.

"Here's my driver's license, Officer. Examine it if you like, but don't look at the picture. It's really bad."

There was no disputing that. Cora's eyes were closed, and her mouth was twisted in a criminal sneer. The woman on Cora's driver's license did not look like someone who sold breakfast cereal to children. She looked like someone on *America's Most Wanted*.

The young cop seemed to put her in that category. "What are you doing here?" he snarled.

Cora could not have smiled more sweetly had the young officer been her son. "Well, that's just the point. We were looking for evidence of employment."

He frowned. "Huh?"

"And so far we can't find any, which is rather annoying."

"They don't work here," the security guard prompted anxiously. "They got no right to be here."

"Is that so?" the cop said. "You don't work here?"

"Well, that's a matter of semantics," Cora said judiciously. "We were actually doing some work when you—arrived."

"How'd you get in?"

"I have a key."

"Where'd you get it?"

"From Mr. Burnside."

"Mr. Burnside gave you a key?"

"In a manner of speaking."

The cop scowled. "Lady, I don't like the way you answer questions. Good thing you called, Chuck. There's something not kosher here." He wheeled on Sherry. "What's *your* name?"

"Sherry Carter."

"You got ID?"

Sherry passed over her driver's license.

The cop examined it, frowned. "This says Sherry Pride."

"That's my married name."

"You don't use it?"

"No."

"Why not?"

"I'm divorced."

"What are you doing here?"

"Helping my aunt."

"This lady's your aunt?"

"That's right."

"Do you work here?"

"Same as she does."

The young cop frowned. "That's no answer. Do you know Mr. Burnside?"

"No, I don't."

"He didn't give you a key?"

"No, he didn't."

"You see him give your aunt a key?"

"No, I didn't."

The cop wheeled back on Cora. "Looks like you're on the hook for this one."

An older cop came in the door. His hair was mussed, his shirt was unbuttoned, and only half tucked in. He had clearly been woken from a sound sleep, and wasn't thrilled about it.

His mouth fell open when he saw Cora.

He groaned.

"I might have known!"

The cop was Sergeant Walpole.

34

BECKY BALDWIN LOOKED LIKE she just stepped out of a fashion magazine. Her makeup was perfect. Every hair was in place. Her tan outfit was miraculously unwrinkled. Looking at her, one could never guess it was two A.M.

One would have known it from Sergeant Walpole. He'd had a cup of coffee—three cups, in fact—but he could have done with a shower, shave, and about twelve hours' sleep. Even so, Becky looked so good, he could barely bring himself to be rude to her.

"Miss Baldwin, I appreciate the fact you drove all the way from Bakerhaven to visit these two, and I'm glad you all had a little chat, but the fact is, the judge ain't coming in till the morning, so there's nothing you can do."

Becky smiled like the cop had just complimented her on her perfume. "Well, that's certainly an interesting starting point for our discussion. Why don't we see what we can do about that?"

"There's nothing we *can* do. That's the point I'm

trying to impress upon you. We don't have night court here in Danbury. You're unlucky enough to get locked up at two in the morning, you're gonna stay in a holding cell till the judge gets here at ten."

"That's why it would be most advantageous for all concerned if my clients were not locked up."

"I'm sure it would. Unfortunately, your clients were apprehended rifling a dead man's office."

"I seriously doubt that, Sergeant." Becky turned to Cora and Sherry, seated at the table in the interrogation room. "Do you think these ladies look capable of rifling anything? I find the idea absurd."

"I saw them myself."

"Rifling the office?"

"In the office."

"Rifling it?"

"No. After they'd been stopped by the security guard."

"The security guard caught them *rifling* the office?"

"Well . . ."

"Wasn't his original impression that they were *working* in the office? Wasn't his only concern that he had never seen them before? And if he *had* seen them before, wouldn't he have been completely reassured that they *were* working in the office?"

"I can't vouch for what the security guard *thought*."

Becky smiled. "Oh, but you are. You just told me these women were caught rifling the office. You also told me it was the security guard who caught them rifling. Now, are you not vouching for what the security guard thought when you characterize their activity as rifling?"

Sergeant Walpole rubbed his forehead. "Come again?"

"So, surely we can clear this matter up."

"I doubt it. I hate to rain on your parade, Miss Baldwin, but I don't care what you wanna call it. These two were discovered in the office of Mr. Burnside, where they had no right to be, after midnight. They pretended they were working, though they do not work there. They claim Burnside gave them a key, though that statement is suspect, since Burnside is dead. You have any problems with that assessment of the situation?"

"I don't think it's true."

Sergeant Walpole scowled.

"Don't take offense. I'm sure *you* think it's true. You just happen to be mistaken."

"And you'd like to point out the error of my ways?"

"No, don't take it like that. We're just having a nice chat. The fact it's two in the morning has nothing to do with it."

"I'll say."

"You say my clients were in the office where they had no right to be. However, they had a key to that office. If they were given a key to the office, they had every right to be there."

"Now you're claiming the dead guy gave them a key?"

"Not at all. I'm merely dissecting your statement. That's the first part that's incorrect. Then you say they pretended they were working. I would think that would be a very hard thing to do. I don't know how one could pretend to work. I would think you would have to work at it. But then you wouldn't be pretending, would you?"

"You know what I mean. They pretended they were working for Mr. Burnside."

Becky's perfect eyebrows arched. "Oh? That's another matter entirely. They pretended they were working for Mr. Burnside? I didn't know the security guard made that claim. Let's get him in here. See if he recalls them mentioning anything about working for Mr. Burnside."

"You're twisting my words," Sergeant Walpole yelped.

"On the contrary, Sergeant. I'm doing my best to take your words literally. So let's push on. Next, you say my clients claimed Burnside gave them the key. I'm sure you'll find they made no such claim. Here's my understanding—and correct me if I'm wrong—the security guard asked Miss Felton where she got the key, and she replied that she got it from Mr. Burnside. But she never said he gave it to her."

"If he didn't give it to her, she got it illegally."

"May I quote you on that?"

"It's gotta be one or the other."

"Don't be absurd. There's lots of legal ways she could have obtained it."

"Name one."

"He could have sold it to her."

"Yeah, sure," Walpole scoffed.

"He could have assigned it to her when he employed her."

"Isn't assigning it to her the same as giving it to her?"

"You really want to discuss semantics at two in the morning?"

"No. Are you claiming he employed her?"

"Not at all. We were talking hypothetically."

"It's two A.M. I don't wanna talk hypothetically."

"Neither do I. I would very much like to go home. I would like to take these two women with me."

"I'm afraid that's not possible."

"Why? What are they charged with?"

"They're not charged with anything yet. They haven't been arraigned."

"What charge did you arrest them on?"

"Breaking and entering."

"They didn't break and enter. They had a key."

"Which they obtained illegally."

"Says who? The security guard? What does *he* know? I can't wait to cross-examine him on how he knew where they got that key."

"Let's not start that again!"

"So what are you going to charge them with? It's clearly not breaking and entering. It's not robbery. There was no attempt to take anything. What else is there? Oh, yes. The security guard's extraordinary claim that they *pretended* they were working. If that *were* true, what would the charge be? Impersonating a file clerk? I didn't know that was illegal in Connecticut."

"The charge is breaking and entering. If they want to advance the defense that they had a key, that's their business."

"And if they want to sue you for false arrest, that's mine. Come on, Sergeant, be a sport. If you can find me two less likely flight risks than Sherry and Cora, I'll buy you dinner. You wanna arraign 'em tomorrow morning, fine, I'll see they show up. But don't hold them overnight in the drunk tank like a pair of hookers. Send them home with me. If you do that, I'll promise not to sue you for false arrest, even if the judge kicks the charge."

Sergeant Walpole bit his lip, considered.

At the interrogation table, Cora surreptitiously

nudged Sherry in the ribs. "He's gonna go for it," she whispered.

"Looks like it," Sherry whispered back.

"If he does, I want you to do me a favor."

"What's that?"

"Ride home with Becky."

35

CORA MADE MORE FIGURE eights than an Olympic-hopeful skater. No one seemed to be following her. Still, she wanted to be sure. She made one more loop and pulled into a back alley two blocks away from Burnside's office.

Cora knew the best way to be unobtrusive was to walk along the street perfectly normally as if nothing had happened. Unfortunately, there was no way to walk along the street normally three hours before dawn. Cora skulked in the shadows, kept her eye out for cars.

There was no police car by the office, at least none in sight. Cora scoped it out from the alley across the street. If there was a cop around, she wouldn't know he was there till she tried the door.

Cora could imagine the look on Sergeant Walpole's face if she was hauled into the police station again.

It was almost worth getting arrested just for that.

Cora smiled, crossed the street.

A car came around the corner. Headlights raked the storefronts next to the office building.

Cora ducked back into the shadows. A no-brainer decision. If the cop saw her, she was dead meat. It wouldn't matter if he saw her hiding, or crossing the street. There was no talking her way out of this one. Not if the cop knew her, and had seen her sent on her way.

Cora crouched in the doorway of a newsstand as the headlights flashed on by.

It was teenagers out joyriding.

Hell, Cora thought. Why weren't the cops busting them? The kids were probably drunk. What could the police be thinking of?

Cora hurried across the street, hoping against hope the cops hadn't locked the front door.

They hadn't.

That was the good news.

The bad news was, they'd kept her keys.

Of course, there was no help for that. She'd had to surrender the keys. If she'd made a fuss, the cops would have figured she planned to use them. They'd have posted a guard. Assuming they hadn't already. But that was a good assumption. She'd already broken into the office. No one would suspect she'd do it again.

If she just had her damn keys.

There was always a chance the office door was open. Cora figured the odds were about a million to one. It was a good thing she didn't bet, because the door was locked.

Cora could have broken the frosted glass, like Sherry was afraid she was going to do earlier that evening. Cora smiled at the thought of considering two in the morning earlier that evening. She also smiled at the thought of breaking the frosted glass. She couldn't recall breaking a frosted-glass window before. Regular panes, sure, but frosted glass was another matter. It had all those little veins in it. Those little hexagons, or octagons, or however many gons it was. Cora wasn't about to count them. Instead she was striding down the hallway to the window at the end.

It opened onto nothing, which was strange. Cora would have expected a fire escape, but there was none. Just an air shaft between this and the next building.

That was interesting. If there was no fire escape there, surely there must be one somewhere else.

Cora made her way back to the elevator, took it up to the sixth floor, and found the stairway to the roof. She pushed the door open and stepped out.

It was a cloudless night. Stars were out. There was a three-quarter moon. Cora knew the Big Dipper. Her fourth husband, Henry, had pointed it out on their honeymoon. At the time Cora had thought of Henry as the big dipper. It was only later when she thought of him as the big dip.

Cora went to the side of the roof where Burnside's office was, looked over the edge. Sure enough, a fire escape ran down the side of the building. Of course, it didn't go to the roof, but it went to the sixth floor. And the sixth floor was close below.

Relatively close.

Somewhere between twisted-ankle and broken-neck close.

Cora looked around the roof. Oddly enough, there was no twelve-foot ladder one could lower over the side. Cora couldn't understand the shortsightedness of the building's maintenance staff. She made a mental note to speak to the super.

The stairwell wasn't that far from the edge of the roof. Cora went back, looked down the stairs.

On the wall of the sixth-floor hallway was a fire hose on a metal wheel.

Cora went down the stairs, grabbed the hose just below the nozzle, and pulled.

The hose obviously hadn't been uncoiled in years. The metal wheel proved mightily reluctant to turn. It squeaked in protest. Yielded each inch of hose grudgingly.

Cora pulled it all out, and made sure the end was securely attached. How the hell they got water in it was beyond her, but that wasn't Cora's problem.

The length of the hose was.

Cora wrestled the hose up the stairs, pulling it tight behind her. Was gratified to see she still had plenty left when she reached the roof. She dragged it to the edge, dropped it onto the fire escape.

Or at least tried to.

The hose was long, but not that long. The nozzle stopped halfway down. A good six or eight feet from the fire escape. It was hard to tell in the dark. Cora told herself it might be closer than that. Hell, holding on to it, her feet might reach the bottom.

Only one way to find out.

Cora looped her drawstring purse over her neck, so that it slung down her back and wouldn't get in her way. She pulled herself up over the parapet, and, holding on to the hose, lowered herself over the side.

The fire escape was a lot farther below than she figured. Or maybe it just seemed a lot farther because she was crawling down the side of the building holding on to the hose. The rough bricks were scraping her knees, the fire hose was rubbing her fingers raw, and the purse was strangling her.

And it was windy. Why hadn't she noticed it was

windy before? All she'd noticed was what a nice night it was. Not that a cold north wind was chilling the hands of anyone attempting to defy gravity by clinging on to a—

Cora lost her grip and fell.

She was high enough that the fire escape rattled as if a subway car had just jumped the rail into a swimming pool of cookie tins.

She was low enough that neither bones nor metal broke.

Her glasses fell off, however. Cora groped around for them on the fire escape. Had a moment of panic that they had fallen through.

Her purse was weighing her down like an anchor. She extracted her head, got to her hands and knees.

Cora couldn't see a thing. Hell, how could she find her glasses without her glasses?

Her left hand hit them, almost knocked them off the fire escape. Cora grabbed the glasses, jammed them on her face. Found she couldn't see with them, either. It was too dark. No matter. She could hold on to the rail, feel her way.

Cora retrieved her purse, slung it over her shoulder, and worked her way down the fire escape to the second floor.

There. This was Burnside's window. Assuming she'd calculated correctly. Assuming it wasn't the window of someone else.

Someone alive.

Cora put her hands on the bottom of the window, pushed up.

It opened.

Cora raised the window, scrambled through.

She emerged on the top of a desk. There was a loud clatter as pencils and pens went flying.

Cora expressed her opinion of the situation in a brief exclamation that would have made Ozzy Osbourne blush. She fumbled in her purse for her cigarette lighter, jerked it out, and fired it up.

Yes. The desk she had just decimated was indeed the property of the late detective.

Cora dropped to the floor and began gathering up the pens, pencils, ruler, stapler, paper clips—what the hell had they been in? Ah, an unused ceramic ashtray? Could that be it?

It was a moment before she remembered the detective whose office it was wouldn't be around to notice if anything was out of place. It didn't matter if everything was exactly as it was, just so long as it was neat.

Cora finished tidying up the desk, turned to the bulletin board on the wall.

And the lighter went out.

Cora spun the wheel, encouraging the flint to produce the spark to light the gas.

There was no gas. The damn thing was empty. It wouldn't light.

Cora rummaged in her purse for another lighter. Or a book of matches. Or two Boy Scouts to rub together. But it was no use. The only thing she found capable of producing a spark was the gun. Cora could imagine herself firing several bullets for illumination as she worked her way across the room.

She shoved the gun back in her bag, along with the useless lighter, and groped her way toward the bulletin board on the wall.

Cora knew she needed something to stand on. She seemed to remember folding chairs somewhere in the room. But way over on the other side. A million miles away.

And here she was, bumping into the desk.

The desk over which the bulletin board hung.

If this was the right desk.

Cora leaned out, groped the wall.

Yes. There was the edge of the frame. Now, if there was just something to stand on.

Just beyond the desk was the computer stand. In front of it was a typing chair, the kind that revolves on wheels, has no arms, and has a back that tilts down.

The least steady chair imaginable.

Cora grabbed it, jammed it into the corner between the desk and the wall. She climbed up on the seat, reached out, and grabbed the edge of the bulletin board.

The bulletin board went one way, the chair went the other.

Cora wound up on the floor in a heap. At least this time she didn't lose her glasses. Merely bruised a few more bones.

Cora struggled to her feet, gained her bearings, headed off in the direction she imagined the chair had gone.

She made out a curve that might have been the back of the chair. It was. She realized her eyes were becoming accustomed to the dark. She grabbed the chair with both hands, marched it back to the desk, and jammed it into place.

This time, when she climbed up on the seat, she could make out the edge of the desk. She put one foot up on it, and tried transferring her weight. Evidently the legs were closer to the middle, because she could feel the desk tip down.

Cora cursed her luck and moved her foot. With a lunge that sent the desk chair rolling across the room, she stepped up onto the center of the desk. She flailed her arms, gained her balance.

Cora lifted the wire off the hook, slid the bulletin board down the wall, and rested it on the desk.

Okay. There was the safe. Now, what was the combination?

Cora glanced across the room at the computer. It was off. It was also across the room. It was also a computer. The odds of Cora getting a combination out of it were infinitesimal.

On the other hand . . .

It was left, right, left. Cora remembered that because her fourth husband, Henry, had gone to West Point, and that was the way the soldiers marched, left, right, left.

And the numbers were . . .

Twenty-four. Hours in a day.

Forty-eight. If you double it.

Fifteen. Minutes of fame.

Cora hoped like hell that was right. She reached up, spun the dial.

Couldn't see the numbers.

Of course she couldn't. Idiot. And here she was, balancing on the top of a desk.

Cora eased herself to her knees and groped around the desk, but there was nothing useful. She jerked open the top drawer and pawed through pencils, pens, and assorted office junk. She had no idea what most of it was, she just hoped it wouldn't stab her.

Her hand encountered thin cardboard. She grabbed it, pulled it out.

A book of matches.

Cora's biggest problem now was not to tip over the

desk in her excitement. She stood up carefully, struck a match, spun the dial.

Left twenty-four.

Right forty-eight.

Left fifteen.

The safe clicked open.

The match went out.

Cora struck another, held it up to the open safe.

It was empty.

Cora rolled her eyes in disbelief. That goddamned gumshoe. Who the hell has a hidden wall safe with nothing in it? No one. No one but what's-his-face dead P.I. No wonder someone offed him. Cora felt like offing him herself.

Cora closed and locked the safe. She bent down, picked up the bulletin board, hung it from the hook. In the dark, she couldn't tell if it was straight. She lit a match, saw the bulletin board was tilting a bit to the right, and evened it up.

Just before the match went out, however, a folded piece of paper caught her eye. Cora had a feeling she'd passed over it the first time around. She lit another match and took a look.

The paper was blank. It was pinned to the bulletin board with a pushpin. Cora pulled out the pin, unfolded the paper.

It was a check made out to Peter Burnside for five hundred dollars. Evidently checks were infrequent enough, Burnside had to pin them to his bulletin board to make sure he didn't lose them until he got to the bank.

The check was signed *Valerie Thompkins.*

It took a moment for Cora to remember who that was.

The woman with the teased hair and the toy poodle.

36

It was easy to find Valerie Thompkins's house. It was the only one on the street with its lights on. Cora could see it two blocks away. There was a light on the two-car garage, and a light over the front door. And there were lights in the upstairs and downstairs windows.

The toy poodle was barking when Cora came up on the front step, a high-pitched *yip, yip, yip*. She wondered if it had heard her car. The house was fairly far back from the road. She'd been quiet coming up the walk. But the dog was yapping to beat the band.

Cora rang the bell. That spurred the poodle to new heights. It managed to hit high F above C. But no one came to the door. That was odd. Cora could imagine someone not hearing the doorbell. She couldn't imagine them not hearing the dog.

It occurred to her Valerie Thompkins might be out. Cora hoped she was.

Cora tried to peer through the living room window, but the drapes were closed. So were those on the next window.

Cora worked her way around the house. All the drapes were closed, and all the doors were locked. The only window not curtained was in the kitchen. All Cora learned there was Valerie Thompkins had a gas stove instead of an electric one. Sherry would have approved.

Cora completed a circuit of the house, rang the doorbell again. No one answered but the dog.

Cora stepped back, looked at the upstairs windows. One was open. And not that far from an elm tree branch.

No way. Cora'd had quite enough climbing for one night.

Were there basement windows? The lights would have been out, so she wouldn't have noticed. She didn't see anything in front of the house. Perhaps she should check around back.

Cora jabbed at the bell one more time. Of course, there was no response.

Cora tried the doorknob.

It opened.

Cora kicked herself in the head for being so stupid. She consoled herself with the fact it was four in the morning, and she'd been given a sedative after someone dropped a body on her. Still, you try the door. After all, she'd tried every *other* door. Why not the front one?

Cora pushed it open, went in.

She was immediately jumped on by a yapping little dog, which set new decibel records as it darted in and out like a deranged hornet, clawing at her legs and snapping at her feet. Cora didn't know whether to defend herself or pet it.

The dog wasn't sure, either. He scooted halfway up the front stairs, bounded down again, shot through Cora's legs, and whizzed into the living room.

That seemed like an invitation to her. Cora followed the poodle through the doorway.

The body of Valerie Thompkins lay sprawled in front of the coffee table. Valerie had somehow managed to sweep everything off the table and onto the floor. An ashtray was overturned, strewing cigarette butts on the white shag rug. A whiskey glass had fallen, leaving an amber stain. Magazines were strewn about, including *Cosmopolitan, People,* and the *TV Guide.*

Valerie lay on her back, with her head lolling crazily to one side. Blood had stopped flowing from the gaping gash in her neck. There was a fairly good pool of it soaking into the white carpet.

The minute Cora was in the room, the poodle barked even more insistently. *All right, I got you here, now do something about it. Make Mommie better.*

Cora knew there was no way in the world she could make Mommie better, and yet she felt for a pulse. Was not surprised to find none. The poodle skidded around the room in crazy circles, romping through the pool of blood, which he somehow had managed to avoid before. Little red paw prints appeared on the rug, tracing the path of the lunatic dog, as it attempted to coax its owner back to life.

Valerie Thompkins was wearing a white blouse and black slacks. There was nothing in her pockets. Nothing clenched in either hand. Cora felt sheepish for looking. Of course there was nothing in her hands. People didn't die clutching clues. Or write messages in blood. Though there was certainly enough to do it. And—

Good lord!

Was she seeing things?

No, there was a smear of blood on Valerie's right index finger.

Good lord!

Cora bent down, tried to peer under the coffee table. She couldn't see a thing. Not from that angle.

Cursing, Cora lay down flat on the rug, trying to avoid the cigarette ash, the whiskey stain, and the blood. Wriggling on her back, she inched her way under the coffee table.

There, on the bottom of the table, not twelve inches from her nose, was scrawled the word BUD, in what appeared to be blood.

Cora felt a cold chill.

She also felt foolish as hell.

Here she was, living out some childhood fantasy from a Nancy Drew novel. The killer's name in blood? What next?

The poodle romped over her stomach. It didn't weigh much, but the nails hurt.

Cora started, banged her head on the bottom of the table. She groaned, rubbed her forehead, knocked off her glasses. She fumbled for them, rammed them on again. Looked at the bottom of the table to make sure she hadn't just imagined BUD.

She hadn't.

But she *had* smudged it.

The midline of the *B* was gone, smushing together the upper and lower loops.

At a casual glance, the message now read DUD.

Cora wondered if it was an editorial comment.

Cora rolled her head away from her handiwork, squirmed out from underneath the coffee table, sat up, and took stock of the situation. She knew what she had to do. She had to call the cops, wait till they arrived, apologize, and explain. It wasn't much, but it was all she could do. At least she could straighten them out on when the bloody paw prints were made.

And how BUD became DUD.

And why she'd gone there in the first place.

And where she got the check.

Cora'd gotten about that far in her list as she wiped her fingerprints off the front doorknob and hurried to her car. She started the engine, pulled out with her lights off, just in case anyone was watching.

Cora drove out of town, stopped at a filling station. There was a pay phone next to the road. Cora dropped a quarter in, dialed 911. When the operator came on, she said, "There's been a break-in at three twenty-five Hickory Road."

"Who is this?"

"This is a good Samaritan, reporting a break-in. I think the owner may be in trouble. Get a car out there at once."

"Can you confirm the identity of the owner of the house?"

Cora slammed down the phone, hopped in her car, and drove as if the devil were at her heels.

37

Sherry Carter moaned, "For Christ's sake, what time is it?"

"Time to get up."

"You've gotta be kidding."

"Come on, come on," Cora chided. "You gonna sleep all day?"

Sherry raised her head from the pillow, focused bleary eyes on the clock. She blinked, rubbed them, looked again. "Six A.M.?"

"Yeah, I was going to let you sleep till six in the evening, but you'd have missed the fun."

"Aunt Cora—"

Cora's face was hard. "Get up. Now. You got some explaining to do."

"I do?"

"Don't play innocent with me. Splash some water on your face and make some coffee."

Sherry rolled out of bed, stumbled into the bathroom. She took time to brush her teeth, before joining Cora in the kitchen.

Sherry found her aunt staring at the coffeemaker as if it were some technological marvel that surpasseth human understanding. Cora had filled the pot with water, and was squinting at the coffeemaker sideways, looking for someplace to pour it. "Where the hell does this go?" she demanded.

"How many times have you seen me make coffee?"

"One too few." Cora thrust the pot into Sherry's hands. "And hurry up with it. I'm dead on my feet."

"No kidding."

Sherry poured the water into the coffeemaker, saw that Cora had taken the bag of ground coffee from the freezer, but had failed to find and wash the filter. Sherry swung it out now, dumped the coffee grounds, washed it in the sink. She measured out the coffee, swung the filter back into the machine, switched it on. She turned back to find her aunt sitting at the table smoking a cigarette.

Sherry put her hands on her hips. "All right. I did what you said. I rode back with Becky. And believe me, that was no treat. She used me for a punching bag most of the way. And what could I say in my defense? After all, we had broken into the damn office."

"We got in with the key, Sherry."

"Which you picked from the dead man's pocket."

"That's not the point."

"Well, then, tell me the point. Because I have a hard time recognizing it on two hours' sleep."

"I've had none."

"Is that my fault?"

"I don't know. Is it?"

"Cora. What have you done?"

"You know that office we broke into?"

"Don't tell me."

"Okay." Cora took a drag on her cigarette, tried to blow a smoke ring. It looked like Picasso drew it.

The coffee burbled. Sherry yanked two cups out of the cupboard, grabbed the milk from the refrigerator, slopped in the coffee. "I think I'm going to need this. Here's yours. Now, what did you do?"

"I went back in that office."

"I thought they took your keys."

"What's your point?"

Sherry sighed. "All right. What did you find?"

Cora reached in her drawstring purse, flopped the check on the dining room table. "This."

"You brought it home? Why didn't you put it back?"

"I was afraid I'd fall off the desk."

"Come again?"

"I didn't want to."

"Better. So what are you gonna do? Give it to Chief Harper?"

"I don't think so."

"Why not?"

"Because she's dead."

"Dead! What are you talking about? Who's dead?"

"The woman who wrote the check."

Cora told Sherry about finding the body of Valerie Thompkins.

"My God, Cora! And you didn't call the police?"

"Sure I did. I just didn't say it was me."

"You reported a murder?"

"Good lord, no. How would I know that? I reported a break-in."

"You didn't give your name?"

"Of course not."

"You made up a name?"

"No, I hung up the phone."

"You called from the house?"

"Do I look stupid?"

"Well, you don't look like a Mensa candidate. What's wrong with your hair?"

"I washed it."

"Why?"

"To get the blood out."

"Blood?"

"The woman's blood. From the secret message, naming her killer."

"Are you kidding me?"

"I wish I were."

Cora told Sherry about finding the message on the coffee table.

"You changed *Bud* to *Dud*?"

"I'm afraid so."

"That's about the worst thing you could have done."

"I suppose I could have written *Chud*."

"You didn't tell the police any of this?"

"No. I just reported a break-in, and got the hell out of there. Actually, I got the hell out of there first. I called from a pay phone."

"You think they believed you?"

"I hope so. I'm worried about the dog."

"What dog?"

"The toy poodle. It's yapping its head off. It's very upset."

"Cora, you have bigger problems right now than a poodle."

"Yes, I do. That's why I woke you up. Before I talk

to anyone. Before I figure out what I'm going to say to the chief. Or the Danbury cops, for that matter. There's one thing I gotta know."

"What's that?"

"How much of this is your fault?"

38

SHERRY'S MOUTH FELL OPEN. "Aunt Cora—"

"Don't play innocent with me." Cora's eyes were hard. "How dumb do you think I am? A guy croaks, and whaddya do? Drive me to Danbury. Help me break into his office."

"You had a key."

"That's not the point."

"It's your own argument."

"Don't change the subject. Why'd you drive me to Danbury?"

"I didn't want you to go alone."

"I *couldn't* have gone alone. Dr. Feelgood's shot hadn't worn off yet. I was still woozy. I should have gone home to bed. Instead, you drove me to Danbury. Which is entirely out of character. You wanna tell me why?"

"Why do you think?"

"I don't think, I know. I've been depressed lately. Ever since the wedding didn't come off. Which is putting it mildly. Down in the doldrums. Whatever the hell they are. So you decided to cheer me up. Decided a little detective work was just what the doctor ordered."

"For Christ's sake, Cora. What's the difference why I gave you a ride? The fact is, I did, and now we have to deal with the result."

"I'm not talking about you giving me a ride."

"Then you're in worse shape than I thought, because that's exactly what you just said."

"That was an *example*. Of what you've been up to."

"What do you mean?"

"You know damn well what I mean." Cora took an angry drag on her cigarette. "Becky Baldwin's gonna take a case without interviewing the client? She's gonna send me out instead?"

"What's wrong with that?"

"Everything. I'd have seen it before, if I wasn't as depressed as you say. If I hadn't wanted the work. Why did you do it?"

"Aunt Cora—"

"Why did you do it?"

Sherry took a breath. Sighed. "For your birthday."

"What?"

"I wanted to do something nice for your birthday. Ah, hell. It was really Harvey Beerbaum's fault."

"Harvey?"

"He was doing everything wrong. Knocking himself out, giving you something you'd hate. I wanted to give you something you'd like."

"So you went to Becky Baldwin?"

"It didn't seem such a bad idea at the time."

"You hired Becky Baldwin?"

"I didn't hire her. I gave her money to hire you."

"How much money?"

"Two hundred dollars."

"Two hundred dollars? Good lord, Sherry. You mean you sent the check? You signed the sister's name to a money order?"

"Of course not."

"Then what *did* you do?"

"I went to Becky Baldwin, asked her if she had anything you could work on. Of course, she didn't. She has a small practice, does most of her own work. I prodded her, so she came up with this. She'd had a phone call from a woman who wanted to get her brother out of jail. For two hundred bucks she'd agreed to look into it, make a recommendation. The money order'd just arrived in the mail. Becky was planning on visiting the guy in prison. That seemed perfect. I said, let you do it. She said, no way, it was a two-hundred-buck job, she wanted the two hundred bucks. I said, fine, I'd give her two hundred bucks to pay you to do it."

"Oh, for—"

"It was a birthday present."

"How is it a birthday present if I don't even know I've got it?"

"You knew you had it. You just didn't know who gave it to you."

"I didn't know *anyone* gave it to me. When were you planning on telling me? My birthday's over."

"Your birthday ended with a murder. That kind of preempted things."

"Like telling me what you'd done?"

Sherry said nothing.

"You weren't gonna, were you? Not if you didn't have to. So how is that a present? I'd never know you gave it to me."

"Does that make it any less of a gift?"

"I don't know, and I don't care. I gotta sort this out.

Jesus Christ, Sherry, help me here. Just how much of all this are you responsible for?"

"Nothing. I got Becky to hire you, and that's it."

"You didn't embellish it in any way?"

"Like what?"

"The rock through our window, for instance. You didn't get someone to throw that rock?"

"Through our living room window? Get serious."

"You didn't pay someone to follow me in a car?"

"Hell, no."

"No, of course not. 'Cause the woman with the dog wound up dead. Now how does that make any sense?"

"I don't know, but you better figure it out fast."

"Why?"

In the driveway, a police car screeched to a stop.

39

CHIEF HARPER WAS REMARKABLY calm. "I didn't expect to find you ladies up."

"We're not only up, we've made coffee." Sherry led him into the kitchen. "There happens to be a cup left."

"I'm glad to hear it. The fact there's a cup left. Not the fact you're up."

Cora, seated at the kitchen table, said, "What's the matter, Chief? Don't you ever get up at six in the morning?"

Chief Harper slid into a chair opposite Cora. "I'm up now. But I've had some sleep. I didn't go rushing off to Danbury last night to burgle a dead man's office."

Cora smiled. "I don't want to pull wordplay on you, Chief, but doesn't *burgle* mean to take something?"

"It's a matter of intent. If you *meant* to steal something, it's burglary. But you're right. I believe in this case you're merely charged with criminal trespass." The chief included Sherry in his gaze. "Both of you, I understand."

"Now, don't go blaming Sherry," Cora said.

"Oh, don't worry. I think I know who to blame." He dumped milk and sugar in his coffee. "It's my understanding the Danbury police confiscated a set of keys."

"Oh."

"Now there's a choice comment. May I quote you on that?"

Cora said nothing, lit another cigarette.

"One of those keys opened Burnside's office, which is not surprising, since that's where you were found. You have any comment on that?"

"I'd like to help you, Chief. But my attorney has advised me to refer all inquiries to her."

"I'd hate to wake Becky up on such a minor matter. So never mind telling me about the keys, I'll tell you. The rest were for various doors in his private home. His home being a third-floor walkup in the suburbs of Danbury. One key was for the front door, one key was for the kitchen door, one key was for the garbage."

"The garbage?"

"The Dumpster in the alley was locked. Why, I don't even want to begin to speculate. One of the keys unlocked it. You weren't aware of this?"

"How could I be?"

"I was just wondering if you dropped in on the gentleman's apartment before you tried his office."

"Now, why would I do that?"

"I don't know, because I don't know what you're looking for. I was just wondering if you did."

"I can neither confirm nor deny that, Chief."

Harper frowned for the first time. "You're gonna take that attitude?"

Cora smiled. "If I answer some questions, it's not gonna fool you much when I refuse to answer others."

"But if you didn't do it . . . ?"

"Exactly. I didn't do it, so I say I didn't do it. Then you ask me something else and I say I can't comment."

"God save me." Chief Harper leaned on the kitchen table. "I'm going to tell you the situation. Then you can decide if you want to comment, or you want to wake up Becky Baldwin. The Danbury police searched Burnside's apartment and they didn't find anything of interest. They also searched his office, with the same result. Of course, there they had the disadvantage of being the second ones to search it."

"So what? Sherry and I didn't take anything."

"No, you didn't. You were interrupted before you had a chance to."

"Whereupon the police searched the office. And found nothing. Because there was nothing to find. You're beating a dead horse, Chief."

"Is there anything else you'd like to tell me?"

"I'll ask Becky Baldwin. If there is, I'll be in touch."

"I'm glad to hear it. Now, would you like to know why I'm calling on you before the sun rises?"

"You like our coffee?"

"No, I like you. I would hate very much for you to get in trouble."

"So would I."

"Which is why I would like to give you one last opportunity to tell me anything significant that might have happened in Danbury last night."

"Can't think of a thing," Cora said.

"I can. Nine-one-one call about four A.M. Report of a break-in. Police investigated, found the owner dead."

"Natural causes?"

"Throat cut. Bled like a stuck pig. All over her living room rug."

"Why are you telling me this?"

"You like murders. I thought it might interest you."

"Sure, Chief. Sherry and I were just sitting here hoping you would come in and tell us a story."

"The woman had a dog."

"Big dog?"

"No, a small dog. Toy poodle. The dog was very upset, as you might expect. Ran all around the room. Trotted through the blood."

"Sounds messy."

"It was. Left bloody footprints all over the floor. Except for one spot. Right by the coffee table. A gap, about a yard wide. Where the tracks leave off and then pick up."

"Maybe the dog jumped."

Chief Harper shook his head. "Too wide. It's a little dog. No, it ran over something. Something that moved. Something that's not there now."

"Like the killer?"

"That's what the Danbury police thought. Then they tried to figure why the killer would lie down next to the corpse. One of the cops laid down and looked, and, wouldn't you know it, there's a message written on the bottom of the coffee table in blood."

"Like a bad mystery."

"Exactly."

"And what was the message scrawled in blood? Was it the killer's name?"

"Not unless the killer's name is Dud."

"That hardly seems likely."

"Upon closer examination, the initial *D* in *Dud* appears to have been altered, either accidentally or intentionally, from some other letter. Most likely a *B*. Which would make the killer's name Bud."

"That's still pretty far-fetched."

"Yeah, but a lot more likely than Dud. Anyway, it raised the question, why was the *B* changed to *D*? Was it done deliberately, to throw us off the track? Or was it done accidentally, perhaps by someone brushing against it with their head."

"Interesting theory."

"I notice you washed your hair, Cora. Isn't that a little unusual for someone who's been up all night? Wouldn't that be the last thing on your mind?"

"That sounds like a song lyric, Chief."

"Are those scratches on your ankles? It looks like something scratched your legs."

"You're a married man, Chief. You shouldn't be noticing a woman's legs."

"You have any comment to make on any of this?"

"Sounds like the Danbury police have their hands full."

"I'm giving you a chance to come clean. You know anything about this second murder?"

"You haven't even told me who the victim is."

"Name's Valerie Thompkins. Ring a bell?"

"Why don't you ring it for me."

"That's the license plate you had me trace. Of the car that was allegedly following you."

"Really?"

"Yeah, really. And there is *absolutely* nothing to connect Valerie Thompkins's murder with the murder of the private investigator, Burnside." His eyes grew hard. "Except for one thing. His license-plate number happens to be the one you gave me to trace yesterday afternoon."

"Oops."

"Isn't that a nice howdy-do. You give me license-plate numbers to trace, and the owners of the cars wind up dead."

"There's absolutely no connection."

"I'm glad you're so sure. But I can't take the chance. It so happens you gave me *three* license-plate numbers. I had the Danbury police check out the address of one Ida Blaine. They're dying to know why."

"How is the young lady?"

"I'm assuming if she were dead, I'd have heard. So, if I were you, I'd have a nice, long talk with Becky Baldwin. Be sure you cover withholding evidence and conspiring to conceal a crime. You might want to touch on accessory after the fact. Then, if either of you have anything to tell me, I'd be more than happy to listen."

Chief Harper pushed back his coffee, got up, and stalked out.

"Well, of all the nerve!" Cora fumed.

"Give the man a break," Sherry said. "He's a friend, but he's the chief of police. He can't cover up a murder."

"Oh, *that*. I'm not mad about that. It's what he said about the dog jumping over the person on the floor." Cora snorted angrily. "A yard wide, indeed!"

40

BECKY BALDWIN WAS INCREDULOUS. "I can't believe you did that!"

"I've done worse," Cora told her.

"I'm sure you have. I mean telling me about it. You know what you've done? You've made me an accessory to murder."

"No such thing. You're only an accessory if you aid someone who's guilty. I happen to be innocent."

"You may be innocent of the murder, but you're guilty of obstruction of justice. Appropriating checks. Rubbing out dying messages. At two separate crime scenes, no less."

"Burnside's office isn't a crime scene."

"Oh, excuse me. I suppose stealing his keys doesn't count."

"It shouldn't. The police have those keys. There's no harm done."

"I can't believe I'm having this conversation."

"Then you should never have passed the bar. I got

news for you. Most clients are guilty. I'm a breath of fresh air."

Cora was smoking. Becky had been too upset to notice. Reminded, she pointed to the window.

"Yeah, yeah." Cora got up, flung the window open, came back, and sat down. "You were saying?"

"I wasn't saying anything. I was sitting here dumbfounded that you would pull such a cockamamy stunt and then lie to the police about it."

"I didn't lie to the police about it. I said I couldn't make any statements until I talked to my lawyer. Okay, I've talked to my lawyer. What's your advice?"

"You should have lied to the police about it."

"Are you kidding me?"

"Only slightly. If you'd lied to the police, I couldn't contradict you. Now any statement you make is with my blessing."

"What statement do you advise me to make?"

"None. I advise you to shut the hell up."

"Channel 8 news crew's in town. Rick Reed is going to want something."

"Tell him, 'No comment.'"

"That's not going to satisfy him. You may have to take him out to dinner."

"Thanks a lot."

"He's going to ask you anyway. It might as well be for a good cause."

"Cora, you want to curb your irrepressible self for a minute, and look at what we've got?"

Cora pursed her lips. "I'm not sure you can curb something irrepressible."

"God save me!"

"That's what Chief Harper said."

"Cora—"

"Okay, I'll tell you what we've got. You and Sherry conspired to give me a job interviewing Darryl Daigue. The job was bogus in more ways than one. Sherry was paying for it. Darryl Daigue's sister wasn't. Either she's lying about it, or somebody used her name."

"Now why the hell would they do that?"

"So they wouldn't have to use their own."

"Exactly. But what does this have to do with the two killings?"

"Four killings. You've got four killings here. The murder of Anita Dryer. The quote 'accidental' unquote death of Ricky Gleason. And the two murders you just mentioned."

"You're saying they're related?"

"If they're not, why did they happen? Assuming all of this is cause and effect. It's certainly linked. Darryl Daigue's in jail for murder. Someone retains you to get him out. You hire me." Cora waggled her hand. "Or whatever. I start investigating. I find that one of the witnesses to the original crime, and perhaps the actual perpetrator, died in a questionable car crash. The doctor who ruled the death accidental is Darryl Daigue's doctor, and a member of the parole board that turned him down. Another member of the parole board is having an affair with the good doctor. She's being watched by a private investigator. The private investigator is snuffed. When I call on the doctor, I find myself being tailed by another woman. She is subsequently killed. The private investigator is in possession of a check signed by the woman who is subsequently killed."

"We don't know that for sure," Becky interjected.

"I have the check right here."

"No, no, you don't," Becky protested. "You have a

check that *purports* to be signed by the woman who was subsequently killed. For all you know, it could be a fake. A false clue that someone has planted. You certainly don't wish to make any allegations based on this unsubstantiated evidence that may prove to be fake."

"Does that cover our asses?"

"I believe that's the correct legal term. The woman who purportedly wrote this check is a middle-aged widow with no known connection to any of the parties in the case."

"With the possible exception of me," Cora pointed out.

"You do seem to be the unifying factor. Not that I'm willing to concede the point."

"God forbid. So the sixty-four-dollar question is, why should anyone want to kill a harmless woman with a little dog?"

"Sixty-four-dollar question?"

"Pre-inflation. Before your time. What happened to the dog, by the way?"

"How the hell should I know? I didn't know there *was* a dog."

"I didn't mention the bloody paw prints?"

"I think you left that out."

"Oh. Well, the toy poodle was running all over the place."

"I don't want to hear this."

"Okay. But find out about the dog, will you? I'm worried about the dog."

"How can I ask about the dog? I'm not even supposed to know about it."

"You're a lawyer, for Christ's sake. Can't you be devious?"

Becky sighed. "To think I was just trying to do

something nice for your birthday. Listen, why don't you go home and get some sleep. You look terrible."

Cora gave her the evil eye. "My ex-husband Melvin used to say that. It's one reason he became my ex-husband Melvin."

"This is a big mess, Cora. Don't make it worse. Go home, take it easy, stay out of trouble. Can you do that?"

Cora nodded emphatically.

"Absolutely," she lied.

41

CORA SMASHED THE LOWER right pane of glass on Peter Burnside's kitchen door. All things considered, that seemed the best pane to smash. It was small and conveniently located right next to the doorknob. Cora figured ninety-nine out of a hundred burglars would choose that pane. She broke it with her gun butt, reached in, unlocked the door.

The kitchen didn't look like it had been searched. That meant the Danbury police had done either a very superficial job, or a very thorough one, putting everything back where it belonged. Cora would have bet on the former. She went to work, tearing the place apart.

The nice thing about burgling an apartment in the daytime was, you didn't need a flashlight. Cora worked quickly, emptying the sugar canister into a bowl, making sure there was nothing in it but sugar, and dumping it back. She did the same with the flour, a slightly messier undertaking, which sent up puffs of powder, and turned her hands white. Cora had to be careful not to leave floury fingerprints. She washed her hands in the sink, took a dishrag, and cleaned the counter. It was the most kitchen work she'd done in years.

Cora continued her search. There was nothing in the cereal boxes, nothing taped to the bottoms or backs of drawers. The ice-cube tray appeared to hold ice cubes. If there were diamonds frozen in them, as in some story or other she'd read, Burnside could keep them.

Cora moved on to the living room. Burnside had a TV with rabbit ears. Cora couldn't recall the last time she'd seen rabbit ears. Everybody had cable or satellite, or something. At least he had a VCR. He didn't appear to have any tapes, though. The TV was on a simple metal stand, with the VCR on the bottom shelf. There was no other place to hold tapes. Still, Cora would have expected some. Maybe with the rabbit ears the guy got such bad reception he never taped any shows, and just rented movies now and then. Anyway, it was odd.

The living room furniture had either come with the apartment or been gathered off the street. Cora couldn't imagine anyone actually buying it. The couch was metal-framed, with burlap cushions. The coffee table was rickety wood. It occurred to Cora that Burnside must be a very poor detective. Aside from being dead.

There were no messages scrawled on the bottom of the coffee table. The sofa cushions did not have zip-on slipcovers. The burlap was stitched on. There was nothing under the couch, nothing under the cushions. It was not a convertible couch. There was no place to hide anything.

An oil painting hung over the couch. There was nothing taped to the back of it.

The easy chair, if one could call it that, had a sterile, vinyl back and seat in a metal frame. Unless the chair itself was a clue, it held no secrets.

In the bedroom, Cora looked under the mattress, under the bed. In and under every drawer in the six-drawer dresser. The pile of junk in the bottom of the closet. The magazines in the bedside table.

The drawer in the bedside table held a tape for the VCR. Not a prerecorded tape, just a plain tape box. Cora turned it over, looked at the side of the cassette. On it was labeled in pen, BEST IN SHOW. Cora knew the movie. It was one of Christopher Guest's mockumentaries, a takeoff on dog shows. She couldn't imagine why Burnside had it, but it made her feel a little warmer toward the deceased detective.

Cora completed her search of the bedroom. Had to agree with the police's assessment that it held absolutely nothing.

Except for the video. Why would a man who didn't even have a decent aerial, have a TV and a VCR just to watch a comedy about a dog competition?

Cora took the tape into the living room, shoved it in the VCR, turned on the TV, and sat down on the couch.

The video played. It was the beginning of the movie *Best in Show*. It occurred to Cora unless Valerie Thompkins's toy poodle was in the movie, the video probably had nothing to do with anything. She figured she should watch a little just to make sure.

There was a remote control on the VCR. If she had it she could speed through the tape. But that would mean getting up and getting it. Which would require moving. Making an effort.

Cora hadn't been to sleep in over twenty-four hours.

Not since her birthday. Which meant she'd never been asleep at her age. The thought amused her. Not her age, but the thought that she hadn't been asleep since she turned it. Cora wasn't admitting her age, even to herself. It was a generic birthday, happened all the time, it didn't mean a thing. Nothing to it.

So what was it she wanted to do? She wanted to get something. But for what purpose? Ah, yes. She needed to get the zapper, so she could speed through the cross-word-puzzle clues. Find out who Harvey Beerbaum killed. Falling on them from a great height and squashing them like a bug. Or bugging them at great length, and squashing them in the fall. Hey, that was wordplay. It should earn her bonus points. Win her the grand prize. The blue ribbon. Best in show.

Cora's eyes snapped open.

She had a panic attack. What happened?

With a rush it came flooding back. Murders, break-ins. Puzzles, real, and real life.

Where was she? What was she doing there? What time was it?

It was three-fifty. In the afternoon, since the sun was out. She was in Peter Burnside's apartment. She'd broken in.

Why?

What was she doing there?

Looking for evidence.

Had she found any?

No. She was watching TV.

No, she wasn't. The TV was off. That confused her. Had she turned it off and gone to sleep? Cora couldn't imagine doing that.

Cora stumbled to her feet, negotiated her way around the coffee table to the TV.

It was off, all right. It hadn't just blown a fuse, fried a tube, or had a power failure. It was switched off.

The tape had probably finished playing and re-wound. Cora pushed the button, ejected it.

Nothing happened.

Was the VCR off too? Yes, it was. Cora snapped the power on, pushed EJECT again.

Nothing.

Cora stuck her hand in the slot.

The tape was gone.

42

SHERRY CARTER WAS SITTING on the couch watching the five o'clock news when Cora burst in the door.

"Sherry! I'm in trouble!"

Aaron Grant came down the hall from the direction of the bathroom. "What's the matter?"

"Jesus Christ!" Cora said. "What are you doing here? Don't you *ever* work?"

"Are you kidding?" Aaron flopped down on the couch next to Sherry. "That detective bit the cake too late for this morning's paper. I've been writing it up all day for tomorrow."

"Get the hell out of here, will you? I need to talk to Sherry."

"Aunt Cora."

"Don't 'Aunt Cora' me. Can't you tell I'm upset?"

"If you're in trouble, I want to help," Aaron offered.

"You're a reporter."

"Off the record."

"*You're* telling *me* 'off the record'? That's a switch."

"Hey," Aaron said. "All kidding aside. You said you're in trouble, and I believe it. I'll print only what you tell me to print. What's wrong?"

"What isn't?" Cora slumped into a chair. "I'm holding out on the cops. I'm holding out on my lawyer. I'm charged with breaking and entering, and I happen to be guilty. I'm also guilty of a lot of other things I haven't been charged with yet. But that doesn't bother me. What bothers me is, I think I blew it."

"What do you mean?"

"I think I bungled the case."

"Wanna tell us how?" Aaron asked.

"I like how you include yourself," Cora said. "I'll tell you how, and you would not *believe* how off the record this is."

Cora told of her adventure with the videotape.

"*Best in Show*?" Aaron said. "I like that movie."

"So do I. But not enough to steal it. The tape's important. I had it in my hand. I let it get away."

"Because you can't function on no sleep at all?" Aaron said. "That's a serious drawback. Why don't you go to Chief Harper, tell him what happened?"

"I can't do that."

"Why not? He'd understand."

"It would put him in a position where he'd have to arrest me."

"He wouldn't do that."

"Yes, he would. I haven't told you everything I've done, Aaron."

"There's more?"

"The hits just keep on coming," Cora said grimly.

"Wanna tell me about it?"

"No." Cora shrugged. "What Sherry decides to tell you is her business. But if you print it, I'll never talk to you again. And if you tell Becky Baldwin, *Sherry* will never talk to you again."

"Hold on, here it is," Sherry said, pointing to the TV.

The face of Rick Reed filled the screen. The young, handsome, and generally clueless on-camera reporter stood in front of the Bakerhaven police station holding a microphone.

Sherry grabbed the remote control, turned the volume up.

"Once again, murder in Bakerhaven," Rick Reed was saying.

"He better not have anything I don't," Aaron said.

Sherry shushed him.

"It happened late last night at a surprise party to celebrate the birthday of Bakerhaven's most celebrated citizen, Miss Cora Felton, the beloved Puzzle Lady."

"If he gives my age, I'll kill him," Cora declared.

A picture of Cora Felton filled the screen.

"It was a surprise all right," Rick Reed's voice-over continued. *"The body of Peter Burnside practically fell in her lap."*

"See," Cora bragged. "He couldn't get me. He had to use a publicity photo."

"You got a publicist?" Aaron asked.

"Naw. The ad agency for the cereal commercials."

"Will you two shut up," Sherry said. "I want to hear."

"Ah, another Rick Reed groupie," Cora said.

"Shhh!"

"Complicating the bewildering investigation is the fact that Peter Burnside was a resident of Danbury, Connecticut, with no ties to the town. Dale Harper, the Bakerhaven chief of police, is cooperating with the Danbury police force, but so far there are no suspects."

On the TV screen, Chief Harper eyed the microphone as if it were some particularly odious vegetable his mother said was good for him. *"We are cooperating with the Danbury police, and we are cooperating with the media. As soon as we know anything, we'll pass it along."*

"Is there any connection between this crime and the murder of Valerie Thompkins last night in Danbury?"

"Only that both victims lived there. But the crimes themselves happened miles apart."

"Weren't both their throats slit, Chief?"

"I have no comment at this time."

"Does that mean you don't know anything?" Rick Reed persisted.

Chief Harper's eyes smoldered, but his voice was steady. *"This is a picture of the victim."*

Peter Burnside's face filled the screen. It had been carefully cropped at the chin so as not to show the slash in his neck. Still, the eyes were dull, glassy. The man did not look well.

"This is the dead man, Peter Burnside. We're asking anyone who recognizes him, anyone who's seen him in Bakerhaven, particularly yesterday—more particularly, last night—to get in touch with the police and tell us what you know. It goes without saying we're particularly interested in anyone Mr. Burnside might have been with," the chief said.

"And there you have it," Rick Reed summed up. *"The police, clueless, appealing for help. This is Rick Reed, Channel 8 News."*

The TV went to commercial.

Sherry picked up the zapper, switched the TV off. "See? He's got no more than you do."

"Yeah, he didn't even mention the stolen videotape," Aaron said.

"Very funny," Cora snapped.

The phone rang. Cora went into the kitchen, scooped it off the wall.

It was Becky Baldwin.

"Hi," Cora said. "You see your boyfriend on TV?"

"Who?"

"Rick Reed."

"He's not my boyfriend."

"He's taking you out to dinner."

"A girl's gotta eat."

"I'll say. What's up?"

"You wanted me to find out about the dog."

"You did?"

"Uh-huh."

"How?"

"Called and asked them."

"Whoa! They fall for that clever strategy?"

"Actually, they wanted to know why."

"What did you tell them?"

"That I heard it was a break-in murder, and was it possibly a negligence case?"

"Cops like that?"

"It made me as popular as the plague. I managed to ask if there was a guard dog involved. I went all mushy when it turned out to be a toy poodle."

"So where's the dog?"

"The neighbor's feeding it."

"A neighbor took the dog in?"

"No, she's just feeding it. I suppose the ASPCA will step in."

"Who's the neighbor?"

"Hey, how much interest could an ambulance chaser show? I got the name of the next of kin, but the name of the dog feeder is a little remote. If you really care, how hard can it be? It's the next-door neighbor. There can't be more than two."

"Thanks, Becky."

"You mind telling me what's so important about this dog?"

"I told you. I'm concerned for its welfare."

"Well, it's fine."

"And it's going to stay that way," Cora muttered, as she hung up the phone.

43

CYNTHIA MAYBERRY WAS THE type of person who regarded every tragedy as an imposition upon them. A stout woman, with a habit of sticking her nose in the air, Mrs. Mayberry had taken the demise of her neighbor particularly hard. Police cars, ambulances, and news vans had tied up the street most of the day. Mrs. Mayberry hadn't even been able to get out to market.

Plus she had to feed the dog.

"Not that I mind, you understand," she whined. "But these are large lots, our houses are *not* that close together, and it's an inconvenience to go traipsing over there twice a day."

"Why didn't you bring the dog here?" Cora asked.

She might as well have suggested strychnine. "*Here?* In my home?" Mrs. Mayberry glanced around the foyer, which was neat as a pin. Cora imagined the rest of the house was the same, though there seemed little chance she would get to see it. Not that she gave a damn. It had taken fast talking to get this far. "You should never have been put in that position," she commiserated.

"I suppose I shouldn't complain," Mrs. Mayberry said, then proceeded to do so. "But if the woman's made *no* provisions for the dog—and from what everyone can tell, she *hasn't*—well, that's just not right. If you live alone, you have to consider what might happen."

"That's certainly true." Cora had a vision of the decedent sitting at her makeup table thinking, "If I get killed today, what's going to happen to my pooch?" She converted her smile of amusement into one of benevolence. "Well, I'm glad I can help you out."

"Yes. And just what relationship were you to Mrs. Thompkins?"

"Oh, Valerie used to follow me around." Cora hated lying, prided herself on her misleading truths. She smiled fondly. "Last time I saw her was with that poor dog. It's hard to believe she's gone."

That was good enough for Cynthia Mayberry. "Well, I'm glad you're willing to take him. He needs a home."

"He certainly does," Cora agreed, heartily. "Now, then, you've been imposed upon enough. If you want, I'll just go over and get him."

"You can't get in. I have the keys."

"I could bring them back," Cora ventured. It was a tactful offer, not suggesting the woman give her the keys, but merely alluding to their safe return.

Cynthia Mayberry wasn't biting. "No. I'll have to go with you. You can drive me over."

"Actually, my car's parked out on the road."

"You walked in?"

"I walked to Valerie's. When I couldn't get in, I cut across the lawn. I hope that's all right."

"That's how I go to feed the dog." Cynthia Mayberry made it sound like a lifetime chore. Cora figured the woman had done it twice at the most.

"If you want to keep the dog, I quite understand," Cora said.

Mrs. Mayberry fell all over herself rejecting the suggestion. "No, no, no. I'm not equipped to do that. Actually, I'm not really a dog person, you know what I mean? Let me get my keys, I'll take you over."

Cora followed Mrs. Mayberry across the lawn. There was not exactly a path worn between the two houses. They had to find a break in the hedge that separated the properties.

Mrs. Mayberry headed for the back of the house. "The police closed the front door. You must have seen the ribbon. But I have a key to the back."

Cora could hear the dog barking through the kitchen door.

"Quiet!" Mrs. Mayberry cried. Defensively, as if that had sounded too harsh, she added, "He yaps a lot." Then, lest Cora change her mind, she added hastily, "I'm sure he'll be fine with you."

"Oh, I'm sure he will," Cora agreed.

Mrs. Mayberry stuck her key in the lock. "Now, the main thing is to get in the door without him getting out."

"You don't let him out?"

"Just on a leash. Otherwise, I don't know if he'd come back."

"I wouldn't," Cora muttered.

"What?"

Cora, realizing she'd actually voiced her thought, said, "I wouldn't let the dear little thing off the leash, either."

Mrs. Mayberry unlocked the door, and they eased in.

The dog was bouncing all over the kitchen. He seemed more happy to see Cynthia Mayberry than any living creature had any right to be. He was equally happy to see Cora. Evidently he had no bad memories of tracking blood on her legs.

Cora bent down, petted the dog. "Isn't he a sweetheart? You know, I used to lie on the floor and let him climb over me."

"His leash is on the doorknob," Cynthia Mayberry said, making no move to touch it. "His bowls are by the kitchen sink. There's a bag of dry food on the counter, if you want to take it."

That didn't suit Cora's purposes. Everything she needed was in the kitchen, including the dog. Unless she could get him to run away, she was going to have to take him and go.

"Is there a carrying case?" Cora asked.

"What?"

"A dog carrier. I'm not sure he should travel in a car without a carrying case. Is there a case?"

"I have no idea."

"Some dogs freak out. I'm sure I remember Valerie saying he wasn't terribly comfortable without his case." Cora had to admit she wasn't *always* able to avoid the direct falsehood.

"I don't see one. You'll just have to take him on the leash."

"I'd really rather not. Perhaps it's in the closet."

"Oh, for goodness' sake." Mrs. Mayberry threw open the door to a broom closet. "No, none here."

"Of course not," Cora said. "She'd take him out the front door. It would be in the coat closet in the foyer."

"We are *not* searching the house," Cynthia Mayberry declared.

"Oh, all right." Cora bent down to the dog again. "Sorry. You have to stay."

Mrs. Mayberry's eyes widened. "You're *not* taking him?"

Cora stood firm. "Well, if I can't have his carrying case . . ." She let it hang in the air, then smiled. "I'm not asking you to search the house. I'm merely asking you to look in the foyer closet, where it should be. If it's not there, I'll take him on a leash. But if it is there, I want to use it. Some dogs throw up in cars. If he does, I guarantee you he'll have a carrier by the door. I don't mind taking him, but I don't want him throwing up on my backseat."

Mrs. Mayberry eyed the poodle as if trying to determine if he'd be ornery enough to do that. "Fine. We'll look in the closet, but that's it. We're not going anywhere else. Whether we find it or not, you take the dog."

"It's a deal," Cora said.

Mrs. Mayberry marched down the hall to the foyer with Cora and the dog right on her heels. She switched on the light, flung open the coat closet door. "Well, if it is here, it's not in plain sight." She moved some hatboxes to see the top shelf, pushed aside some coats to see the closet floor.

Cora managed to sidle up to the front door, reach behind her, and undo the lock. She stepped away just as Mrs. Mayberry finished rummaging in the closet.

"See, nothing here."

"I must have confused him with another dog," Cora said. "I know there was someone who always used a carrying case. I thought it was her. Don't worry, I'll take him off your hands."

Cora headed for the kitchen, hoping Cynthia Mayberry would follow before she noticed the front door was now unlocked.

In the kitchen Cora grabbed the leash, knelt down, crooned, "Here, boy."

The dog jumped up on her and licked her face.

"That's a good boy."

Cora snapped the leash on. She stood up, tucked the dog under one arm, grabbed the bowls and dry food in the other, just as Mrs. Mayberry came into the kitchen.

"Hey, this is terrific," Cora said. "If you could just open the door for me. Thanks. I'll get out of your hair, you can lock up and go home. You don't have to worry about the dog anymore."

Cora talked her way out the kitchen door, hurried around the house, and down the long asphalt driveway. At the bottom she turned right, walked along the road.

Cora's car was a block down the street, not right in front of the house. That was one reason she'd left quickly, because the car was not where she'd said.

The other was because Sherry and Aaron were in it.

Cora slipped into the backseat of the car, and held up the dog. "Look what I got."

"You stole the dead woman's dog?" Sherry said.

"The one that made bloody paw prints all over you?" Aaron said.

"The very same."

"Why did you steal the dead woman's dog?" Sherry persisted.

"I had to get into her house."

"Couldn't you think of any other way without kidnapping her pet?"

"No, I couldn't. I haven't slept in days. My mind is barely working. You wouldn't let me drive out here, if you'll recall."

"Of course not. You're clearly not in possession of your faculties."

"Hey, I got into her house, didn't I?"

"Yeah, and now you've got her dog."

"Actually," Cora said, handing him to Sherry, "*you've* got her dog. I've got work to do."

"Work?" Sherry said. "What the hell are we going to do with a dog?"

Cora smiled and patted Sherry on the cheek.

"Least of our worries."

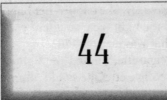

44

CORA CREPT UP THE driveway, crouching low behind the sight line of the hedge, just in case the annoying neighbor was watching. She didn't think Mrs. Mayberry was suspicious, but in Cora's diminished capacity she wasn't sure she could trust her own judgment.

There were no lights on in the dead woman's house. The light in the kitchen had been only for the dog. Mrs. Mayberry had turned it off when she left.

There was a crime-scene ribbon across the front door. Actually, two, crisscrossing, forming an X. Cora reached through, tried the knob. It turned, just as it had the night before. The only difference was, that time the lights were on. And there was a corpse.

Cora hoped there wasn't a corpse now. If there was, she sorta hoped it was Cynthia Mayberry. Cora pushed such facetious thoughts from her sleep-addled brain, stepped carefully through the X, into the house. She closed the door quietly behind her, and plunged herself into total darkness.

Did she dare risk a light?

Cora knew she didn't. On the other hand, she couldn't see a damn thing.

Cora fumbled in her purse, came out with her new cigarette lighter. She fired it up, was amazed at how much light it gave off. She cupped her hand around the flame. Wished the light were smaller.

Actually, that was no problem.

Cora lit a cigarette, doused the lighter. There. By puffing on the cigarette she could illuminate things with the glowing end.

Of course, if anyone showed up, the smoke would alert them that there was someone in the house. But then, Cora figured, if anyone showed up, she was dead meat anyway.

Cora puffed the cigarette, headed upstairs.

Valerie's bedroom was the large one on the right. It was a no-brainer—there was virtually nothing in the bedroom on the left. Valerie's had a makeup table loaded to the gills. An unmade bed. Clothes hurled in all directions. At first glance, it appeared the bedroom had been ransacked. Then Cora realized that was just how the woman lived.

The bedroom's two windows had lace curtains and roller blinds. The curtains were tied back, the roller blinds were up. Cora made her way to the windows, pulled the blinds down.

Cora's cigarette was burning her fingers. She dropped it in a cup of water on the makeup table, took out the lighter.

Cora jerked open the drawer of the makeup table, discovered nothing but cosmetics.

She moved on to the dresser. The top drawer, as she had expected, held undergarments, ranging from lacy to extra support. Cora imagined the decision as to which to wear related not so much to weight fluctuation as to state of mind.

The rest of the bureau drawers held nothing of interest. Slacks, blouses, and sweaters. A gray-and-white pullover looked particularly attractive. Cora wondered if it was in her size. Considered trying it on.

Cora remembered where she was, put the sweater back, closed the drawer.

Cora moved on to the closet. As she pawed through the hanging clothes, it occurred to her that if a man had been killed, she would be searching his office. Since it was a woman, she was searching her bedroom. That seemed sexist to Cora.

Cora took off the hat she'd tried on and put it back.

Cora found nothing in the bedroom. Nothing relating to the crime, at any rate.

She checked out the other bedroom. It had obviously belonged to the departed husband, and Valerie had clearly washed that man right out of her hair. There was a spread on the bed, but no sheets. There was nothing under the mattress.

The bed rested on a large area rug. Cora rolled back the corners, hoping for something.

A business card caught her eye. She picked it up, just as the light flickered out.

Cora snapped the lighter again, to no avail. She was furious. A brand-new lighter. Cora ascribed some activities to the lighter it could not possibly enjoy, then crammed it and the business card into her purse. She flipped the rug back into place.

Cora groped her way downstairs, holding the railing, headed for the living room. The crime-scene ribbon assured her she had the right door. She ducked under, and stood up.

Ghostly moonlight filtered in through the front windows. That, coupled with the fact Cora's eyes had become accustomed to the dark, enabled her to make out silhouettes. There was the couch. There was the coffee table with the message DUD. And there was the outline where the woman had lain. Not chalk, on the shag rug, but tape of some sort, luminescent tape, an eerie outline in the room of death.

Cora shivered, wondered where to start.

She dug in her purse, came out with the book of matches from Burnside's office. She struck one, cupped it, looked around the room. It occurred to her it would be a bitch searching under the couch.

Across from the couch was a TV and VCR. Cora hadn't noticed it before—but then, she'd been busy. On a hunch, she clicked the VCR on, pushed EJECT. It was empty.

Cora moved on to the end table. It held a bunch of magazines. She wasn't sure, but she thought some of them had been on the coffee table. Yes, there was nothing on it now. The police had moved the magazines to turn the table over to photograph DUD.

Cora tipped the table up, peered under. It was still there. The same misleading message, leading no one anywhere.

There was a bookcase on the side wall. Cora was not surprised to find it jammed with romance novels and an occasional trashy best seller. Cora tried not to be too judgmental, particularly since she noticed one or two trashy best sellers she'd read.

Before Cora's match burned out, she noticed the bookcase's bottom shelves held videotapes. She struck another match, and scanned them. Apparently, the woman never recorded any shows. All the tapes on the shelves were prerecorded movies, in their original colorful boxes.

Cora ran her finger down the rows, looking for the one odd tape, the one hand-lettered box. But there were none. Every single tape was a store-bought movie. Cora noted that, here, too, the trend ran toward sudsy romance and tearjerkers: *An Affair to Remember, The English Patient, Bridges of Madison County, Unfaithful*. The theme of infidelity also seemed to be running rampant. And—

Cora stopped.

Best in Show.

Not a duplicate tape, like Burnside's. Like all the rest, this was a professional copy.

Cora pulled it out.

Yes, there were all the dog people on the cover. Of course, that movie didn't have to be in the box.

But it was.

Cora slid the tape out, read the title. It was exactly what it purported to be. A movie about dogs.

The match went out.

Cora shoved the tape back in the box.

Her finger hit something sticky.

She frowned, lit another match.

Slid the movie out of the box again.

There was a piece of Scotch tape around one end of the videocassette. Not all the way around, but just over the far end of the long thin side with the title.

The Scotch tape covered a small, rectangular indentation in the plastic.

Headlights flashed through the window, lit up the room.

Two cars hurtled up the drive.

Cora blew out the match, headed for the back of the

house. Too bad about the crime-scene ribbon. She plowed right through as she went out the living room door.

She sprinted down the hall to the kitchen, fumbled with the back-door lock. It clicked. Cora jerked the door open, shut it behind her.

Cora could hear footsteps pelting toward the house. She dived into the bushes, raced for the house next door. The other one. Not Cynthia Mayberry's.

There were lights on in the house, so the people were still up. As Cora worked her way behind it, lights came on in Valerie Thompkins's house.

Cora stayed in the bushes, reached the far end of the adjoining property. It was a tall hedge, wider and thicker than the one between Valerie's and Cynthia's houses. Cora kept in the shadows, worked her way down to the road.

Her car was gone.

45

"Where are you?" Sherry demanded.

"Where am *I*? Where the hell are *you*?"

"We had to get out of there. The cops showed up."

"Oh, there's a news flash," Cora said. "That must have put you in great danger. The cops might have caught you two lovebirds parking. You'd have never been able to live it down. I, on the other hand, could have told 'em I came back for the dog's toys."

"Incidentally, the dog's getting restless."

"So am I. Where the hell *are* you?"

"We had to find a place Aaron's cell phone would work. Or you couldn't have called us."

"Well, that's just great," Cora said. "You wanna pick me up before the cops do?"

"Where are you?"

"I have no idea."

"What?"

"I'm in a phone booth outside an Exxon station on a corner with no street signs whatsoever."

"Couldn't you walk a block and find a sign?"

"I'm too damn tired. There's cop cars looking for me. Come get me. How hard can it be. I'm within a mile of the house. I think I went in the direction your car was facing. At least at first."

"You want me to cruise around till I find an Exxon station?"

"Yeah, and don't drive off when you don't see me. I hide from headlights."

Sherry and Aaron drove into the station fifteen minutes later. The minute Sherry pulled the car to a stop, Cora slid into the backseat.

"Well, you certainly took your time."

"You want this ride or not?"

The dog jumped all over Cora.

"He's going nuts. Did you walk him?"

Sherry pulled out of the service station. "Are you kidding? Won't the cops be looking for the dog?"

"Only if they're smart."

"You find anything?" Aaron asked.

"Just this."

Cora handed him the videotape.

Aaron held it up by the dashboard lights. "*Best in Show*!" he exclaimed. "You found it!"

"Yes, and no. The tape I lost was a homemade dupe. This is a prerecorded tape."

"Then what's the point?" Sherry asked.

"I think it's evidence."

"How can it be evidence?"

"There's Scotch tape on it."

Aaron slid the videotape out of the box. "You're right. It's taped over."

"Please," Sherry protested. "I'm trying to drive. The word *tape* is really distracting. Videotape. Scotch tape. What are you two talking about?"

"Videotapes have a little plastic tab in the corner you can break off if you don't want them recorded over," Cora explained. "You do that if you've got something you wanna make sure you don't erase. But if you change your mind, and you want to use the tape again, you put a piece of Scotch tape over the hole where the tab was, and you can record on it."

"How do you know that?"

"My second husband, Arthur, was too cheap to buy new tapes. He used to get old discarded videotapes, put Scotch tape over the holes, and use 'em to record TV shows. Some of the tapes he got were pretty steamy. It made for some interesting montages."

"But this is a prerecorded tape. You wouldn't want to record on it."

"Exactly," Cora said, smugly.

"Great," Aaron said. "Let's go home and watch it."

"If we don't get stopped," Sherry pointed out dryly, "with a stolen dog and a stolen tape."

No one stopped them. They drove back to Baker-haven without incident. Cora half expected to see a police car in their driveway, but there was no one there.

The poodle was out the back door of the car like a shot. He ran around the lawn, peeing on everything.

"Marking his territory," Sherry said.

"Think he'll come back?" Aaron said.

"He will if he gets hungry," Cora said. "Bring that bag of food."

They went inside, leaving the front door open. Aaron followed Cora into the kitchen and filled one bowl with kibble while she filled the other with water. They put them on the floor next to the sink. Almost before the bowls hit the floor, the little poodle darted in the door and began to eat.

Cora and Aaron went back in the living room, where Sherry had turned on the TV and the VCR.

"Should I take the Scotch tape off?" Sherry asked. "We don't want to record over it."

"Better not," Cora advised.

Sherry shoved the videotape into the VCR.

"Shall I make popcorn?" Aaron asked.

"Very funny," Cora said. "We're speeding through this before I fall asleep. Go on, start it, Sherry."

Sherry held up the remote control. "We're speeding through this on the condition that you *promise* to go to sleep, no matter what we find on the tape."

"Trust me, if I can sleep, I will."

"That's not exactly what I said."

"So, sue me. If I can't sleep, I can't sleep."

"Girls, can we watch this?" Aaron said.

Sherry hit PLAY. The warning label came on, followed by a host of previews. Sherry fast-forwarded through them all. The movie started. Actors of all shapes and sizes kept dancing across the screen, picking up and putting down dogs of all shapes and sizes.

"Hell of a way to watch a movie," Aaron said.

The movie reached the part where Cora had fallen asleep. At least where she thought she'd fallen asleep. She really had no idea.

The movie continued through more and more dog gyrations. While it was going, the poodle came in from the kitchen, jumped on the couch, and snuggled up next to Cora.

"You're going to let him on the couch?" Sherry said.

"How do you suggest I keep him off?"

"Pick him up and put him down."

"You want me to train a dog? I'm not sure you can train an old dog."

"That's for sure," Sherry muttered.

"What was that?"

"Nothing. I—"

On the screen the image suddenly changed. It was readily apparent because the lighting was different. And because the date and time appeared in the lower right-hand corner.

And because the people on-screen were naked.

Sherry hit PLAY.

The video slowed to normal time.

It showed a man and woman in bed.

The woman was Ida Blaine.

The man was Warden Prufrock.

46

"TELL ME ABOUT THE tape."

Warden Prufrock frowned at Cora. "What?"

"The blackmail tape. Tell me about the blackmail tape."

"I don't know what you're talking about."

Cora smiled. "Yeah, you do. You must have seen it, because, otherwise, what's the point? Who brought it to you?"

"You're being impertinent, Miss Felton."

"Not yet. I'm just warming up. You'll know when I'm impertinent."

"Last I heard, the police were looking for you. Suppose I make a little call."

"Then they might catch me with the tape."

"You keep talking about a tape."

"Yeah. I figured you'd know what I meant. In case there's any confusion, I'm talking about the blackmail tape. The pornographic blackmail tape. The pornographic blackmail tape in which you feature quite prominently. Does that refresh your recollection?"

"You're trying to blackmail me?"

"Heaven forbid. I'm just trying to have a conversation. Were you trying to threaten me with the police?"

"Go on," Prufrock growled.

"Okay," Cora said. "I'm going to assume for the sake of argument that you've seen the blackmail tape. What I'm interested in is what sort of hoops you've been made to jump through."

The warden glowered, said nothing.

"Let me take a wild guess. Would it have anything to do with the prisoner Darryl Daigue?"

"I think this conversation is over."

"That's practically a confirmation. Well, what an interesting situation. You're the warden of a prison. You have a lifer with no possibility of parole. Yet he gets parole hearings. Am I getting warm?"

"You're out of your mind."

"Not only does he get parole hearings, but the woman in the porno tape winds up on the parole board."

The warden's face reddened.

"Didn't handle that one too well," Cora told him. "Probably not that much experience with lying. Never had to before. What was it? 'No-nonsense warden.' 'The iron man.' 'Takes a stand, lets the chips fall where they may.'"

"Damn you."

"So what happens next? A prison doctor winds up on the parole board. A young, impressionable prison doctor. Who is immediately hit on by the woman in the tape. Which is pretty ironic, since the doc's the one who started it all, mentioning to the prisoner that a guy he used to know bought the farm in a traffic accident."

Cora looked hard at the warden. "I know all these

things happened. I just don't know why. I'd like you to tell me. I'd like that to happen before the police pick me up and force me to turn over any evidence I might have in my possession."

"So this *is* blackmail."

"What, you wearing a wire? You want me to incriminate myself? How many times do I have to tell you this is *not* blackmail. This is just me trying to get the facts. I have no reason to embarrass you. But I'd like to know who dropped the dead detective in my lap and slit the housewife's throat. If you didn't do it, I got no quarrel with you. But I need to know. Can you help me out?"

Warden Prufrock spread his hands helplessly. "I have no idea."

"You know who was blackmailing you?"

"No."

"Did they ask for money?"

"No."

"How did they contact you?"

"Look here—"

"How did they contact you?"

"If I tell you, will you go away?"

"You can count on it. That doesn't mean others won't come. But I won't send 'em."

"It came in the mail. In a plain brown wrapper. To my office. Here at the prison. I didn't know what it was. I almost took it home. Can you believe it? I almost brought it home."

"But you didn't."

"No." He pointed. "Luckily, I have a VCR. I took a look. Jesus Christ!"

"Was there a letter?"

"Yeah. Anonymous. Cut from headlines."

"What did it say?"

" 'Get Daigue out of solitary.' "

"What?"

"Like I told you. Darryl Daigue's a problem prisoner. He spent most of his time in solitary confinement."

"So?"

"So I took him out, put him back in the general population. Which basically meant he got beat up more often."

"What was the point?"

"I don't know, but it was a real pain. Almost immediately an investigative journalist took the opportunity to do a series of uncomplimentary essays on the prison."

"What do you mean, 'took the opportunity'?"

"Oh. Daigue couldn't have visitors in solitary. When he got transferred, this journalist interviewed him for his book."

"What book?"

"I don't know. Something about how inmates are treated. The guy managed to trash the prison."

"Then what happened?"

"Nothing. I waited for demands, but that was it. I thought it was over. Then, out of the blue, another copy of the tape arrives. Just in case I've forgotten. This time it's not 'Get him out of solitary.' This time they want Daigue out of jail."

"They tell you how?"

"Sure. Schedule a parole hearing and sway the board."

"Was the second tape the same as the first?"

"Essentially."

"What was different?"

"I think the tapes were a different brand."

"Aside from that?"

"It was the same footage, if that's what you mean."

"How about the letter?"

"That was different. The first one was cut from newspaper headlines. The second one was typed."

"Really? Didn't you think that was strange?"

"Strange? It's a nightmare! I can't eat. I can't sleep. My wife thinks I'm having an affair."

"Perceptive of her."

"Don't be dumb. That was over a long time ago. Anyway, I scheduled a parole hearing for Darryl Daigue. Naturally, they turned him down. Two days later I got another letter. 'Rig the board,' it said."

"That's when you put Ida Blaine on the board. And told her how to vote. She couldn't swing it herself, so you had her go to work on the doctor. Or did you add him too?"

"Both. What could I do? I was in a terrible position."

Cora snorted. "You don't know from terrible positions. Two people died in the last forty-eight hours. Each one of them had a copy of your videotape."

Warden Prufrock's face went white. "Are you kidding me?"

Cora nodded approvingly. "Nice reaction. Just as if you didn't know."

"I didn't."

"Well, now you do. Next time someone tells you, you won't have that nice reaction."

Prufrock frowned.

"The worst of it is, the killer appears to have been looking for the tapes."

"How do you know?"

"He got one of them."

"He?"

"Or she. I don't mean to be sexist. Though I hope a woman wouldn't slice a man's throat and heave him over a rail."

"Do you have the other tape?"

"I certainly hope not. If I did, I can't imagine how many laws I would have broken."

"Oh, hell," Warden Prufrock moaned. "What am I going to do?"

"Uh! Uh! Steady there. Remember. 'Iron Man.'" Cora struck an Arnold Schwarzenegger pose, then ducked out the door.

47

"I'VE SEEN YOU NAKED."

"I beg your pardon?"

"You didn't look bad. Of course, you were a year or two younger, but even so."

Ida Blaine started to slam the door in Cora's face.

Cora lowered her shoulder and pushed. "You don't want to do that."

"Get out of here!"

Cora shook her head. "You don't know how bad a move that is. If someone told me they'd seen me naked, I'd want to know where. Just in case I'd married them accidentally when I was drinking."

"You've been drinking? That explains it. Will you please leave?"

"The first time I came by you were wearing a mud pack. And the dead detective was watching your house."

"Dead detective?"

"He wasn't dead then. He died on my birthday. You know anything about that?"

"Of course not."

"That's funny. It's been in all the papers. Not to mention on TV. Anyway, the dead detective has a videotape of you. That's how I happened to see you naked. Which got me thinking. Why would a detective with a videotape of you still be watching you? Could it be he showed that tape to your husband to justify his employment?"

"You're way off base."

"I'm not surprised. This case has so many twists and turns I can't even keep the players straight. Except the dead ones. They tend to stay put."

"Lady, are you on something? You're acting mighty weird."

"I just had a nice talk with Warden Prufrock. Wanna know what he said?"

"You're bluffing."

"Yeah, well, it's a good bluff. I wanted to know if the warden called you. Evidently he didn't. Which is interesting. He doesn't consider you a partner, just a pawn."

She frowned. "What do you mean?"

"Did he tell you what he wanted *before* he put you on the parole board?"

Ida Blaine said nothing.

"That must have been a shock. Out of the blue the guy calls and says you're in trouble. I mean the plural *you,* as in both X-rated video stars. Did you believe him? Did you ask to see the tape? Were you surprised to learn there was one?"

"I don't believe you. I think you're making this up."

"Okay. I'll ask your husband."

Cora started for her car.

Ida chased her down the walk. "No, wait."

"Ah, the magic words. So, what's the story?"

"I don't want you talking to my husband about the detective."

"Why? Because he hired him?"

"No. Because he didn't."

Cora frowned. "What?"

"I hired him."

"Why?"

"To watch my husband."

"Why?"

"Why do you think?"

"Who's the other lady?"

"That's not important."

"You tell me it's Valerie Thompkins, I'm gonna lose it."

"It's not Valerie Thompkins."

"Then who is it?"

Ida Blaine exhaled. "Damn it. All right, you win. There is no other lady."

"Then why do you want your husband watched?"

"To see if he's watching me."

Cora considered that. "I like it. I'm not sure I believe it, but I like it."

"It's the truth."

"Well, the nice thing is, the dead detective can't deny it. But how'd he come to have in his possession a videotape of you carousing in the altogether?"

"Says you."

"According to Warden Studly that tape was influencing your vote. And was helping you influence the good doctor's."

"Jesus, what a mess."

"Well, at least we agree on one thing. So, where is this famous husband of yours? The one who's footing all the bills, keeping you in this nice house? The one you don't want me talking to?"

"He's out of town."

"Where out of town?"

She took a breath. Exhaled. "Australia."

"Australia?" Cora chuckled. "That will make him hard to contact. How long has he been there?"

"The past month."

"Really. Then hiring a detective to have him watched was sort of an empty gesture."

"Yeah, I knew that wasn't going to fly."

"So who hired the detective?"

"I don't *know* who hired the damn detective," Ida Blaine snapped. "You say he was watching my house, well, whoopee for him. I don't know what he expected to find. I can't explain the detective. I don't know a damn thing about him."

"You *tried* to explain the detective."

"I didn't want you to think he was watching me. That's creepy."

"It's more than creepy, considering the guy had a nude video of you. Did he approach you with it?"

"No."

"Maybe offer to sell it back to you?"

"Absolutely not!"

"You tell him you had to get your hands on some money? Offer to meet him somewhere? Like the library stacks?"

"No, I did not."

"Your denial might carry more weight if you hadn't already given me so many versions. What was your relationship with the gentleman?"

"I didn't *have* a relationship with the gentleman. The fact he was watching my house was news to me. I should have just said that. Instead, I panicked, and tried to brush it off as something else."

"Why did you panic?"

"Why did I panic? You come here and threaten me with videotapes and conspiracies to subvert the penal system, and then you dangle a dead detective in front of my face and wonder why I panic?"

"You made up things. All you had to do was say, 'I know nothing about it.'"

"And that would have satisfied you, and you would have gone away and left me alone, and we wouldn't be having this conversation," Ida said, sarcastically. "You threatened me with my husband. The fact is, I don't want you talking to him. Even long distance in Australia."

"But if you don't know anything . . ."

"You're just going to ask him about the shadow? You're not going to bring up the videotape? See, I don't want you talking to him at all. I tried to say something to get you to stop. It was a stupid lie. You gonna hold me to it?"

"You know the detective who was watching your house?"

"Hell, no."

"What do you suppose he was looking for?"

"I don't know that, either."

"You know a woman named Valerie Thompkins?"

"No, but I've heard the name. Now, where did—" Ida Blaine broke off. "You. You mentioned her. About my husband. What was that all about?"

"Don't blame me. That was in response to your lie that you hired the detective to stake out your husband."

"Yeah, but—"

"How about Bud? You know anyone named Bud?"

"Bud? Who the hell is Bud?"

"I have no idea. Do you?"

"Aren't you supposed to be good with words? When I say, 'Who the hell is Bud?' it's a hint I don't have a clue who he is."

"Thanks for the tip. Do I have to point out you haven't been scoring a hundred percent in the veracity department?"

"Yeah, well, you say the detective was watching me. If that's true, I don't know why, but we've only got your word for it."

"Luckily, I believe me. I don't give a damn what you think. How about Dr. What's-his-name? Was he in on it? Or an unwitting dupe?"

"Dr. Jenkins is just a friend!"

Cora sighed, shook her head. "Now, how did I know you were going to say that?"

Cora stomped down the path, got in the car, and drove home.

The police were there waiting for her.

48

BECKY BALDWIN WAS INCREDULOUS. "Dognapping?"

"I don't believe there is such a crime. On the Connecticut books, I mean."

"Oh? You're telling me I drove all the way down to the Danbury lockup for a crime that doesn't exist?"

"I think they're charging me with theft."

"What makes you think that?"

"The prosecutor came in and said, 'We're charging you with theft.'"

"Petty theft?"

"No, grand larceny. Unfortunately, the dog is a purebred. You wouldn't believe how much he cost."

"Yeah, I would. But they don't claim you broke in to steal him?"

"No."

"Why not?"

"Because they can't *prove* I broke in."

"Cora."

"I didn't break in to get the dog. I already *had* the dog."

"You admit you stole the dog?"

"Not at all. A neighbor *gave* me the dog."

"Because you lied and deceived her in order to illegally obtain the dog."

"Does that make me guilty of stealing?"

"Well, it doesn't qualify you for a medal. Why did you steal the dog?"

"The dog shouldn't have been left there in the first place. What, are they nuts? Leave an animal alone? I don't care if the neighbor is feeding it. The owner is dead. Someone should have taken charge of the dog."

"You're right. They paid entirely too much attention to the dead woman on the floor."

"You've been watching too many lawyer shows, Becky. Lawyers don't *have* to be sarcastic with their clients. It's possible to just *discuss* the crime."

"Then, by all means, let's discuss it. Just don't confess to anything illegal that puts me in an impossible position."

"No position is impossible when you're young and healthy."

Becky's mouth fell open.

Cora laughed. "That's from *What the Butler Saw,* by Joe Orton. My third husband, Frank, took me to it, largely because he felt guilty for running around with the hatcheck girl. Sorry. I've had no sleep. I keep free-associating. Where were we?"

"You ripped off a dog."

"Surely we'd gotten past that by now."

"Unfortunately, the police haven't. You're going to be arraigned on it."

"Then what?"

"You'll be released on bail. If they're serious about

pursuing this, the A.D.A. will schedule a probable-cause hearing."

"That's where you get the charge thrown out?"

"No, it's just a formality. All they have to show is the police had reasonable grounds to think you might be guilty of a crime. There's more than enough. The dog was found at your house, the neighbor saw you take the dog. The only way to settle a case at a probable-cause hearing is to make a deal."

"You mean plead it out?"

"Exactly."

"I plead guilty to something?"

"Well, you *are* guilty, aren't you?"

"That's not the point. I have a career built on a reputation. You run 'Puzzle Lady Cops Plea' in the tabloids, and there go my TV ads."

"You should have thought of that before you swiped the dog."

"Hey! You saying you can't handle this? I gotta fire you and bring in the Dream Team? I'm not copping a plea. There must be another way to beat it at probable cause."

"We'll be lucky if we can beat it at trial. You wanna consult another attorney, I'll bet you a nickle they say the same thing."

"I'm sure they would. Listen, am I just charged with the dog?"

"That's not enough?"

"It's plenty. But is it all?"

"It's all I heard of. Why?"

"Oh," Cora said airily, "you know how the police like to pile on charges."

"Well, if they consider taking the dog obstruction

of justice, they haven't let on. With regard to your fraudulent representation—"

"What fraudulent representation? Is there a statute on the books about impersonating a friend of a poodle owner?"

"It may not be an additional charge, but I know how it's going to look to a jury."

"We're not getting to a jury. We're beating it on probable cause."

"Right," Becky agreed.

Her enthusiasm was decidedly lacking.

49

SHERRY CARTER DIDN'T MINCE words.

"You look awful."

Cora made a remark reflecting on Sherry's lineage, demeanor, and intelligence, and suggesting a romantic interlude she might experience alone.

"I can't help it," Sherry said, "if you refuse to eat, sleep, or even change your clothes, Aunt Cora. You look like holy hell. Getting arrested is just the icing on the cake."

Cora didn't want to think about cakes. "Where's the dog?" she demanded.

"The police have the dog."

"Are they treating it right?"

"How the hell should I know?"

"Why are you cranky? I'm the one in jail."

"Yes, and is that my fault? When you go running all over the place getting into trouble?"

"That isn't what got me into trouble. I got busted for coming home. Listen, Sherry, find out where the dog is. See if they'll let you take him. The poor thing's been through enough."

"They're holding the dog for evidence."

"Oh, come on. Are they afraid we'd switch dogs on them? Or wouldn't bring him back? See if they'll let you keep him."

"Asking for the dog is just going to confirm the fact you took him."

"So what? They don't *need* confirmation. They found him at our house. Come on, Sherry. I'm having a hard time thinking this out. Just get that off my mind."

"Fine. Consider it off your mind. Go ahead and concentrate on the crimes. You'll have a lot of time. I understand you're not making bail until tomorrow."

"What! Becky didn't mention that!"

"She's down there pushing, but the judge went home. I don't think he's in any hurry to come back."

"Son of a bitch!"

"So it looks like you're here for the night."

"Who told you this?"

"Becky."

"Well, she didn't tell me!"

"She probably had other things to discuss."

"Some birthday present!" Cora grumbled. "Listen, do me a favor. Next year give me a watch."

Sherry took out a folded paper. "Speaking of birthday presents, you got another card."

"Oh, give me a break!"

"No, you'll like this one."

"Don't count on it."

Cora unfolded the paper.

" '*Misnomers,* by Hillary Mustache'? Who the hell is Hillary Mustache?"

Sherry grinned. "Yes, that's the point."

MISNOMERS
by Hillary Mustache

ACROSS

1 Role, so to speak
4 Works at the Met?
10 Move one's mandible, maybe
14 Program file name suffix
15 Luggage piece
16 Pueblo dweller
17 Kids' Christmas special, perhaps
19 Tennessee's state flower
20 Cut from copy
21 Tatting-eschewing
23 Ere modern days
25 Cleansed
26 Tuxedo, often
28 1997 novel by Lorrie Moore
33 Comedian Philips
34 Deems culpable
36 EPA concern
37 Drove and drove?
39 Door word
40 ___ nous (in confidence)
41 With a bow, in the pit
42 Muscular
44 Goldfish-swallowing, once
45 How taxes might reduce income
47 Bittern's kin
49 Poet Hughes
50 Drink that may be hard
51 Sing a note, Sinatra-style
56 Literary miscellanies
59 Modem speed measure

60 Witch on a broomstick	22 Wheels for 51-Down
62 Pinza of "South Pacific"	24 Cotton ball applications
63 Copland, Spelling, etc.	26 Physiatrist's field, briefly
64 Bygone period	27 Board for nails
65 Breather	28 Set right
66 Least well-mannered	29 Endangered goose
67 Jam ingredient?	30 Coward's agent would do it
	31 Notorious Bugs
DOWN	32 Malamute tows
	35 Mideast pooh-bah
1 Mind	38 Kind of puzzle in which kids
2 Hot rod rod	connect?
3 Killer that would be slippery	40 Checked out
4 They might make up a Caesar	42 Citrus cocktail
salad	43 Blanches
5 Country singer Lee Roy ___	46 Leghorn lady
6 John who sang "Daniel"	48 Type of time
7 Laugh and a half	50 Its paddlings don't hurt
8 Commencing	51 Handle holder
9 Married *mujeres*	52 Level
10 UNICEF beneficiaries	53 Monet's okays
11 Wedding ring-action	54 *Wiener* wife
12 "The Lord of the Rings," for one	55 Top of the feud chain
13 Start to crack?	57 Do that might block a view
18 Bean Town hoopster	58 Deer sir
	61 Abbr. on Nova Scotia skeds

"What do you mean?"

"Believe it or not, there *is* no such constructor as Hillary Mustache."

"Sherry, I'm in no mood for this."

"Yes, you are. It's fun."

"Why is it fun?"

"Hillary Mustache is an anagram for Cathy Millhauser. And do you know who that is?"

"Was she the Bond girl in *Thunderball*?"

"No."

"Then I guess I don't."

"Cathy Millhauser is famous for her word games.

Punning and gimmickry. She's a gas. I have her book, *Humorous Crosswords*."

"I'm happy for you. So what?"

"There are word games in this puzzle even you would like."

"Pardon me for not falling on the floor, but I've had a rather busy day, what with getting arrested and all."

"Look the puzzle over in your spare time. See if you notice anything about the long answers."

"I notice they're not filled in."

"I brought a pencil."

"Dream on!"

"Cora, you got all night. Why not give it a shot?"

"You want me to give *you* a shot? All I need is some goddamned puzzle."

"Okay, be that way." Sherry dug in her purse. "Here's the solution. Check it out if you get a chance." Sherry handed Cora a book. "I also brought you some light reading."

"What's this? *Lifer*?" Cora snorted. "That's a hell of a thing to give someone in jail. Wait a minute! A. E. Greenhouse! Is this the book you Googled?"

"Right. That's the book Darryl Daigue was in. *Lifer*, by A. E. Greenhouse. I bought it on the Advanced Book Exchange."

Cora grinned. "Well, that's more like it!"

50

CORA'S ENTHUSIASM FOR *Lifer* was short-lived. Despite its exciting premise, the book was dull as dishwater. A. E. Greenhouse was a dry writer, and no new facts were revealed. In just a few pages, Cora's eyes began to glaze over.

Greenhouse had interviewed Darryl Daigue in prison. Daigue had spun his usual web of lies. Except, in this version, Ricky Gleason had nothing to do with the murder. In fact, Gleason wasn't even mentioned. Instead, Darryl Daigue blamed the murder on one of Anita Dryer's classmates.

Though A. E. Greenhouse didn't actually say so, it was clear that the author didn't place much credence in Darryl Daigue's assertions.

Supporting material was skimpy at best. Stacy Daigue expressed the opinion that her brother was pure as the driven snow, but there was nothing anyone could do about it. Darryl Daigue had no other friends or relatives, at least none uncovered by A. E. Greenhouse.

Interviews with the family of the deceased were equally unrevealing. Anita Dryer's mother and father were dead. Her younger sister could not be found. The only available relative, her brother, Jason, was a notorious thief and drug addict, who had actually served time at the Brandon State Penitentiary.

That woke Cora up.

Before she could get too excited, A. E. Greenhouse spoiled her fun with the news that brother Jason had died of a drug overdose just a few weeks after the interview.

Which was too bad. Because Jason had stated in no uncertain terms that he would gladly have killed Darryl Daigue with his bare hands if he'd run into him in prison. The only reason he hadn't was that the son of a bitch was in solitary, and Jason had been paroled before he got the chance.

Cora skimmed through the rest of the book, but found nothing useful. A. E. Greenhouse acknowledged Warden Prufrock, among others, for granting him access to interview the prisoners, but that was about it. There were no other references to Darryl Daigue.

Cora sat on the edge of her cot to figure things out. All she could think of was how tired she was. The facts of the case circled through her head, making absolutely no sense.

Cora absently picked up the puzzle. "*Misnomers,* by Hillary Mustache." And Hillary Mustache was actually somebody else. Big deal.

Cora picked up the pencil and read the clues. Her eyes began to glaze over. It occurred to her she'd have to get a life sentence to finish the damn thing.

Cora put down the puzzle and picked up the solution. There. That was better. Now, what was it Sherry wanted her to see?

Cora studied the long answers: 17 Across, *Kids' Christmas special,* was ELF CARTOON. That didn't do much for her. Then 21 Across, *Tatting-eschewing,* was NOT FOR LACE. So *tatting* must be lace, and *eschewing* must be not having any. And this had made Sherry's day. Cora's mind boggled.

Sing a note, Sinatra-style, 51 Across, was CROON E FLAT. The less said the better. And 60 Across, *Witch on a broomstick,* was CRONE ALOFT.

Cora stopped. Wait a minute.

CRONE ALOFT was awfully close to CROON E FLAT.

Cora looked back at ELF CARTOON and NOT FOR LACE.

Son of a bitch! Each answer had the same letters. They were all anagrams of each other. And the word *anagrams* was in the puzzle.

But why was the puzzle called "MISNOMERS"? Didn't that mean wrong name? So why was ELF CARTOON . . . ?

Oh!

Cora felt like an idiot. The long answers were anagrams, all right. They were all anagrams of her name.

Cora might have been amused, if she weren't in jail.

Okay. Now that Cora had honed her wits on the puzzle, she could tackle these little murder cases.

All right. A detective and a housewife were murdered. Each one had in their possession a pornographic videotape being used to blackmail a warden into letting a prisoner out of jail. That certainly pointed to the convict's sister. Or the convict's girlfriend, assuming she was still in the picture.

MISNOMERS
by Hillary Mustache

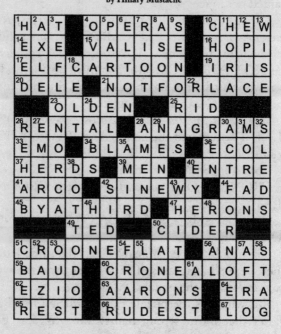

¹H	²A	³T		⁴O	⁵P	⁶E	⁷R	⁸A	⁹S		¹⁰C	¹¹H	¹²E	¹³W
¹⁴E	X	E		¹⁵V	A	L	I	S	E		¹⁶H	O	P	I
¹⁷E	L	F	¹⁸C	A	R	T	O	O	N		¹⁹I	R	I	S
²⁰D	E	L	E		²¹N	O	T	F	O	²²R	L	A	C	E
		²³O	L	D	E	N			²⁵R	I	D			
²⁶R	²⁷E	N	T	A	L		²⁸A	²⁹N	A	G	R	A	M	³⁰S	³¹	³²
³³E	M	O		³⁴B	L	³⁵A	M	E	S		³⁶E	C	O	L
³⁷H	E	R	D	S		³⁹M	E	N		⁴⁰E	N	T	R	E
⁴¹A	R	C	O		⁴²S	I	N	E	⁴³W	Y		⁴⁴F	A	D
⁴⁵B	Y	A	⁴⁶T	H	I	R	D		⁴⁷H	E	⁴⁸R	O	N	S
			⁴⁹T	E	D		⁵⁰C	I	D	E	R			
⁵¹C	⁵²R	⁵³O	O	N	E	⁵⁴F	L	⁵⁵A	T		⁵⁶A	⁵⁷N	⁵⁸A	S
⁵⁹B	A	U	D		⁶⁰C	R	O	N	E	⁶¹A	L	O	F	T
⁶²E	Z	I	O		⁶³A	A	R	O	N	S		⁶⁴E	R	A
⁶⁵R	E	S	T		⁶⁶R	U	D	E	S	T		⁶⁷L	O	G

ACROSS

1 Role, so to speak
4 Works at the Met?
10 Move one's mandible, maybe
14 Program file name suffix
15 Luggage piece
16 Pueblo dweller
17 Kids' Christmas special, perhaps
19 Tennessee's state flower
20 Cut from copy
21 Tatting-eschewing
23 Ere modern days
25 Cleansed
26 Tuxedo, often
28 1997 novel by Lorrie Moore
33 Comedian Philips
34 Deems culpable
36 EPA concern
37 Drove and drove?
39 Door word
40 ___ nous (in confidence)
41 With a bow, in the pit
42 Muscular
44 Goldfish-swallowing, once
45 How taxes might reduce income
47 Bittern's kin
49 Poet Hughes
50 Drink that may be hard
51 Sing a note, Sinatra-style
56 Literary miscellanies
59 Modem speed measure

60 Witch on a broomstick
62 Pinza of "South Pacific"
63 Copland, Spelling, etc.
64 Bygone period
65 Breather
66 Least well-mannered
67 Jam ingredient?

DOWN

1 Mind
2 Hot rod rod
3 Killer that would be slippery
4 They might make up a Caesar salad
5 Country singer Lee Roy ___
6 John who sang "Daniel"
7 Laugh and a half
8 Commencing
9 Married *mujeres*
10 UNICEF beneficiaries
11 Wedding ring-action
12 "The Lord of the Rings," for one
13 Start to crack?
18 Bean Town hoopster

22 Wheels for 51-Down
24 Cotton ball applications
26 Physiatrist's field, briefly
27 Board for nails
28 Set right
29 Endangered goose
30 Coward's agent would do it
31 Notorious Bugs
32 Malamute tows
35 Mideast pooh-bah
38 Kind of puzzle in which kids connect?
40 Checked out
42 Citrus cocktail
43 Blanches
46 Leghorn lady
48 Type of time
50 Its paddlings don't hurt
51 Handle holder
52 Level
53 Monet's okays
54 *Wiener* wife
55 Top of the feud chain
57 Do that might block a view
58 Deer sir
61 Abbr. on Nova Scotia skeds

Cora made a mental note to check if Valerie Thompkins's maiden name might be Tambourine.

But that would make the girlfriend the victim, not the killer.

Okay, back to the drawing board.

The problem was that there was way too much information to process. Did Darryl Daigue murder Anita Dryer? If not, who did? Ricky Gleason, the other counter boy? If so, did someone kill him and fake a car accident? Was Dr. Jenkins covering it up? Did Dr. Jenkins fake the car accident? Or did Warden Prufrock fake it? Did Valerie Thompkins or Peter

Burnside have anything to do with the car accident? They had something to do with the blackmail tape. Were Valerie Thompkins and the detective killed for the blackmail tape? Did the blackmail tape have anything to do with the car accident? The connection was Ida Blaine, who was having an affair with Dr. Jenkins, who might be lying about the accident, and who worked at the prison of Warden Prufrock, the star of the blackmail tape.

Cora yawned.

Who threw the rock through her window? And why was Valerie following her? If she *was* following her, and not just parking at the vet. How about Ida Blaine's husband, Quentin Hawes? Or Valerie Thompkins's deceased husband, for that matter? Whose name was Fleckstein.

How did any of that make sense? Why did it all happen? For starters, why did someone hire her? More to the point, why did someone hire Becky? Was the twenty-year-old murder of a young girl by Darryl Daigue connected in any way to what was happening now?

Cora had the feeling the answer was right there, if she could just put her finger on it.

Her eyes closed, and she immediately fell asleep.

51

Cora Felton stomped out of the Danbury courthouse to the camera whir of the paparazzi. "Damn it to hell," she muttered.

"Smile," Becky Baldwin told her.

"I don't feel like smiling."

"Choose the expression you'd like to see in tomorrow's paper. Preferably one that won't end your commercial career. Unless you're planning on auditioning for an acid reflux ad, that one's not going to fly."

Cora plastered a lopsided grin on her face, snarled out of the corner of her mouth, "If we weren't on camera now, I'd wring your neck."

"When clients do that, I usually refuse to represent them."

"What do you mean, usually? You're barely out of diapers."

"Oh, how witty," Becky said through a frozen smile. "If you can just hang on till we get in the car, I'll rip your head off."

"I *usually* fire lawyers who do that."

"You'd have to hire them first, wouldn't you? I don't recall you paying me any money."

"Picky, picky. Where's your car?"

"Right down the street. You want a ride?"

"No, I want to be left on foot in Danbury."

Cora stomped off toward Becky's car.

Becky caught up. "I bail you out, and this is the thanks I get?"

"Well, did you have to look like that?"

"Like what?"

"It's ten in the morning. You're dressed for a dinner party. I slept in my clothes."

"That's one of the downsides of getting arrested."

Cora and Becky pulled out as flashbulbs blazed.

"Why didn't Sherry and Aaron come?" Cora asked Becky.

"They had a little spat."

"About what?"

"You. The end result is, Aaron isn't covering your arrest."

"That puts him in a majority of one. So this won't make the *Gazette*?"

"It will. They sent another reporter."

"Wonderful."

The women drove in silence a while, then Becky said, "What is it you're not telling me?"

"What do you mean?"

"The buzz around the courthouse is they'd charge you with breaking and entering if they just had a little more evidence."

"*More* evidence? You mean they have *some*?"

"They have suspicions. Valerie Thompkins's house was broken into. A neighbor says he saw an elderly woman running through the bushes."

"Elderly?" Cora fumed.

"What do you care? It wasn't you."

"Right. Even so, I'd pin the jerk's ears back."

"You want to tell me exactly what you were doing last night?"

"I was sleeping in a cell."

"I mean the night before."

"According to the police, I was stealing a dog."

"After that."

"I really don't recall."

"Yeah. So, here's the deal: I'm driving you home so you can take a shower and get cleaned up."

"Sounds good."

"Stay there, and stay out of trouble."

"Killjoy."

"You've got to, Cora. At least until you beat this dognapping charge."

"You gonna baby-sit me?"

"No, I trust you to follow my advice."

"Fine. Take me home."

Cora was quiet until Becky turned into the driveway. Then she said, "Hey! Where's Sherry?"

"I have no idea."

"The car's gone."

"I see that."

"You're not leaving me here without a car."

"Why? You're not going anywhere."

"Oh, for Christ's sake."

Cora jerked the door open and stormed out.

"Hang on. I got something for you." Becky reached to the floor of the backseat, picked up a paper bag, and pulled out a gift-wrapped box. "Happy birthday. Sorry it's late, but I've been kind of busy."

Cora's mouth fell open. "Are you kidding me?"

"Well, actually, it took me a while to find something you haven't got." Becky pulled the car door shut. "See ya."

Cora stuck her head in the window. "Are you sure we shouldn't wait for Sherry?"

"Very sure."

Becky gunned the car down the driveway.

Cora went inside, flopped down on the couch. She lit a cigarette and contemplated her present. What had Becky gotten her?

She picked the box up and shook it. It rattled, like there was something small inside. She tore the wrapping off, lifted the lid, peered inside.

It was a single piece of cardboard, about the size of a business card. Except it was orange and it was blank.

Cora picked it up and turned it over. Her eyes widened.

It was a Chance card from a Monopoly set.

A Get Out of Jail Free card.

Cora leaned back on the couch and grinned. Well, wasn't that nice? Becky was right. It was the one thing Cora needed: a pro bono lawyer. Cora figured she'd better cut Becky a little more slack.

Particularly since she wasn't planning on taking her advice.

Cora got up and went into the study. The computer was on. Now, how did Sherry Google people? By pulling up a word browser. But which one?

Cora clicked on an icon, and there it was. The word *Google* and an empty slot.

She typed in *Cynthia Mayberry,* the neighbor.

There were only two hits. Cynthia Mayberry had come in second in a pie-baking contest. She was also mentioned in her mother's obituary.

Cora was disappointed. She would have loved to have nailed the woman with something.

Cora leafed through the book *Lifer* by A. E. Greenhouse, and Googled everyone associated with Darryl Daigue.

This was not particularly gratifying, either.

Darryl's sister, Stacy, scored three hits, each of which consisted of some person named Daigue being mentioned in the same article as some other person named Stacy.

Jason Dryer, on the other hand, yielded forty-eight thousand, eight hundred seventeen hits. This seemed promising, but turned out to be due to the fact that the name Dryer was also a word. Cora narrowed her search, checking only news instead of the whole Web. That yielded twelve hits. Scrolling down the page, Cora found one article actually relating to the man: an obituary notice.

The deceased was identified as Jason Dryer, of New York City. The address listed in the Bowery was most likely a none-too-reputable single-room-occupancy hotel. Jason's age was reported as thirty-two. He was survived by his younger sister, Gwendolyn, of Boulder, Colorado. No other living relative was mentioned, nor was there any allusion to his murdered sister, Anita.

Cora tried *Gwendolyn Dryer,* with even less luck. A housewife named Gwendolyn was suing the manufacturer of a cordless hair dryer, an actress named Dryer was playing the part of Gwendolyn in Oscar Wilde's *The Importance of Being Earnest,* and a meteorologist named Gwendolyn seemed to be of the opinion the weather might become dryer, but that was about it.

Cora tried *A. E. Greenhouse*. She came up with thirty-five hits, all of them relating to the book. There were a few reviews, lukewarm at best. Aside from that, most were from local libraries simply listing the fact they had the book.

Cora dug in her purse again for her cigarettes. A card came out with the pack. At first she thought it was Becky Baldwin's Get Out of Jail Free card, but then she remembered. It was the card she'd found under the rug in Valerie Thompkins's spare bedroom. What with finding the porno tape, she'd completely forgotten it.

Cora turned the card over.

It was a business card, all right.

The card read:

A. E. Greenhouse
Author

52

MASON WESTBOURNE, THE EDITOR of Pilgrim Publishing, couldn't have been more irritating. "I'm sorry, I can't help you."

"But I need to talk to Mr. Greenhouse."

"I'm not allowed to discuss the affairs of my authors."

"I don't give a damn about his affairs. I just want to get him on the phone."

"I'm sure you do. But you need to follow the proper procedure. You can write to Mr. Greenhouse care of Pilgrim Publishing. Give your name, address, telephone number, fax number, and e-mail address. If Mr. Greenhouse wishes to contact you, he may."

"Whoa! Should we start over? Did I explain to you who I was?"

"Yes, you did."

"Did I explain to you what this was with regard to?"

"I trust that is a rhetorical question. Because this

conversation has not been sufficiently long for me to have forgotten the gist of it."

"You're an editor?"

"Yes."

"I hope your books don't read like you talk."

"Miss Felton, I'm not going to take offense. I know who you are. Someday Pilgrim Publishing would be honored to publish a collection of your work. Something your agent might wish to discuss—"

"Gee, I'd love to talk business, if it weren't for a minor homicide case or two."

"Miss Felton, if you were my author, you wouldn't want me giving out your information to everyone who asked for it."

"Fine," Cora said. "Call Mr. Greenhouse. Tell him what I told you. Give him my phone number. Tell him to call me."

"I really can't do that. I strongly suggest you handle this the way I said. Now, if you'll excuse me, I have to take another call."

"We're not done."

"Then I have to put you on hold."

"No! No! No! You goddamned son of a bitch!"

"Gee, what did I do now?" Sherry said, coming into the kitchen.

"Where the hell have you been?" Cora snarled.

"Aaron and I went to lunch."

"How can you eat, with me in jail?"

"Well, if I can't, I sure hope you get a light sentence. What are you so worked up about?"

"Publishing nerd on the phone."

"Not so loud. We may need to get published."

"That's what *he* said."

"What did you say?"

"Told him I'd rip his lungs out, and— Well, Mr. Westbourne, it's about time. Are you going to listen to reason, or do I have to sic my attorney on you?"

"Actually, that's probably the best way to handle it. Have your attorney contact my attorney. Pardon me, but I have this other call."

Cora's face purpled. She slammed down the phone.

"I'd like to point out whatever that man said to you is not my fault," Sherry said mildly.

"You took my car," Cora accused.

"You weren't here."

"I'm here now."

"So's your car. Where are you going, anyway?"

Cora started to flare up angrily. She exhaled and collapsed into a chair. "Damn it, I don't know. It's so frustrating. Everything's a dead end. See what Becky gave me?" She pointed to the card. "Free legal services. Unless *you're* paying her and not telling me."

"Don't be paranoid."

"You paid her before and didn't tell me. And she didn't tell me. And you didn't tell me I was having a birthday. You even sent me a murder puzzle to trick me into going down there. You're not paranoid if people really are out to get you."

"No one's out to get you."

"Right. The fact I'm a criminal defendant is entirely coincidental."

"That's hardly a conspiracy. You've been charged with stealing a dog. Why? Because you stole a dog. Boy, is that unfair."

"Where is Fido, by the way?"

"The police have him."

"I thought you were going to get him."

"They wouldn't give him to me."

"The police are keeping the dog?"

"No, they're boarding him at a kennel."

"So pick him up there."

"You think I didn't try? The kennel owner would like to know on what authority I was taking the dog. I was hard-pressed to tell him."

"Did you say the dog had been living at your house?"

"I did. The kennel guy wanted to know how long. My answer wasn't good. Even in dog years, four hours is a pretty short time. It might have helped if I'd known the dog's name. I had to keep referring to him as 'Mrs. Thompkins's dog.' "

"Jerk probably didn't notice."

"Jerk probably did."

"What makes you think so?"

"He said, 'You don't even know his name, do you?' "

"How'd you bluff that one through?"

"I said, 'No, what's his name?' "

"That fool him?"

"I don't think so. He hung up on me."

"What's the number?"

Cora called the Carlyle Kennel.

Mr. Carlyle was not moved. "Miss Felton, I can't believe you're asking for the dog. The reason the police boarded him here is because he'd been stolen."

"Not at all. His owner got her throat cut. Don't you read the paper?"

"Yes, I do. It says you're the one who stole him."

"Nonsense. I was given the dog to look after. This is just a misunderstanding."

"Well, you can take that up with the police. Until I hear otherwise, Buddy's staying here."

Cora blinked. "Buddy?"

"His name is Buddy." Mr. Carlyle's tone was withering. "You didn't even know that, did you?"

Cora Felton slammed down the phone and raced out the door.

53

BECKY BALDWIN'S SMILE WAS superior. "Cora. It's a probable-cause hearing."

"Yes, I know."

"You can't subpoena witnesses for a probable-cause hearing."

"Why not?"

"It isn't done."

"It's done if we want to do it."

"We don't want to do it. It won't accomplish anything. All it will do is make me look like a rank amateur."

"Whereas actually you've had decades of experience."

"That's not the point. The point is, we look bad."

"I don't care how we look. I want to get out of jail."

"I understand. I hope you understand that Get Out of Jail Free card was not a license to order every legal procedure in the book."

"You don't want to do it unless you're paid?"

"I don't want to do it at all. It's a terrible legal move."

"I didn't know this was a restricted gift. What legal procedures *am* I entitled to?"

"It's not a matter of money."

"You don't care how much it costs?"

"I care how much it costs. It's not a determining factor."

"What is? Looking good?"

"It's not a case of looking good, Cora. It's a case of following proper legal procedure. Because if we don't, the judge is going to shut us down."

"I really think you worry too much."

"Cora, do you know what abuse of process is?"

"It's when you call witnesses for no particular reason. I assure you, *I* have a reason."

"Could you tell me what it is?" Becky requested dryly.

"Probably better not."

"Cora—"

"Hey, if you don't know, it's not your fault." Cora smiled. "Becky, sweetie, just do what I say, and everything will be all right."

"And just what do you want me to do?"

"I told you. Subpoena people."

"Who?"

Cora considered. "Practically everybody."

"What?"

"Well, I need them all there."

"Why? What do you expect to prove?"

"That's difficult to say."

"Why?"

"Because I'm not entirely sure."

"Damn it, Cora, that's *exactly* what is meant by

abuse of process. You can't just subpoena people on a whim. The prosecutor will object, and the judge will demand to know what you expect to prove by the witness. If he doesn't like your answer, you can go to jail."

"Well, I'm already going to jail."

"Cora, this isn't funny."

"Look, I need those witnesses. Can you help me out?"

"As your attorney, I advise you not to call them."

Cora nodded. "Okay. You're fired."

"What?!"

"I'm relieving you of your duties. You're no longer responsible for my defense."

"You're *firing* your *pro bono* lawyer?" Becky said incredulously.

"What, I can't fire you unless I pay you?"

"Hey, I'm not *refusing* to do what you want. I'm only advising against it. Why are you firing me?"

Cora smiled, and patted Becky on the cheek.

"Because I don't want to get you disbarred."

54

JUDGE TRILLING LOOKED DOWN from his bench, shook his head, and sighed. It had not occurred to the venerable jurist to ban cameras from his courtroom. For a simple probable-cause hearing, there was no need. As a result, Rick Reed and the Channel 8 news team had commandeered the entire spectator section behind the prosecution table. A camera on a tall tripod straddled a row of seats, and an operator with a headset stood by ready to mount a stepladder when it was time to film. A handheld camera and sound crew snaked through the rows, scouting out locations to get the best shots. Since there were no jurors present, the crew had cast a covetous eye on the jury box, which would have had a better angle on the defense and prosecution tables, but the judge had drawn the line.

Also out-of-bounds was the section behind the defense table. That side of the courtroom was packed. Many of the people were merely spectators, but lots of them were witnesses. None of whom knew why.

Judge Trilling didn't know why, either. Trilling

was, in fact, baffled. The defendant, a little old lady in Miss Marple tweed, looked incapable of speeding, much less the crime for which she was charged. Her defense attorney looked more like a fashion model than a lawyer.

Judge Trilling settled back on his bench, slapped on his most kindly but judicial smile, and said, "All right, what have we here?"

A.D.A. Goldstein rose, adjusted his tie, and cast a glance at the unruly scene across the aisle. His gaze was contemptuous. "*People vs. Cora Felton,* grand larceny, involving the theft of a purebred poodle valued at sixteen hundred dollars. Defendant has pled not guilty and requests the prosecution show probable cause."

"Are you ready to proceed?"

"*We* are, Your Honor."

"Is the defense ready?"

Cora Felton and Becky Baldwin rose.

"Yes, Your Honor," Cora said.

Judge Trilling frowned. "Miss Felton, that question was directed to your lawyer. Please let your lawyer answer."

"Yes, Your Honor," Cora said. "The fact is—"

"Miss Felton, perhaps you did not understand me. I do not want a statement from you. I want to hear from your lawyer."

"Yes, Your Honor. The fact is—"

"Miss Felton! I will thank you not to call me 'Your Honor' and tell me 'the fact is.' It is the height of rudeness, assuming I, a judge, need to be lectured on courtroom procedure. Am I making myself clear?"

"Perfectly, Your Honor. However—"

Judge Trilling banged his gavel. "That will do! Miss

Baldwin, I will thank you to control your client. Do you think you can do that?"

"No, Your Honor."

Judge Trilling's eyes widened in disbelief. "I *beg* your pardon! Did you just say *no*?"

"Sorry, Your Honor, but I am no longer Miss Felton's attorney, as she has been attempting to tell you."

"You are not representing the defendant?"

"That's right, Your Honor."

"Why? Why won't you represent her?"

"She fired me, Your Honor."

A loud murmur ran through the courtroom. The Channel 8 news crew filmed gleefully. The mobile team was torn between getting an angle on Cora and Becky, and focusing on the judge's stupefied expression.

"If you are not representing the defendant, why are you here?"

"I feel ethically bound to offer what legal advice she might need in presenting her own defense."

"*What* defense? This is a probable-cause hearing. You don't put *on* a defense."

"That's what I told Miss Felton, Your Honor."

"What did she say to that?"

"She fired me, Your Honor."

Judge Trilling frowned. "Miss Felton, you claim you are acting as your own attorney?"

"That's right, Your Honor."

"I'd like to point out the folly of such a move. Granted, this is a preliminary hearing. Even so, you could get yourself in trouble. Has your lawyer advised you of the pitfalls of such actions? I mean, your former lawyer?"

"Yes, Your Honor."

"Yet here you are."

"Well, it's just a probable-cause hearing. I don't see what's so hard."

"It isn't. Unless you're not a lawyer." Judge Trilling cleared his throat. "Miss Felton, it has come to my attention that you have served several subpoenas in this case."

"I'm surprised you noticed. Like you say, it's such a minor matter."

"It has come to my attention because several people are not happy about it. Particularly the policemen you have seen fit to call into court."

Cora shrugged. "Sort of goes with the territory, though, doesn't it? If you're a cop, you're going to get subpoenaed."

"Not by the defense in a probable-cause case. Which is in itself sufficient reason to show you need an attorney."

"I fail to see why, Your Honor."

"This is a probable-cause hearing. *You* don't call witnesses. The *prosecution* calls witnesses. To show that there are reasonable grounds to proceed."

"Yes, Your Honor. I'm going to show reasonable grounds that there *aren't.*"

"No, you're not."

"I beg your pardon?"

"Miss Felton, is this your first probable-cause hearing?"

"Yes, Your Honor."

"Then perhaps you will allow yourself to be instructed. If not, you will be instructed anyway, but I would like to avoid unpleasantness. Am I making myself clear?"

"Yes, Your Honor."

"Now, then. You do not *need* witnesses at a probable-cause hearing. You are *not* going to put on a defense."

"I'm not, Your Honor?"

"No, you're not. You therefore have summoned witnesses you do not need to call. There is a judicial term for such an action. Do you know what that would be?"

"Is Your Honor referring to 'abuse of process'?"

"Yes, I am. Which is something I do not take lightly in my court."

"I'm thrilled to hear it, Your Honor."

"So, since this is your first probable-cause hearing, and you are perhaps overzealous, I would like to give you an opportunity to reconsider your position before such charges might be made. I am willing to quash these subpoenas without prejudice, and give you the opportunity to avoid the charge of abuse of process. With that in mind, Miss Felton, do you have any statement you would like to make with regard to the witnesses you've summoned here today?"

"Yes, Your Honor."

"Proceed, Ms. Felton."

"I want a bench warrant issued for the Carlyle Kennel."

Judge Trilling could not have been more surprised had Cora ordered a pepperoni pizza. "You what?!"

"I have served the Kennel with a subpoena *duces tecum,* ordering them to bring a toy poodle into court, and they have failed to do so. I need a warrant."

Mr. Carlyle, a lanky young man in the second row, stood up and adjusted his glasses. "That's not true, Your Honor. The animal's outside in my van. I can get him on a moment's notice. But I see no reason to subject a dog to these proceedings any more than is necessary."

Judge Trilling blinked his eyes, rubbed his head. "I wish someone had been so considerate of me. Miss Felton, you subpoenaed a dog into my courtroom?"

"Not just any dog, Your Honor. This is the dog that I'm accused of swiping."

"Is that true, Mr. Goldstein?"

"Yes, Your Honor. It is the dog the defendant is accused of stealing, because it is the dog that was recovered in the defendant's possession, and it is the dog the defendant was observed removing from the premises. Which can be shown by competent witnesses if I am just allowed to call them. There is no question as to probable cause."

"Says you," Cora snorted. "Luckily, the judge here requires more than just your assurance."

The prosecutor's angry retort was silenced by the judge's gavel. "That will do! Do I understand that you have subpoenaed the stolen property?"

"Yes, Your Honor."

"For what purpose?"

"To make sure we'd have it." Cora jerked her thumb at the prosecutor. "You see how F. Lee Bailey here expects us to take his word for everything? I couldn't count on him bringing the dog into court."

"That's not what I meant. You subpoenaed a dog. What did you expect to prove by it?"

"That I'm innocent of the crime."

Judge Trilling could feel a headache coming on. He repressed a groan. "Miss Felton, I am not sure if you are willfully misunderstanding me, or simply missing the point. I am going to give you the benefit of the doubt. Unfair though it may seem, your guilt or innocence is not at issue here. We are not trying the case. There is no reason to call these witnesses, since all the prosecution is attempting to establish is probable cause."

"Phooey, Your Honor. Suppose the prosecutor puts on a police officer who claims he found the dog at my house. Suppose I have six reputable witnesses who saw that police officer picking up that dog from the crime scene and *taking* it to my house. Wouldn't that show the officer *didn't* have probable cause?"

"Do you claim such is the case?"

"No. I was stating a hypothetical. But excluding my witnesses out of hand is unacceptable, and grounds for appeal."

"You intend to appeal a probable-cause hearing?"

"Not at all, Your Honor. I intend to win it."

"God save me." Judge Trilling cocked his head at the prosecutor. "Mr. Goldstein, is there the least doubt as to probable cause?"

"Not at all, Your Honor. If I can just be allowed to make my case . . ."

Cora waved her hand. "Who cares about your darn case? As the judge here pointed out, that's not at issue. The defense will stipulate that you could call a cop who would testify to finding the dog at my house, as well as the next-door neighbor who would testify to seeing me take the dog. She would also have to testify that she *gave* me the dog."

"That's justification that should be argued at trial," the prosecutor protested. His cheeks were getting red. "All we need to show is that the defendant took it."

"You don't have to *show* I took it," Cora retorted. "I'm offering to *stipulate* I took it. I can't believe you're not willing to stipulate in return."

Judge Trilling banged the gavel. "Miss Felton! Are you willing to stipulate as stated?"

"Yes, Your Honor. On the condition that I be allowed to call my witnesses."

"For what possible purpose? You just stipulated to the theft."

"No, Your Honor, I stipulated that I was *given* the dog. But that's not why I want to call these witnesses. I would point out, Your Honor, that I have been threatened with abuse of process. That is an extremely serious charge. But I didn't do it. As I can readily explain, if given the chance."

"Your Honor, I must object most strenuously to this highly unorthodox procedure—"

"Oh, keep your shirt on, Goldstein," Cora said. "You've already won your case. Wouldn't you like to know what's going on?"

"Miss Felton," Judge Trilling began, "I don't want to warn you again."

"Sure, Your Honor. But could we move things along? He just made his case. Now it's my turn. Can I call my witnesses?"

"Objection, Your Honor!" A.D.A. Goldstein snapped. "The defendant is making a mockery of this courtroom. These witnesses have no bearing on the case. I object to them being called!"

In the back of the courtroom Sergeant Walpole of the Danbury police force stood up. "Your Honor, I have been subpoenaed as a witness in this case. I would like to state that I have absolutely no evidence that would bear on the theft of the dog in question. I ask that I be released from this subpoena."

"This is flagrant abuse of process, Your Honor," A.D.A. Goldstein contributed.

Judge Trilling frowned. "Miss Felton. Once again, the question of abuse of process has been raised. I ask you now, are you willing to release Sergeant Walpole from his subpoena?"

"No, Your Honor. But thank you for asking."

"Are you willing to release any of the other people you've called?"

"No, Your Honor."

"Very well, Miss Felton. Then will you please tell the court just exactly what you hope to prove by these witnesses?"

Cora Felton smiled.

"Thought you'd never ask."

55

CORA FELTON STRODE OUT into the middle of the court-room, doing her best Perry Mason. There was no jury to address, but she managed to play to the cameras and the house. She shrugged her tweed jacket open, put her hands on her hips, and smiled. If she'd had suspenders, she'd have hooked her thumbs.

"If it please the court," she began, "before I explain what I expect to prove by these people, I'd better tell you who they are."

Cora gestured to the front row. "First off, that scruffy-looking man with the black eye and the scab on his chin is Mr. Darryl Daigue, lifer at Brandon State Penitentiary. The gentlemen seated next to him are not under subpoena. I would suspect they are prison guards."

"You subpoenaed a life prisoner?"

"Yes, Your Honor. I would say that Darryl's appearance here is a dramatic demonstration of the effectiveness of our legal system in general and our courtroom summons system in particular, which is even capable of getting a life prisoner *out* of jail."

"That's not exactly how I would view it," Judge Trilling said dryly. "It would appear that the abuse of process is even more egregious than I thought."

"Not at all, Your Honor. Darryl Daigue is central to the whole affair, as I shall demonstrate. Mr. Daigue has been behind bars for twenty years for a murder he swears he did not commit, that of a young girl named Anita Dryer. My attorney, Miss Baldwin, was asked to look into this situation by the prisoner's sister, Miss Stacy Daigue, though she now denies it. That's Miss Daigue over there in the red bandanna and the leather jacket, and, if she'll forgive me, a little too much makeup. She's a waitress from New Haven, finds it a huge imposition to be here. She's one of the people pushing abuse of process. Yet her presence here is key.

"That gloomy man in the three-piece suit who manages to look angry and apprehensive at the same time, is Warden 'Iron Man' Prufrock, of the Brandon correctional facility, where Darryl Daigue currently resides.

"That attractive woman sitting next to him is Ida Blaine, wife of industrialist Quentin Hawes, currently on vacation in Australia. She and her husband take separate vacations, not an essential point, except for the fact Quentin is not here. Mrs. Blaine is important because she is on the parole board that considers Darryl Daigue's case.

"Also on the parole board is Dr. Jenkins. Dr. Jenkins is the prison doctor, one of his patients is Darryl Daigue. Dr. Jenkins is also the doctor who performed the postmortem on one Ricky Gleason, killed in an automobile accident last summer. Mr. Gleason is reputed to be the counter boy who was on duty the night twenty years ago when Anita Dryer met her death.

"Sergeant Walpole, who just objected to this procedure, is the officer who investigated Ricky Gleason's accident. He also examined the crime scene where Valerie Thompkins was murdered."

"Objection, Your Honor!" The prosecutor shot to his feet. "None of this is relevant."

"Oh, keep your trap shut," Cora told Goldstein. "I'm trying to answer the judge's question."

"Miss Felton," Judge Trilling said severely. "Do I need to remind you it is not your place to admonish counsel? That's my job."

"Then go ahead and do it, Judge. He's got it coming."

The prosecutor sputtered angrily.

Laughter rippled through the courtroom.

Judge Trilling banged the gavel. "That will do. Your indignation is noted, Mr. Goldstein. Miss Felton, if we could move this along . . ."

"Sure thing, Your Honor. Now, where was I?" Cora looked around the courtroom. "Oh, yes. That gentleman in the Brandon State Penitentiary uniform is the prison guard I spoke to the first time I called on Darryl Daigue.

"The woman next to him with the pretty grim hairstyle and radical face-lift who looks like she swallowed a bottle of castor oil is Valerie Thompkins's next-door neighbor, Cynthia Mayberry, who was in charge of feeding Val's dog.

"The plump gentleman next to Cynthia, the guy with the curly thinning hair, is Mason Westbourne, editor of Pilgrim Publishing. He has been served with a subpoena *duces tecum,* ordering him to bring into court any and all contracts entered into between Pilgrim Publishing and A. E. Greenhouse, author of the book *Lifer,* which has a section on Darryl Daigue. Mr. Greenhouse is not here today, all attempts to serve a subpoena on him having failed.

"Also not here is Jason Dryer, brother of murder victim Anita Dryer, and recent inmate at Brandon State Penitentiary, where Darryl Daigue is incarcerated. Mr. Dryer died of a drug overdose shortly after being released from prison, but not before giving an interview to Mr. Greenhouse, which wound up in Greenhouse's book.

"Also under subpoena are cruciverbalist Harvey Beerbaum, Bakerhaven Police Chief Dale Harper, Officer Sam Brogan, *Bakerhaven Gazette* reporter Aaron Grant, my niece, Sherry Carter, and my former attorney, Becky Baldwin."

"Is that *all*?"

"For the moment, Your Honor. I can't promise more witnesses may not arise."

"I *can*. Miss Felton, you're not calling any of these people. So far, you have listed them. And if there is a *germ* of an idea in that list, I have yet to see it. So I suggest you get your act together. What do you expect to *prove*?"

"By Sergeant Walpole, I expect to prove that Ricky Gleason died in a traffic accident. I expect to prove that Dr. Jenkins was the medical examiner who examined Ricky's body and ruled it an accidental death. I expect to prove that Dr. Jenkins was Darryl Daigue's prison doctor, and that he communicated this fact to Darryl Daigue. I expect to prove that Darryl Daigue is an opportunist, that upon hearing a coworker from the old diner had kicked the bucket, Daigue immediately began to blame the crime on him, since Gleason was dead as a doorknob and couldn't deny it. I expect to prove that this is absolute hogwash, a complete fabrication, and has absolutely nothing to do with the price of corn."

Judge Trilling leaned forward. "Wait a minute. You are now *admitting* you summoned witnesses *knowing* they had no relevant testimony?"

"Not at all, Your Honor." Cora smiled. "The fact that some of these people are lying makes their testimony no less relevant."

"It does to *me,* Miss Felton. You are bordering dangerously on contempt of court. What do you expect to *prove?*"

"I expect to prove that these lies were *told.* I expect to prove that they are *lies.* And I expect to prove that these lies precipitated the current situation.

"It all goes back to the writer, A. E. Greenhouse, who, as I say, I have been unable to dig up. I have, instead, his book, his editor, and his contract. I expect to prove that Mr. Greenhouse was an author researching a book on life prisoners in the American penal system; that Mr. Greenhouse wanted to interview Darryl Daigue, who was serving a life term for the murder of a seventeen-year-old named Anita Dryer. Initially, Mr. Greenhouse was unable to do so. Why? Because Darryl Daigue was one of the least savory individuals in Brandon prison, an antisocial troublemaker who spent most of his time in solitary confinement.

"In the interim, Greenhouse spoke with Anita Dryer's brother, Jason Dryer, who was also an inmate at Brandon prison. Jason was a junkie, who died of an overdose shortly after getting out of jail, but not before giving Mr. Greenhouse an interview in which Jason stated frankly he would have killed Mr. Daigue with his bare hands had he encountered him in prison.

"I expect to prove with the records kept by the Brandon prison guard that shortly after Darryl Daigue was released from solitary he was interviewed by A. E. Greenhouse for the book *Lifer,* published by Pilgrim Publishing.

"I expect to prove that after the publication of the book, A. E. Greenhouse vanished off the face of the earth."

"I beg your pardon?" Judge Trilling exclaimed.

"Oh, that one's easy, Your Honor. That's why I have his editor here with his book contract. I expect to show that A. E. Greenhouse was not the author's real name, but merely a pseudonym. I expect to find his real name on the contract."

"What significance, if any, would that have in the case?"

"Just this: I expect to be able to show, Your Honor, that A. E. Greenhouse was the pen name of Marvin Fleckstein, husband of Valerie Thompkins, the murdered woman from whom I am accused of stealing the dog."

"Really?" After he disentangled this, Judge Trilling sounded interested for the first time since entering the courtroom.

"I submit that none of this has any bearing on the crime, Your Honor," A.D.A. Goldstein complained.

"Maybe not, but I intend to hear it. Go on, Miss Felton. You claim the author of this book was married to the decedent dog owner?"

"Yep."

"Do you have any grounds for making this statement?"

"I certainly hope so, Your Honor. The editor has refused to cooperate with me. That's why I've subpoenaed him."

"So this is mere conjecture?"

"It's the only thing that makes sense, Your Honor. See why I need to call the witness?"

"I see nothing of the sort. What bearing could this possibly have on the theft of the dog?"

"The proof is cumulative, Your Honor. I'm just getting started."

"God help us."

"It's really quite simple. Greenhouse, or Fleckstein, if you will, wanted to interview Darryl Daigue. I expect to prove Greenhouse used his influence to get Mr. Daigue out of solitary."

"How do you expect to prove that?"

Cora caught Warden Prufrock's eye. "I suspect it is not unusual for writers and journalists to be afforded accommodations. I expect that Warden Prufrock will testify to the fact that Greenhouse was given access to Darryl Daigue. This is corroborated by the fact this interview is reported in his book. Unfortunately, we are not able to find Mr. Greenhouse to verify that. If my theory is correct, we will never be able to find Mr. Greenhouse, because the real author, Marvin Fleckstein, husband of Valerie Thompkins, had a heart attack right after turning in the manuscript, and died before the book was published."

"Miss Felton, do you have a point?"

"Yes, Your Honor. I expect to prove that on his death, the influence Marvin Fleckstein used in order to see the prisoner transferred to his wife, the late Valerie Thompkins. I expect to prove that she, in conjunction with Danbury private investigator Peter Burnside, conspired to wield that influence in an attempt to get Darryl Daigue paroled. Obviously, Thompkins and Burnside were not acting on their own, but carrying out the instructions of a third party.

"Who might that be? Who might have a motive for wanting Darryl Daigue out of jail?"

"His sister immediately comes to mind. She allegedly hired attorney Becky Baldwin for just that purpose. Becky hired me, and the rest is history."

"The hell it is!" Stacy Daigue cried indignantly.

"Silence!" Judge Trilling glowered at Stacy. "One more outburst like that, and I'll find you in contempt of court. Is that clear?"

Stacy Daigue was not intimidated. "Do I have to sit here and listen to this?" she demanded.

"No, you don't. I can have you removed and held in custody until you are called. It's entirely up to you."

Stacy showed her disdain with the trademark Daigue sneer, but held her tongue.

Judge Trilling turned his attention back to Cora. "If what you say is true, why were Mrs. Thompkins and the detective killed?"

"Simple. They were trying to get Darryl Daigue out of jail. Someone wanted to stop it."

"Who would have such a motive?"

"That remains to be seen, Your Honor. But we do have a clue. By the testimony of Sergeant Walpole, I expect to show that when the police processed the crime scene of the murder of Valerie Thompkins they discovered the word *Bud* scrawled on the underside of the coffee table, in the victim's blood."

"How the *hell* do you know that!?" Sergeant Walpole cried indignantly. "We haven't released that information!"

"Is that true?" Judge Trilling asked, fascinated.

"*I* only found out this morning!" A.D.A. Goldstein blurted out. "Your Honor, this *proves* the defendant was at the crime scene!"

Cora waved her hand breezily. "That's not at issue, Your Honor. The point is, there's a good chance Valerie Thompkins wrote the word *Bud* just before she died. She was definitely trying to name her killer."

"Nonsense!" A.D.A. Goldstein scoffed.

"Hold on," Judge Trilling said. "Miss Felton, if this is true, do you know who Valerie Thompkins meant by *Bud*?"

"Not for certain, Your Honor. But I do know Anita Dryer had a younger sister. That sister is not quoted in the Greenhouse article. In fact, she's not even mentioned by A. E. Greenhouse. Yet, according to Vital Statistics, Gwendolyn Dryer did exist. And there is no record of her death."

"Have you subpoenaed Gwendolyn Dryer too?"

"No, Your Honor. I can't find her. Nor can I find Cindy Tambourine."

"Who?"

"Darryl Daigue's childhood girlfriend. She, too, has vanished off the face of the earth."

Judge Trilling's head was swimming. "Wait a minute. Why would *she* have a motive to keep Daigue in jail?"

"I'm not saying she would, Your Honor. I'm just saying I couldn't find her."

"Oh, Your Honor," A.D.A. Goldstein objected. "I fail to see what any of this has to do with the dog—"

"Do you care about the murders?" Cora asked.

"We're not trying the murders. We're dealing with grand larceny."

"I can connect it up. I'm merely laying the ground-work."

"I think the connection should come *first,*" Goldstein blustered.

"I think so too," Judge Trilling agreed. "Miss Felton, I've given you as much leeway as possible. The prosecutor is right. Interesting as all this background may be, I need to hear something relevant to the current charge."

"Sure thing, Your Honor. The charge is that I swiped the dog. I can disprove that in a moment. I subpoenaed the dog. He's right outside. Let's bring him in."

"I thought you weren't going to let her put on witnesses," A.D.A. Goldstein howled.

"I'm not going to put on witnesses. I just want to see the dog."

"Why?"

"To make sure he's okay, for one thing. He's had enough trauma without being locked in a cage."

"That's not a legal reason," Goldstein snapped.

Cora smiled at the TV cameras. "I'm sure the dog lovers in the audience will appreciate that comment."

The A.D.A.'s furious retort was drowned out by the judge's gavel. "That will do! Let's bring in the animal. Then, Miss Felton, you may continue with your offer of proof. But I sincerely hope you will come up with something that will relieve me of the responsibility of locking you in a cell."

Mr. Carlyle went out and returned with the dog in a small carrying case. Whether it was the cage, the Kennel, or the lack of human companionship, Buddy looked despondent.

"There, Your Honor," Cora said. "You don't have to take my word for it. This is *not* a happy dog."

Buddy, however, perked up at the sound of Cora's voice. He jumped to his feet, let out a high-pitched *yip,* and began clawing at the bars.

"See?" Cora said. "The dog likes me."

"That's irrelevant," A.D.A. Goldstein protested.

"Not to the dog. If I may beg your indulgence, Your Honor?"

"You've had it for some time," Judge Trilling said dryly. "Let him out before he breaks a nail."

Cora walked over to Mr. Carlyle, lifted the latch, and swung open the door of the cage.

Buddy immediately leaped into her arms.

"The fact the dog likes her means nothing," A.D.A. Goldstein fumed.

"It means something to me," Cora said. "And I would imagine it means something to someone else."

Cora turned her back on the judge's bench, and walked around the defense table, up to the spectators' section. The TV cameras followed her as she walked along the rail, the toy poodle in her arms.

Buddy tensed. His lip curled.

As he neared Ida Blaine, he began to growl.

Suddenly, with a snarl of rage, he sprang into the air, hurtled over Ida Blaine, and sank his teeth into the forearm of Darryl Daigue's sister, Stacy.

56

CORA FELTON STOOD ON the front steps of the courthouse holding a dog, while Rick Reed pushed a microphone in her face. *"Miss Felton. Were you surprised the prosecution dismissed the charges?"*

"Not at all. The prosecutor is a reasonable man, only concerned with justice. I think you can count on him to vigorously prosecute Stacy Daigue for murder."

"How did you know she was the killer?"

Cora scratched the dog under the chin. *"I didn't. Buddy did. As you saw in court."*

The TV screen cut to a replay of Buddy leaping from Cora's arms and biting Darryl Daigue's sister.

"Yay, Buddy!" Cora cheered. Sherry and Aaron, watching with her, echoed the sentiment.

"How did you know the dog would do that?" Rick Reed asked.

"Valerie Thompkins wrote the word Bud *at the murder scene in her own blood. That told me two things. One, she didn't know her killer's name, or she would have*

written it. And, two, the dog knew. Val tried to write his name, 'Buddy.' She got as far as 'Bud' before she died. Valerie named Buddy, and Buddy named the killer."

"But why did Stacy Daigue commit the alleged *crimes?*" Rick Reed asked.

"Oh, they're real crimes, all right," Cora assured him. *"It's just her guilt that's alleged. But I imagine it will be easy to prove. The new bite mark on her arm is identical to the ones on her legs. I doubt if the police will have much trouble breaking Stacy down."*

"But why would she do it? Why would she commit these crimes?"

Cora shrugged. *"I really couldn't say. But I'm sure it will all come out in her trial."*

"And there you have it. The sudden, dramatic courtroom accusation by a canine."

The footage ran again of Buddy springing from Cora's arms and sinking his teeth into Stacy Daigue.

"Live, from Danbury, this is Rick Reed, Channel 8 News."

Sherry picked up the remote control, snapped the TV off.

Aaron Grant said, "You're sure the motives will come out in the trial?"

Cora scratched Buddy behind the ears. "Actually, I'm sure they won't. The prosecutor hasn't a clue, and I doubt if Stacy Daigue's going to spill the beans. But convicting her shouldn't be a problem. The Daigues aren't the smartest of criminals. She probably left fingerprints all over the place. She's got no reason at all for being at Valerie Thompkins's house. One fingerprint will hang her.

"Same thing with the private detective. Bet you

a nickle Stacy left her fingerprints in the library stacks."

"It's a public place," Aaron pointed out.

"And her lawyer will argue that. But it's a tough sell. A waitress from New Haven using the Bakerhaven Library? That'll require some fancy footwork. Particularly if her license plate turns up among the ones Dan Finley took the night of my party."

"I forgot about that."

"Yeah, well, the police won't. I bet they're running the numbers now. She probably also left her prints in Burnside's apartment, and that's *not* a public place."

"You mean when she stole the videotape?"

"Videotape? What videotape?"

"Best in Show."

"She didn't steal that videotape." Cora pointed to the shelf under her VCR. "See? It's right there."

Aaron's eyes widened. "You didn't get rid of it?"

"Why should I get rid of it? I just bought it yesterday."

"You switched tapes?"

"I don't know what you're talking about. I just bought a movie. They're real cheap now. Everyone's switching to DVD. I got it new for under ten bucks."

"Why did you buy one at all?"

"To see if anyone would steal it. The killer stole Burnside's. I figured they'd watch it, see what movie was on it, and go looking for the original at Valerie's. When they didn't find it, they'd come here."

"But they didn't."

"No. Because I served a subpoena. Otherwise, Stacy Daigue would have looked for this while I was in court."

Outside, a car door slammed.

"That's probably Chief Harper, wanting a post-mortem."

"You going to tell him about the tape?" Sherry asked.

"What tape? I haven't got a tape."

"Have it your way."

Sherry opened the front door.

"Oh," Ida Blaine said. "I was looking for her. Cora Felton. Is she here?"

"I'm her niece. Please come in."

Cora Felton smiled when she saw Ida. "Come on in. Take a load off. You met my niece, Sherry. This is Aaron Grant."

"Could I talk to you alone?"

"These guys are family. They've seen the tape."

"Aw, hell." Ida Blaine slumped into a chair. Her high-fashion clothes seemed wilted, as if all the energy had drained out of her body. Her perfectly made-up face showed the lines of age. She took a breath, said anxiously, "What's going to happen?"

"Stacy Daigue's going to be prosecuted for murder. I would expect she'll go to jail."

"No. I mean about me."

"Nothing's going to happen. Nothing will come out."

"Won't the prosecution connect it up?"

"They have no evidence."

"Won't the defense?"

"They have even less."

"What about you?"

"What *about* me?"

"What are you going to say?"

"I've already said it. In court. You were there. You heard."

"Yes, but . . ."

"But what?"

"You didn't mention the tape. Why not?"

"I didn't think it was fair. I didn't think you deserved that. No matter what you've done."

A spasm twisted Ida Blaine's face. She looked at Cora with scared eyes. "How much do you know?" she asked wretchedly.

"Actually, very little. The rest I can merely guess. Which is good. I can't testify to suppositions."

Aaron Grant frowned. "What are you two talking about?"

"He's a reporter," Cora explained to Ida. "But don't mind him. He's not writing this."

"How do you know?"

"He's got the hots for my niece."

"Aunt Cora!"

Cora got up. "Come on. Let's take a little walk. Leave these lovebirds together."

Cora took Ida Blaine out back, where the autumn wind was chasing the brown leaves around the picnic table. Cora sat on the tabletop, motioned Ida up beside her.

Ida pulled her coat around her shoulders, more for protection than warmth. "Please. What do you really know?"

"I'll tell you what I *think*. If you want, you can tell me where I'm wrong." Cora caught a dry leaf, crumbled it in her hand. "Twenty years ago Darryl Daigue committed a brutal, mindless crime. There's no question about the fact he did it. He's scum, he's filth, he should rot in hell. Instead, he gets a life sentence. A *life* sentence. Anita gets death, Darryl gets life. There's gotta be some irony there.

"Here's another irony for you: Anita Dryer's family never recovers from the killing. Her parents waste away and die. Her brother embarks on a life of crime to support his drug habit. He's busted, goes to jail. The same jail that Darryl Daigue is in. The brother's interviewed before he gets out. That interview is quoted in the book. The brother would have killed Darryl Daigue if Daigue hadn't been in solitary.

"That's the key. That's where it all began. Anita Dryer's brother in prison dying to whack Darryl Daigue. It came very close to happening. The writer, A. E. Greenhouse, got Daigue out of solitary so he could interview him for his book. How did he accomplish that? Greenhouse blackmailed the warden. He blackmailed him with a videotape. A videotape of the warden and you.

"The question arises, where did that tape come from? Logically, from the private eye, Peter Burnside. Where did Burnside get it? He took it. He set up a secret camera and filmed the two of you.

"But how could he do that? How would he know where to put the camera? How would he get you there?" Cora smiled. "You see what I mean?"

"This is all speculation," Ida protested feebly.

"Of course. There are no facts being thrown about here. Anyway, there's only one way it works. You're in on it. You set the warden up. You helped the P.I. make the tape."

"Why in heaven's name would I do that?"

"To get Darryl Daigue out of jail."

Ida Blaine sucked in her breath.

Cora nodded. "See, I Googled your name. And I can't find anything beyond ten years back."

"There wasn't an Internet then."

"Yeah, there was. Granted, not like today. But it existed. Anyway, facts go back. People didn't spring full-blown on this planet with the dawn of the computer. You Google other people, you get their life story."

"What's your point?"

"It's real boring in jail. The night I got busted I had a crossword puzzle for company. By a woman named Hillary Mustache. Ever hear of her?"

"No."

"That's not surprising. She doesn't exist. Hillary Mustache is just a pen name for the real constructor."

"So?"

"It got me thinking about people using other names. Like A. E. Greenhouse, for instance."

Cora crumpled another leaf. "Or Ida Blaine."

Ida sniffed. "I don't know what you're talking about."

"*Two* women disappeared right after Darryl Daigue's murder trial. One was Anita Dryer's sister, Gwendolyn. The other was Cindy Tambourine."

"Who?"

"I think you know who. I'm talking about Darryl Daigue's girlfriend. Cindy Tambourine. Who, to all intents and purposes, suddenly ceased to exist."

"So what?"

"We're looking for someone with a reason to get Darryl Daigue out of jail."

"Right," Ida Blaine scoffed. "His childhood sweetheart, who waits twenty years before coming to get him."

"A lot of things happen in twenty years. People grow up. Get married. Put themselves in positions of power."

"You're way off base."

"Maybe. But what about Gwendolyn Dryer? A. E. Greenhouse didn't interview her. He doesn't even mention her in his book."

"He probably couldn't find her."

"Oh, I doubt that. I think *she* found *him*."

"Huh?"

Cora nodded. "Try this on for size. Jason Dryer's in jail with Darryl Daigue, but he can't get at him. A writer, also trying to get to Darryl Daigue, interviews Mr. Dryer. Jason reports this to his sister, and a light-bulb goes on. The sister goes to the writer, tells him her story."

"It wasn't in the book."

"The sister made a deal," Cora said. "If the writer agrees not to mention her, she'll get him an interview with Darryl Daigue. The writer's hesitant at first, but he really wants his interview. He gets sucked in.

"The sister provides him with the means of squeezing the warden. The writer uses it, and interviews Darryl Daigue.

"Irony of ironies, before Daigue gets out of solitary, Jason Dryer gets paroled.

"I would imagine his sister was pretty steamed at him, after all the trouble she went through. I mean, how hard would it have been to screw up parole? One misbehavior would have done the trick. I suppose Jason did it for the drugs. Cold turkey was wearing him down. He wanted his fix. He made parole, scored drugs, and O.D.'d.

"Well, imagine how his sister must have felt.

Her elaborate scheme had failed. Back to the drawing board. If she can't get to Darryl Daigue in jail, she'll have to get him *out*. She'll have to get him paroled.

"Small problem. Darryl Daigue isn't a candidate for parole. He doesn't *have* parole hearings. But that's just in theory. He'll have 'em if the warden wants him to. She just needs to pressure the warden again.

"But there's another teeny problem. The sister doesn't have the videotape anymore. She goes to the detective. He doesn't have it, either. It was given to the writer to blackmail the warden. And, guess what? The writer has had a heart attack and died.

"So the sister approaches the writer's wife. Valerie Thompkins. Valerie is a recent widow with a need for money, and her eye on the main chance. Val's willing to listen to the sister's spiel. She's pleased when she hears it's about the videotape. She suspected it was. Yes, she has it, and, no, she's not giving it up. She's willing to cooperate for a price. What does Gwendolyn want?

"What the sister wants, of course, is to bombard the warden with copies of the videotape until he paroles Darryl Daigue.

"That's fine with Valerie Thompkins. She'll send the tapes herself, as long as the sister keeps paying. But there's no way she's letting Gwendolyn get her hands on the tape, or the money will dry up.

"By now Valerie Thompkins is somewhat paranoid, and who could blame her? She takes her copy of the videotape and she hides it where she thinks no one will ever look. In the middle of a store-bought copy of *Best in Show*. Once she's sure her dupe came out, she destroys the original. The tape is Valerie's gold mine. She figures it's safe.

"Now she has to blackmail the warden. She's not too keen on doing it herself. She goes to the detective who worked with her husband. The detective who made the tape in the first place. Valerie verifies that he doesn't have a copy—which, of course, he doesn't, or the sister wouldn't have needed Valerie—and she hires him to do the dirty work. Prepare the packages and letters, and send them to the warden of the jail.

"To do that, she has to give Burnside a copy of the tape. She's not giving him *her* copy; she runs a dupe. Not just the porno part—she copies the whole movie. It's a neat way of hiding it, and she doesn't want anyone finding it at his place, either. She gives him the copy to run dupes and send them off. Which he does.

"You know the rest. The warden grants Darryl Daigue parole hearings. Naturally, no one wants to let Daigue loose, so the warden has to stack the board. He puts you on it. Has you line up the doc.

"For a while no one notices. Because no one cares.

"With one exception.

"Darryl Daigue's sister.

"On one of her infrequent visits, brother Darryl tells her he's having parole hearings. Stacy Daigue is no dope. She smells a big, fat, odoriferous rat.

"So what does she do? She hires me to look into it. Well, not me directly—she hires the attorney who hires me. Hires her through the mail with a money order. So if asked, she can deny doing it. Which she did, by the way, the first time I questioned her."

Cora smiled. "Here's another irony for you. I shouldn't have been a problem. The woman was only spending two hundred dollars. For that type of money, at best I look into the thing, interview a few people, and report back there isn't a chance in hell of Darryl Daigue ever getting paroled.

"But no one will leave it at that. The minute I start investigating, everyone and his brother acts guilty as hell. Warden Porno-star hauls me into his office to find out what I'm doing and suggest I do it elsewhere. And Valerie Thompkins and the private dick start following me around town."

Cora dug a cigarette out of her purse. "You smoke?"

"No."

"Keep this up and you will. Where was I? Oh, yeah, I'm being tailed." Cora lit up, inhaled a big drag, blew it out. "This is an ironic side effect of gilding the lily. I would imagine attempting to spring Darryl Daigue was rough sledding. So the conspirators tried to give the process a nudge. Among the good doctor's many postmortems there just so happened to be one of a guy who used to work with Darryl Daigue, a Mr. Ricky Gleason, who smashed himself to hell in a drunken car wreck. Next time Dr. Jenkins examined Darryl Daigue, he made a point of bringing it up, knowing Daigue would immediately blame the crime on Ricky. Since Gleason was dead and couldn't deny it, that would be one more thing to argue at the next parole hearing.

"Here's the ironic side effect. When I interview Darryl Daigue, he tells *me* about Ricky Gleason. I check it out. Doing so leads me to Dr. Jenkins, who performed the postmortem.

"And here's where the comedy begins. You, also, are calling on Dr. Jenkins. Now, Valerie Thompkins doesn't trust you. I can't imagine why. You're the woman *in* the videotape. You want the videotape sent to the warden. And you want the warden to name *you* to the parole board. Whatever you're paying Valerie Thompkins, it isn't nearly enough.

"Toward that end, she has her detective friend tailing you. So far, he has uncovered a less than appropriate relationship with the doctor. Interesting, but probably not the real bone of contention. Anyway, the P. I.'s following you when you call on the doctor. Which is the exact same time *I* call on the doctor.

"The warden has already complained to you that I'm snooping around. The detective listened in on that call. How, I don't know, but it wouldn't surprise me to learn your phone was bugged.

"Anyway, I'm a public figure." Cora waggled her hand. "Semi. My picture's in the paper. I'm on TV. The detective recognizes me. He whips out his cell phone, calls Valerie Thompkins. 'Guess what, that woman the warden complained about is still nosing around in the case. She just called on the doc.'

"Valerie Thompkins hops in her car, hightails it down there, and when I leave the doctor's, she falls in behind. She's rather upset when I give her the slip."

"How do you know all this?"

"I ran her license plate, for one thing. It's standard procedure when you're being tailed. Double back and get a plate number." Cora felt no need to mention she thought it was the *wrong* plate. The point was, she got it.

"Anyway, that might have been the end of it. Except the detective goes back to shadowing you. And when I find out you're on the parole board, I come to your house. That's enough to convince our friends that I deserve a little more attention. The dick drops you and starts tailing me. He was tailing me when he died."

"How delicately you put that."

"Don't I?" Cora took a drag. "You prefer 'when someone slit his throat and dropped him in my birthday cake'?"

"Stacy Daigue?"

"Yes." Cora sighed. "That's why this case was so hard to figure out. It's always been upside down. Stacy Daigue should be the one blackmailing the warden, trying to get her brother out of jail. It's a kick in the face when she isn't. She claims she didn't hire me. Maybe she didn't. Maybe she doesn't know a damn thing about it.

"But what if she does? What if she *was* the one who hired me, but she *wasn't* the one trying to get her brother out of jail? So what was her angle? She's trying to keep her brother *in?*

"I played with that for a while. Stacy Daigue knows her brother's a psychopath, knows he's a cold-blooded killer, knows if Darryl gets out he'll kill again. She knows he belongs in prison, and she needs to stop any misguided bleeding-heart liberal who wants to spring him.

"Having met the woman, I find that hard to buy. Because Stacy Daigue has the same hereditary characteristic as her brother. It's impossible to imagine her committing an unselfish act. No, Stacy is just as ruthless and cunning as brother Darryl.

"She is also damn smart. Something is going on. She wants to know why. So she starts with the parole board. That leads her straight to you and the doc. Add in the fact the doctor is the source of Darryl's current scapegoat, Ricky Gleason, and a nasty picture begins to emerge. Stacy pokes into your past, and she's much quicker than I to figure out who you really are. Of course, she's about your age, was around back then, might have even known you. No matter. The fact is, she makes the connection and starts tailing you. Runs into Valerie Thompkins and the private eye. This is pay dirt and she knows it, particularly when the P.I. starts tailing me. When he knocks off, she puts a brick through my window just to see what I'll do.

"What I do is show up in her diner. The very next day. Stacy nearly plotzes. How the hell did I get onto her so fast? She's amused and relieved to find out I think she hired me. She denies it, of course. But when I leave, she tags along.

"Burnside the detective is on my tail too. But he's not the swiftest tool in the drawer. He doesn't spot Stacy, she spots him. So what happens? I lead him right to the police. What the hell is that about? Actually, it's just my niece's way of conning me to my surprise party. But the detective doesn't know that, and neither does Stacy. When Harper and I head for the library the detective follows.

"Which is when the guy makes his fatal mistake. He doesn't dare walk into the library right behind us. He goes around to the back door. Creeps up the stairs to the stacks.

"Stacy Daigue is right on his tail. She walks up behind Burnside, puts a razor to his throat, and asks him what he's doing."

Cora made a face. "I only met the guy once, but he struck me as the type who'd spill his guts. I imagine when it penetrated his thick skull that Stacy Daigue really did have a razor at his throat, he told her everything she wanted to know.

"Unluckily for Burnside, this did no good. As soon as Stacy's got the goods, she slits his throat and drops him in my birthday cake.

"The only thing she didn't get was the location of the videotape, or she would have stolen it when she knocked off Valerie. Destroying the tape, you see, would have ended your leverage with the warden. It was the only way to keep from killing you."

"Killing *me*?"

"Yeah. I don't think she wanted to do that."

"Why not?"

"Because she knows who you are." Cora sighed. "I do, too. I know from the porno video. Only two women had enough motive to set up the warden by appearing in that tape. If you were Cindy Tambourine, you could have wanted to free your boyfriend. If you were Gwendolyn Dryer, you could have wanted to get Darryl Daigue out of jail . . . and, once you did, to kill him."

Ida Blaine gasped.

"Stacy knew you were Gwendolyn Dryer. She knew Darryl viciously murdered your sister." Cora shrugged. "I could be wrong. It could be Stacy just wanted you to live in frustration the way her brother lives in captivity. After all, she did mean to thwart your efforts."

"I see."

"Yes, you do. It's dawning on you now, isn't it? But the realization's there. The tapes are gone. Given the scrutiny this case has been under, there's no way of ever getting Darryl Daigue paroled. No way you can finish the job."

"Why are you telling me this?" Ida asked softly.

"I feel for you. Despite what you planned. I want to

give you some advice: Let it go. You got lucky this time. You're not involved. No one suspects you're Gwendolyn Dryer. No one suspects a thing. You got off scot-free this time. Let it go."

Ida Blaine said something unintelligible.

"What?"

"I can't," Ida said, louder.

"Yes, you can. You saw Darryl Daigue in court. You saw his face. He's been beaten in jail."

"So?"

"Darryl's lawyer may not have been much good, but there's one thing he did do. He got him released on bail. It was revoked when the trial started, but Darryl was out free after the murder."

"I remember," Ida said bitterly. "If I'd just done something then."

"Cindy Tambourine didn't testify at the trial. Even as a character witness. Much less an alibi witness. And girlfriends usually do."

"What are you getting at?"

"I figure Darryl went over her testimony with Cindy, and didn't like what he heard. So Cindy disappeared."

"What are you saying?"

"You know damn well what I'm saying. There's no record of Cindy Tambourine anywhere after the trial. She just vanished."

Ida Blaine looked at Cora searchingly. "What are you getting at? You can prove Daigue killed Cindy? Try him again, get him the death penalty?"

"Are you kidding me? I can't even prove she's *dead*."

"Then what's your point?"

"Tambourine's an unusual name. I checked the prison files, and guess what?"

Ida Blaine's eyes widened. "No . . ."

"Yes. Just admitted. Criminal assault. Kenneth Tambourine. Notorious low-life. Two-time loser, and general all-around scum. Dropped out of Bakerhaven High shortly after the Darryl Daigue trial. Been getting into mischief ever since. This is Kenneth's first incarceration at Brandon State Penitentiary. So far no one's made the connection between him and Darryl Daigue. Not the real connection. They just figured Darryl sold him bad drugs."

"You mean Tambourine's the one who beat Daigue up?"

"Among others. Kenneth just made better work of it. The way I understand it, Kenny could have killed Darryl. Instead he beat him bad." Cora shrugged. "I guess he didn't want to kill him—yet. Not when he'll have so many more opportunities to beat Darryl within an inch of his life. Tambourine's serving five-to-ten."

"I hope Kenneth Tambourine never gets out!"

"Well, I got some good news for you in that regard."

"What's that?"

Cora smiled. "You're on the parole board."

Ida Blaine's smile was probably the first genuine one she'd smiled in twenty years. "Damned if I'm not!"

Sherry Carter and Aaron Grant came out the screen door as Ida Blaine drove off. Buddy pelted across the lawn and leaped into Cora's arms. She hefted the tiny dog, which immediately began licking her face.

"Cut it out, Buddy."

"What's her story?" Aaron asked Cora, gesturing at Ida.

"She just wanted to make sure the videotapes are suppressed."

"And that's all?" Sherry said.

"Are you kidding?" Cora said. "You *begged* me to ditch that nude reel of *you*."

"What nude reel of you?"

"She's kidding, Aaron. Can't you tell when Cora's kidding?"

"It's in the middle of *Sleepless in Seattle*," Cora said. "Unfortunately, it got returned to the video store."

"Arf!" Buddy said.

Cora put him down. He bounded around the yard in a large, crazy circle and leaped back in her arms again.

"What are you going to do with him?" Aaron asked.

"Why? You want him?"

"Are you kidding? I can't take a dog. Besides, he seems to like you."

"We have a no-dog policy," Cora said. "We'll have to find him a home."

"ASPCA?"

"I don't know. I hear if they can't place them, they put them to sleep."

"They'd place him."

"He's an old dog. People want puppies."

"Actually," Sherry said, eyeing her aunt, "the no-dog policy was for large dogs. Dobermans. Rottweilers. It hardly applies."

Cora looked at her in surprise. "Really?"

Sherry smiled. "Happy birthday, Cora."

"You hear that, Buddy?" Cora said. "You're reprieved!"

Buddy responded to the news by slobbering all over Cora's cheeks.

Cora chuckled. "You know something? This is turning out to be the best birthday I ever had!"

*If you enjoyed Parnell Hall's latest
Puzzle Lady mystery,*

AND A PUZZLE TO DIE ON,

you won't want to miss any of the hilarious
adventures of Cora Felton: Look for them at
your favorite bookseller's!

And read on for an early peek at Cora's
next investigation:

STALKING THE PUZZLE LADY

by

Parnell Hall

Coming in hardcover from Bantam in
November 2005

"A FUN SERIES FOR MYSTERY FANS AND CRUCIVERBALISTS."
—*USA Today*

STALKING THE PUZZLE LADY

A PUZZLE LADY
MYSTERY

PARNELL HALL

AUTHOR OF *AND A PUZZLE TO DIE ON*

STALKING THE PUZZLE LADY

On sale November 2005

HE COULDN'T BELIEVE IT! She hadn't answered his letter. True, he hadn't left a return address, but there were so many other ways. And a clever woman could find them. And she was not just a clever woman, she was a brilliant woman. When it came to delving, investigating, figuring things out.

So why hadn't she?

The thought that tortured him was, What if she had? What if she'd devised some clever means of communication that he was too slow to grasp? What if she had already answered him in one way or another? What if her answer was waiting for him right now?

But what kind of answer could it be? An ad in the Personals column? What Personals column? And what newspaper? How would he know?

No, there was only one way she could communicate. Only one way he expected her to. Only one way that made sense.

After all, she had a nationally syndicated crossword-puzzle column. And how simple it would be to slip a word or phrase into the puzzle. Meaningless to everyone else, but a wink and a nod to him. And wouldn't that be delicious. To have a secret. Their secret. In plain view, on display, for everyone to see. If only they had the perspicacity to glean the hidden meaning. To crack the secret cypher.

Each morning he snatched up the paper, flipped to the Entertainment section, and solved the puzzle, always in under five minutes. For the next half hour he would study what he'd done, searching for a clue.

Which never came.

It infuriated him. Was it possible she hadn't gotten the letter? He had written care of the paper, not having her address. It was only a local paper, but still, they would forward it, wouldn't they? And the breakfast cereal company. He had written her care of that too. She was the spokesperson for the company. Surely they would send her mail.

If not, he would have to get her home address. He

hated to do it. It would make him seem like an obsessed fan. Like that nutcase who kept showing up at David Letterman's.

And it wasn't that way with him. It wasn't that way at all. He was her confederate, her peer, her equal. Theirs was a true meeting of the minds.

If only he could arrange the introduction.

Should he nudge the breakfast cereal company?

Perhaps.

Or maybe it was time for a special delivery.

2

"I'M TIRED OF LIVING a lie."

Sherry Carter looked at her aunt in amusement. Cora Felton did not look like a liar. The white-haired, bespectacled lady looked like everyone's favorite grandmother, the type that baked pumpkin pies at Thanksgiving, cookies at Christmastime, and cupcakes for no particular reason on any given occasion. Sherry, of course, knew better. Cora smoked, swore, gambled, had only recently given up drinking, and was somewhat hazy on the subject of how many husbands she'd had. "Mine or other people's?" was her usual deflection.

"Good lord, Cora. Do you have another husband I haven't heard of?"

"It's entirely possible, but that isn't what I meant." Cora pointed at the computer screen, on which Sherry was composing a puzzle in Cross-word Compiler. "I'm tired of being the Puzzle Lady. I'm tired of feigning an expertise I have not got."

Sherry nodded approvingly. "See? You even *sound* like the Puzzle Lady. Do you realize how much more elegant and refined your speech has become since you've been doing it?"

Cora responded with a remark that could hardly be considered elegant or refined by any stretch of the imagination.

"Aunt Cora!" Sherry remonstrated.

"Oh, pooh," Cora retorted. "I'm the Milli Vanilli of the crossword-puzzle community. A hollow subterfuge that has stretched way thin."

"You're mixing metaphors."

A toy poodle scampered into the office and yipped around Cora's feet. She bent down, scooped him up. He nestled against her chest, nuzzled under her chin.

"Look at me," Cora complained. "I used to be tough as nails. Now I'm a dotty old woman with a dog."

"We don't have to keep the dog," Sherry pointed out. "He's here on a trial run."

"Shh! He'll hear you!" Cora hissed. "Buddy, don't listen to her. Cut it out, Sherry. I'm not getting rid of the D-O-G just to make a point."

"And just what point are you making, Cora?"

"I'm not comfortable taking credit for something I don't do. I think it's time you were recognized for your work."

"I don't want to be recognized."

"Why not? It's not like you're hiding from your ex-husband anymore. Dennis knows you're the Puzzle Lady. He also knows where you live. What have you got to lose?"

"My privacy, for one thing."

"Oh? But it's all right for me to lose mine?"

"It's not the same thing, Aunt Cora."

"Why not?"

"You don't *do* anything."

"I beg your pardon?"

Sherry shrugged. "I create the puzzles. Losing your privacy is your *entire* contribution to the project."

"Oh, for Christ's sake!"

Cora jerked a pack of cigarettes out of her floppy, drawstring purse.

"I thought you weren't going to smoke in here," Sherry observed.

"That only works when you agree with me," Cora snapped. "When you argue with me, I gotta smoke." Buddy squirmed and yipped. "Oh, was I squeezing too tight?" She set the poodle down. "All right, I'll go outside. You wanna come, too, or should I finish this conversation myself?"

Sherry followed Cora down the hall through

the living room and out the front door of the modest prefab rental she and her aunt shared together. The house wasn't much, except for the location. On a scenic country road in Bakerhaven, Connecticut, with no near neighbors, the one-acre lot was an idyllic setting.

Cora stopped on the front step, but Buddy pelted by and yipped around the yard. It was mud season, and the tiny poodle's white feet were rapidly turning black.

"You'll wash him off before he comes in the house?" Sherry said.

"Why is it always me?" Cora groused. "Why don't you wash him off?"

"I do when you're not here."

"Yeah, yeah. What's this crap about *I* don't do anything? How does that have anything to do with *you* owning up to what *you* do?"

"It's a partnership. I supply the work, you supply the image."

"I *hate* the image. I gotta be decorous in public, while you run around in jeans and a sweater. Is that fair? You're young and attractive and you happen to look *good* in jeans and a sweater."

Before Cora quit drinking she had often appeared far from decorous in public, but Sherry wasn't about to point that out. "What's really the matter, Cora?"

Cora puffed in smoke, watched the dog

cavorting on the lawn. "I told you what's the matter. I'm tired of the deception. I'm tired of pretending to be something I'm not."

"Cora. You've hated the deception from the word go. Why do you want to quit *now*?"

"Oh."

"Ah! There's an *oh*?"

"It's the damn cereal company."

"The damn cereal company that put you on TV? You'd like to give that up?"

"Sherry . . ."

"What have they done?"

"They've come out with a new cereal."

"And they want you to promote it?"

"Yeah."

"That's wonderful, Cora. That probably pays our rent for a year. We might even think of buying this place, knocking it down, and building something better."

"I don't want to do it."

"Why not?"

"Well, for one thing, it's not a *new* cereal. It's the same *old* cereal, it's just *new and improved*."

"So what?"

"I hate that. It's like saying, 'The stuff I've been selling you for years is crap, but, hang on, I got something better.' "

"All products do that. It's called progress."

"It's humiliating."

"No, it's great. The product launch is a gold mine. So you have to tape some TV ads. What's the big deal?"

Cora exhaled an angry drag. "They want me to tour."

"What?"

"They want me to make *personal appearances.*" Her tone was scathing. "They want me to do *supermarkets. Shopping centers. Malls.* They want me to be there hawking their products. They want to let kids meet the Puzzle Lady. Like a Macy's *Santa.*"

"What's wrong with that?"

"I'm not good with kids, Sherry. Kids have sticky hands and snotty noses. And a complete and utter lack of tact. They stand there and tell me to my face I look older than their grandmother. It's all I can do to keep from telling them that's 'cause their mother got knocked up when she was fifteen."

"I see your point. Can you do the ads and not the tour?"

"No. 'Cause they're shooting the ads *on* the tour." Cora snorted. "It's all this goddamned reality TV. They want real kids trying the cereal for the first time. Along with the Puzzle Lady. And I *hate* cold cereal. Give me ham and eggs and a buttered muffin."

Sherry Carter looked at her aunt. "You really

want to do this? Tell people you're a fake, I mean?"

"I got some money put away. Not just from this, but from my alimony and property settlements. If ever there was a time, it's now."

"If you give it up, what are you going to do?"

Cora shrugged. "Hold a press conference. Do the *Today Show*. We could go on *Oprah* together, tell our story. I could abdicate the throne. Like the way I said *abdicate*?"

"I'm not going on TV, Cora."

"You may think you're not, but TV's gonna find you."

"You'd do that to me?"

"I'm not doing it *to* you. You pushed me out front for years. Was that doing it to *me*? It's just the way it goes. Hey, Buddy!" Cora yelled. The little poodle had ventured too far down the drive for her liking. He halted at the sound of her voice, scampered across the lawn.

"Fine," Sherry said. "That's not what I mean. If you're not the Puzzle Lady, what will you do?"

"Pretty much the same as I do now. I mean, it's not like I spend any time on crossword puzzles. All I do is film a commercial or two a year. At least until this damn tour came up."

"I don't think you've thought this through."

"Why not?"

"Right now people cut you a lot of slack because you're the most famous woman in town. Give it up, you'll be the most *in*famous woman in town. You're gonna spend most of your time apologizing to people for duping them. People don't *like* to be duped. It makes them feel stupid. People *resent* a person who makes them feel stupid. They could make her life a living hell."

"I think you're wrong. I think our friends would come around."

"Maybe." Sherry said it without enthusiasm. "You're doing this just to get out of a tour?"

"Would *you* want to do a supermarket tour?" Cora countered.

"Don't be absurd."

"Well, at least we agree on one thing."

The phone rang. Sherry ducked back inside to answer it.

Cora sat on the front step to play with the dog. The concrete stoop was cold despite her tweed skirt. Cora didn't mind. She put out her arms, lifted the little dog up into her lap.

"You going to snub Mommie if she's not a celebrity? No, you're not. You won't care at all."

From the kitchen Sherry shouted, "Cora!"

"Ooh," Cora said. "I hope that's a poker game. Mommie could use a poker game. Come on, Buddy. Let's go in."

Cora set the poodle down in the living room,

and went to answer the phone. "Who is it?" she asked as Sherry handed her the receiver.

"Don't know. He asked for Miss Felton."

"As long as he didn't ask for the darn Puzzle Lady." Cora took the phone, said, "Hello?"

"Miss Felton?"

"Yes."

"This is Charles Coleson, Truestar Investments."

Cora groaned. "Not again."

"Miss Felton—"

"I told you. I don't want to diversify."

"Yes, you did. And we haven't. We've kept all your stock right where you had it. That's why I'm calling."

"What do you mean?"

Cora could hear Charles Coleson take a breath.

"Miss Felton, I'm afraid I have some rather bad news."